Sweet Spot

Laura Drake

FOREVER

NEW YORK   BOSTON

Forever
Hachette Book Group
237 Park Avenue
New York, NY 10017

www.HachetteBookGroup.com

Printed in the United States of America

First Edition: May 2013

10 9 8 7 6 5 4 3 2 1

OPM

Forever is an imprint of Grand Central Publishing.
The Forever name and logo are trademarks of Hachette Book Group, Inc.

The Hachette Speakers Bureau provides a wide range of authors for speaking events. To find out more, go to www.hachettespeakersbureau.com or call (866) 376-6591.

The publisher is not responsible for websites (or their content) that are not owned by the publisher.

SHE'S NO LONGER YOUR WIFE.

Maybe not, but her pheromones still called to him from across a room, touching him places no other woman's ever had.

He wanted her. Sexually, obviously, but also in ways he'd forgotten until he found himself outside her world, looking in. He missed the way she used to look at him: a corner of her mouth lifted in a girl-next-door-centerfold way. He missed the sight of her dancing in the kitchen, when she thought she was alone. He missed having the home she'd created wrapped around him, giving him strength to go out in the world and do things.

He missed all those things. But it was the changes in her that kept him awake at night. She was stronger now. Stronger than before the accident. Stronger than he'd ever seen her. *And he liked it.*

To Lady Beans
Thank you. For everything.

Acknowledgments

This book wouldn't have happened without many hands, reaching back. First, my critique partners, Fae Rowen, Jenny Hansen, and Sharla Rae (thanks for letting me borrow your name!) Thanks to everyone at OCCRWA, the best writer's group on the planet.

Thanks to the bull riding insiders, who helped a city girl get it right: Clint Wade, of Exclusive Genetics, for his time and knowledge of bull husbandry; Cindy Rosser, who gave me insight into the life of a stock contractor; and Joe Scully, for the arena announcer details.

Once written, the book would never have made it out of the drawer but for Sue Grimshaw, who was supportive even after being stuck two hours in an L.A. traffic jam with an aspiring author (so sorry). Thanks to my agent, Nalini Akolekar, of Spencerhill Associates, for taking a chance on me, and to Latoya Smith, my Grand Central editor.

To my mother-in-law, Edith, who is a shining example of how amazing a ranch wife and mother can be.

And always, to my very own hero—my bleed-maroon Texas Aggie, who always believed.

The
Sweet Spot

CHAPTER 1

The grief counselor told the group to be grateful for what they had left. After lots of considering, Charla Rae decided she was grateful for the bull semen.

Charla Rae Denny wiped her hands with her apron and stepped back, surveying the shelves of her pantry. This month's *Good Housekeeping* suggested using scraps of linoleum as shelf paper. It had been a bitch-kitty to cut but cost nothing, would be easy to clean, and continued the white-pebbled theme of her kitchen floor. And for a few hours, the project had rescued her weary mind from a hamster-wheel of regret.

The homing beacon in the Valium bottle next to the sink tugged at her insides.

She sipped a glass of water to avoid reaching for it and glanced out the window to the spring-skeletal trees of the backyard.

Her gaze returned to the two-foot-wide stump the way a tongue wanders to a missing tooth. Tentative grass shoots had sprung up to obscure the obscene scar in the soil.

She hadn't thought that an innocent tree could kill a child.

She hadn't thought that an innocent coed could kill a marriage.

And if those pills could kill the thinking, she'd take ten.

At the familiar throaty growl of a Peterbilt turning off the road out front, Char jerked, realizing minutes had passed. She'd been listening for that deep throb for hours. She always did. As the cab and empty cattle hauler swept by the window, she wound her shaking hands in her apron, as if the sturdy cotton would hold her together.

A ranch wife could stretch a pound of hamburger farther than anyone, but Daddy's new medication cost the moon, and the bills in the basket beside the computer were piling up like snowdrifts in a blizzard. Hands still shaking, she untied the bibbed apron and pulled it over her head. She'd rather clean bathrooms at the airport than ask her ex for money, but, then, most of her choices these days were like that. Sighing, she walked to the mudroom, shrugged into her spring jacket, yanked open the back door, and stepped into the nippy air.

Jimmy had backed the rig to the corral and left the engine running. He stepped down from the cab to stand, one foot on the running board, looking up into the dim interior, unaware of her approach. After all, the past four months she'd made sure that when he was here, she'd been purposely somewhere else.

He looked different. Her Jimmy, but with an older man superimposed, blurring the strong, familiar lines of the body she knew like her own. The mean midday sun highlighted the deep furrows bracketing his mouth and the brown hair curling from under his cowboy hat glinted with silver. His legs were still long and lean, but a bit of spare tire sheltered his huge oval belt buckle. Jimmy wouldn't go anywhere without his State Champion Bull Rider buckle.

She halted ten feet from the truck, thrust her fists in the pockets of the jacket, and forced words past the ball wedged in her throat. "Jimmy, we need to talk."

His head jerked around, face frozen in guilty shock. He looked like Benje as a toddler, caught misbehaving. Yet another reason she'd avoided him was stamped in the features he'd passed to their son.

He spun back to the cab and mumbled. She followed his line of vision to catch a quick flash of sun on bleached blond hair. Charla stopped, stunned to stillness. She'd doubt her vision if that flash of blond hadn't burned in her mind like a smoking brand.

"You brought her here, Jimmy?" she whispered. "To our—to *my* home?" Oh, sure, she'd known about the Cupcake. The whole town knew. The girl was the straw that had finished off their marriage.

Jimmy slammed the truck door and stood before it like a challenging bull. "That's not Jess, Charla. Jess and I broke up months ago. That's Mitzi, Jess's roommate. And before you get any wrong ideas, I'm taking her to the event to watch her boyfriend ride. That's it."

"Do you think I'm stupid? Lies like that only work once, Jimmy."

He ducked his head, strode the length of the trailer, and busied himself letting down the tailgate. She stalked him, anger advancing with every step.

"Do you have that little respect for me?" The pleading

in her voice only made her madder. "James Benton Denny. You *look* at me."

Hands busy, he shot her his I-may-be-wrong-but-I'm-not-admitting-anything look.

Words piled into her throat, and she swallowed. "Aren't you even embarrassed? She could be your daughter, for cripes' sake. People are laughing their heads off—at you—at me." Her traitorous voice cracked.

"Look, I'm telling you the truth, okay?" Jimmy's voice echoed as he climbed into the cattle trailer. "The morning has been a disaster. First, that useless Emilio didn't show, and I had to fire him." The empty metal box amplified his sigh. "I needed to let him go anyway. We're making good money, but now the business has to support two households—" He hesitated, apparently recalling his audience.

"Then we had a flat on that danged retread. I knew better than to buy tires from Baynard's." Eyes down, he scanned the metal floor of the truck bed for anything that could hurt the stock. "I'm seriously late here, Little Bit, can we—"

"Don't you dare call me that!" She charged up the tailgate, her face blazing. "You lost that right two months, two weeks, four days ago."

He trotted by without a word, to the corral. The bulls, who had been watching the proceedings with interest, sauntered to the trailer. Realizing she stood between them and their destination, Char jumped from the tailgate.

Jimmy circled the pen, keeping a wary eye on the bulls, urging them gently toward the gate. "What did you want to talk to me about, Char?"

Slivers of pain shot up her palms. Realizing what she

was doing, she relaxed her fingers until her nails popped out of the skin. *God, I'm a fool.* "Never mind."

"I'll be at the event in Abilene for the week."

Char stepped to the side of the corral to hear over the clatter of hooves on the metal tailgate.

"I've deposited the money from the last semen sale into your account, and I'm dropping the bulls off at the vet to have more collected on the return trip. I should be back with them sometime on the twenty-fifth."

After the last bull, Kid Charlemagne, trotted up the ramp, Jimmy hoisted the tailgate and shot the pins into place. His nonchalance stung more than his hubris. *Just another day dealing with the unreasonable ex.* Her odd, out-of-body objectivity kicked in again as Jimmy closed the corral gate. Why shouldn't he brush her off? What was she but an old coffee stain on his Important Life?

He still had a job, two of them, in fact. One, working as an arena announcer for the pro bull riding circuit and the other as a stock contractor, supplying bucking bulls for the events.

Her only job ended the day Benje died.

Jimmy halted in front of her, his gaze sharpening on her face. "You still taking those pills, Little Bit?" His brow creased like it did when he was considering, and the look in his eye softened to . . . pity? "You've gotta get off those things, Hon. Medicating your life won't make it better."

She wanted to slap the solicitous look off his face. She wanted to run.

Instead, she held her ground, stabbing a finger at the trailer. "Those bulls have nothing on *you* in the balls department. You've got no talking room, Jimmy. Your old life fell apart, so you just threw it away and started a new one. *Your* medication just leans toward blonde and brainless."

Delicious flames licked the inside of her skin, urging her on. "Well, then, you go on and lie in that bed, Jimmy Denny. I don't want to see your face on this property again. Do you hear me?"

Jimmy's mouth dropped. She'd gotten his attention now, all right.

"You can't do that, Char. You may own the semen, but I own the bulls. The land—"

"Is my daddy's. His Alzheimer's hasn't changed that, and I have his power of attorney." The freed flames roared in her ears, and her body shook with righteous crackling heat. "You know very well I can do this, and by God, if you show up here again, I'll call Sheriff Sloan and have you arrested for trespassing."

She crossed her arms over her chest and wished looks really could kill. "Just leave the rig at the vet. I'll pick up the bulls."

"But Char—"

She tipped her chin to the truck cab. "You'd better hurry, Jimmy. Your girlfriend is waiting." Spinning on her heel, Charla stomped stiff-legged to the house, mortification, anger, and fear roiling in her gut.

Giving the door a satisfying slam, she strode to the kitchen, to the fire extinguisher disguised as a prescription bottle.

CHAPTER 2

Reality is the leading cause of stress for those in touch with it.

—Jane Wagner

A blast of warm air hit JB as he hauled himself into the cab and slammed the door. "I apologize for that." Vibration from the idling engine throbbed through the seat as he raised his fingers to the heating vents. *Just my luck. The day I do a favor for someone, Little Bit decides she wants to talk.*

Mitzi flipped a curl of bleached hair over her shoulder. "No apology needed. I'm sorry I brought you trouble. Sam and I owe you a couple of drinks."

The sympathy in her look granted him absolution. For the moment, anyway. "After today, I'll need them. Let's get on the road." He double-clutched and rammed the truck into gear.

The look of betrayal on Char's face had sent a shard of guilt slicing through his gut. He shouldn't have chanced bringing Mitzi. He knew what it would look like to Char. But they were two hours late already, and if he'd had to drive back across town to pick her up...God, he was a shit.

As he goosed the accelerator, the whine of the engine and his thoughts crowded out Mitzi's chatter. Aware that the truck's passenger side would face the kitchen window on the trip out, he considered asking Mitzi to duck, but that horse had already left the barn. Besides, it was a long drive to Abilene, and he couldn't take four hours of cab time with an indignant woman.

Char's words stung like sweat in an open cut. Jess had *not* been young enough to be their daughter. He checked traffic and eased onto the highway, taking it easy on the bulls. Shifting through the gears, he remembered the first time he and Char had made love, the spring of their senior year.

Telling their parents they were going to the baseball game, they'd driven out to the Pedernales River for a picnic. He'd spread a blanket on the bank, and that afternoon, his world shifted. He'd never been inside someone's skin before, in more ways than physically. Char's sharing of her deepest self had loosened his defenses, and that day she'd settled in, next to his heart.

They'd been what, seventeen? Subtracting that from forty? Twenty-three. Crap. That hurt, but not because she'd been right about Jess being young. How long had Char been chewing on this? Long enough to do the math and, he was sure, remember that day at the river.

His thoughts shifted gears again. *How does she think she's going to run things by herself?* Since he'd fired Emilio this morning, she wouldn't even have a hand to help out. He was sure the ramifications still hadn't occurred to her. When Charla got mad, she didn't think.

A traditional ranch wife, she considered her home and family her career, and everything outside the house his responsibility. Not a popular career for a girl in the late 1980s, but it fit him down to the ground. They'd made a good team. He hadn't known a partnership so strong could break so fast.

Benje's earnest, seven-year-old face swam into his vision. *I shouldn't be surprised. When you cut the center out of something, the rest falls in on itself.*

Imagining Char, trying to handle the day-to-day labor of their bucking bull operation, he relaxed. He'd be getting a call from Little Bit by tomorrow.

A call he'd be waiting for.

Charla rolled over, pulling the covers up to block the light, but it was no use. Consciousness was as relentless as the dawn that inched across the ceiling, highlighting the crack above her bed. It had been painted over many times, but the lightning-shaped fissure had been there, even when this had been her parent's room.

She felt around the edges of her mind. She'd forgotten something. Something important. It barreled from a tunnel and slammed her to reality. The hollowness in her chest made her gasp and she hugged herself, afraid she would implode.

Benje is gone.

She pulled the covers up and curled into a ball. Another day to face, when her reason for facing it was gone. *Why bother?*

She heard the answer in the *shush* of slippered feet passing her door. Daddy. The grief counselor pointed out that they still had responsibilities. She had to go on for those. Dashing the tears from her cheeks, she threw back the covers and shouldered the sunrise.

After a quick shower, she donned an old sweatshirt and buttoned jeans that hung loose, gapping at the waist. She made the mistake of glancing in the mirror on her way out of the bathroom. The haggard scarecrow staring back frightened her. *I'm cutting back on the pills today.* She stared down the hag in the mirror. *I am.*

After making her bed, Char walked the hall to the kitchen and stopped in the doorway. Her father, dressed for the day in slippers, jeans, and a blue Western-cut shirt, sat at the table, staring out the window. His red hair had blanched gray over the years, and his beard stubble shone silver in the morning light.

Smiling, she walked around the table, rested her hands on his shoulders, and dropped a kiss on his forehead. "Mornin', Daddy."

He looked up, his brow furrowed, worry in his washed blue eyes. "When's Benje coming home?"

The hope she'd garnered in the mirror blew away. *Another bad day.* She had to quit kidding herself; he was getting worse. Trying to convince Daddy of facts he didn't remember only upset him. "Benje's gone off with his dad. They'll be back by dinnertime." She hugged his neck, resting her head against his as his shaky hand patted her hair. Eyes closed, she took comfort from his touch for a moment, then sniffed and straightened. "Coffee's coming up."

As she filled the carafe at the tap, the sound of an indignant bawl from outside jerked her head up.

The heifers crowded the fence, gazing toward the house. "Now where's that darned Emil—" It all came crashing back. She'd been so mad yesterday that Jimmy telling her he'd fired Emilio hadn't even registered. She fetched two of her mother's Vintage Rose teacups while the coffeemaker burbled and her mind whirled. Their eighty acres was a decent-size spread for Fredericksburg. But between the bucking bulls and the mama cows, they were overgrazed, so JB had to supplement feed. Her shoulders slumped. Scratch that. *She* needed to feed.

Dang him. She'd been naive enough to believe, the first time, that the little buckle bunny perched on his truck seat belonged to a friend. Did he really think she was stupid enough to swallow the same story a second time?

The heifers at the fence bellowed for breakfast.

Focus, Charla. You have bigger problems today.

After yanking out the loaf of bread she'd made the day before, she popped two slices in the toaster, then glanced at her father's profile, his long face slack as he stared out the window. *I can't leave Daddy alone today.* She needed at least part-time help with him, but after Jimmy's comments on their finances yesterday, she was glad she hadn't asked him for more money.

A half hour later, Char stood in front of the open barn door. *Only two sacks of feed? What the heck were you thinking, Jimmy?* The bawl of hungry cattle got her moving. She would have to make do.

"I'll get this, Little Bit." Her father rounded the bed of the pickup. Growing up, she'd worshiped this big bear of a man who'd constructed the world to fit her mother and her. She glanced at his bent shoulders and spindly bowed legs. When had he gotten so fragile?

"We'll do it together, Daddy." They wrestled the sacks onto the battered truck bed. Her father walked to the fence and opened the gate, and she drove through it. After closing the gate, her dad got in the truck, and she drove to the center of the pasture. Jimmy always fed there, not wanting the cows at the front fence, leaning on it, breaking it down.

She turned off the engine and looked around the messy cab for Jimmy's work gloves as her father came around to open the door for her. Giving up the hunt, she stepped out, then hopped into the bed of the truck as the curious cattle trotted up. She had to admit, the infernal beasts were pretty. Their colors were as varied as their breeds: rusty reds, blacks, creams, brindles, and even a few speckled blues. All fat and pregnant.

Char wrestled the cloth bag onto the edge of the tailgate and studied the sewn closure. *I should have thought to bring a jackknife.* "Why the heck don't they make these things easier to open?" She worked a fingernail under the string. A spear of pain shot up her finger. "Oh, dadgum it!"

She inspected the nail, broken below the quick. Something bumped at her backside. Whirling, she saw a heifer back away, breaking a string of drool that stretched from its snout to the rear of her jeans. "Yuk." She glared at the offender. "Y'all just cool your jets, will you? None of you look like you're going to starve to death in the next five minutes."

Her father chuckled as he pulled himself up into the truck bed. "That's what you get when you hang your rump in the wind, Little Bit."

She met his gaze and grinned back. *This* was her dad.

"Scoot over, I'll do that," he said.

"No, I've got it, Daddy. I need to learn this." She bent

over and managed to tear a hole in the bag. Together, they emptied it out of the end of the truck. As the stream of golden feed spilled, the cattle jostled each other to get to it. Her father helped drag the second bag to the tailgate, then jumped down and walked to the front of the truck as Char emptied the feed bag.

She straightened, a stiff breeze lifting her hair. The ancient oak and pecan trees looked dormant face-on, but if she squinted just right, they had a wash of green so delicate she had to look twice to be sure. Not a cloud marred the bluebonnet sky, and she inhaled crisp air, feeling like she'd hibernated the winter away.

Wishing she had.

A bull's outraged bellow snatched her attention. Looking up, her heartbeat stuttered. Her father had wandered fifty yards away and stood staring down a yearling bull that pawed the ground between him and the truck.

Before Char could catch her breath, the bull charged.

"Check one, check." JB tweaked the bass a bit and sang softly into the mike, " 'Women have been my trouble since I found out they weren't men—' " Sound checks had always seemed lame to him, so a year or so ago, he started singing instead.

He looked up, to where Jess's sexy, knowing smile used to be, across the arena, among the riders' wives. They'd met at an event in San Angelo, when his singing had prompted her to ask her friend for an introduction. The gravitational pull that hit when he'd slapped eyes on that innocent face and wicked little body hadn't let go, though, Lord knows, he'd tried. She'd made him feel alive at a time when he'd forgotten what alive felt like.

He shouldn't have been surprised when Char hadn't believed him yesterday. Jess may have gotten him through that horrible time, but his lies had cost him dear.

The arena before him was anthill busy. Workers hung gates on the bucking chutes at one end, while more swarmed in the center, setting up the round shark cage that would house the camera crew. Its flat top would provide a haven from charging bulls as well as a stage for the arena clown.

"Hey, big guy." As if his thought conjured him, Wylie Galt, the arena entertainer of the event, simpered up, waggling his fingers. He hadn't yet dressed in his signature baggy shorts and oversize hockey jersey, but his white-face makeup and huge red smile were in place. And obviously he was playing the clown already. "Oooh, that song has me positively tingly."

"Put a sock in it, Wylie, you idiot. We've got work to do." They'd worked events together, the past two years. Along with being the arena announcer at pro bull riding events, JB had played straight man to Wylie as they entertained the crowd during the breaks in the action. But Wylie was more than a coworker; he was a good friend. Most of the men on the circuit were single—JB and Wiley both knew what it was like to be on the road, missing a family back home. Well, JB used to know what it was like. "The PBR nixed your idea of bringing the fan of the night down on the dirt—too much liability."

"That's okay. I've got a better idea." Wylie scanned the empty seats of the arena. "I'll jump the fence and go to them. Can the camera follow me up there?" He pointed to the seats at the ceiling of the arena.

"The camera can, but it's gonna look bad if you collapse of a heart attack on national TV."

Wylie puffed out his chest. "That might be tough for a lesser man." At JB's snort, Wylie leveled a gaze at JB's midsection. "Shee-it, cowboy, you're the one gone soft as a girl's hands. Either Jess was blind, or you've got the biggest squash in the garden under that bushel." He pointed to JB's crotch.

"You know, you picturing my gourd makes me a little squeamish. I'd wonder if you were going vegetarian if I didn't know Dana was home with a new baby. Now, can we get to work here, so we can trick the fans into thinking you're clever one more time?"

His production manager hollered, "JB, we've got some things to go over."

JB didn't realize how many things the manager referred to until he looked out over the stands and realized they'd filled. Standing behind the sound boards, he shrugged into his Western yoked suit coat and breathed in the excitement and electric pulse of anticipation rolling off the audience. Another packed-to-capacity crowd. He looked out at the colorful swath of humanity: families, cowboys, buckle bunnies, old men, and babies. He felt most alive here, in the arena, his voice the focus of thousands of people. *Time to go to work.*

He flipped the mike. "Hello, Abilene!" The crowd cheered. "I'm JB Denny, and we've got a heck of a show for you tonight. Just like in the olden days, the best bulls in the country have converged on Abilene, and the cowboys waiting to ride them are tougher'n a two-dollar steak.

"We're going live on national TV in a few seconds, so let's show the rest of the country what a Texas crowd sounds like." The crowd murmured as the lights went down. JB went silent, letting the anticipation build. Roadies ran out to light kerosene poured on the dirt in front of the bucking chutes, spelling out P B R.

The evening's potential fizzed under his skin as JB whispered into the mike. "We're live in 3, 2, 1..." His voice boomed. "Welcome, professional bull riding fans, to the toughest sport on earth! This is not a rodeo, this is the one, the only, Peee Beeee Rrrr!" Two of the crew touched torches to the kerosene and the advancing flame revealed the letters in the dirt. Pyro booms concussed the air, flashes of flames and a fountain of sparkly fireworks shot from tubes on either side of the chutes.

The lights came up and the cheer of the crowd lifted and swept him forward in a wave.

The night had begun.

Between calling the rides, reporting stats, and quipping with Wylie during the TV time-outs, two hours passed in a blur.

JB thumbed the mike. "The final ride of the night is the guy with a target on his back, the points leader on the tour, Colby Marcos. He's drawn the bull, Mighty Mouse, from CJ Denny Bucking Bulls. And, in the spirit of full disclosure, yes, that *is* my bull." JB eyed the small cowboy lowering himself on the bull and timed his commentary to end with the opening of the chute.

"Mighty Mouse is a son of the legendary Yosemite Sam and has shown some promise here lately, with a ninety percent buck-off ratio." The rider took the taut rope from his buddy and wrapped it around his fist, effectively tying himself to the bull by one hand. "Colby needs a ninety-point ride to regain the lead. What do you say, Abilene, let's cheer that cowboy on!"

The crowd roared as the cowboy nodded his head, and

the gate swung open. The small gray-and-white-spotted bull burst from the chute, lunging forward before settling into a dizzying left-handed spin. The rider balanced in the middle, taking away the force of the bull's buck by matching it, jump for jump.

If his bull bucked well and advanced to the final round, JB would earn a good bonus. His heart fell as the cowboy started spurring with his outside leg; if he felt in control enough to loosen up and spur, the Mouse was going down.

But at 6.5 seconds, the bull stopped stock still and, as if switching gears, spun in the opposite direction. Colby was caught out of position, and his hand popped out of the rope. The cowboy was ejected to fly ten feet, landing face-first in the dirt. Three bullfighters moved in to distract the fired-up bull by making a better target than the downed rider.

One tapped the Mouse between his formidable horns and danced away. Another shouted and waved his hat. The third stepped up and slapped the bull's tail. Colby scrabbled in the dirt, trying to get up and run at the same time, but not managing much of either. Luckily, the confused animal gave up and trotted to the exit gate.

The crowd groaned. JB looked up at the ride clock. "Seven point three seconds. Looks like the round win goes to Travis Byrd, and Mighty Mouse advances to the short go tomorrow." *Thank you, Lord.* He could really use that bonus check.

After all the drama and pageantry that led up to the event, it ended simply. The quieted crowd filed for the exits as the winner stood in front of the chutes to accept his placard check and be interviewed. The other riders strolled around the edge of the arena to sign autographs and meet the fans. Wylie stood next to JB's platform, joking and talking to a clamoring bevy of kids waiting to meet him and get him to sign their programs.

JB smiled and turned to shut down his laptop.

"'Scuse me, sir?" JB ignored the voice until he felt a tap on his shoulder. He turned, and his lungs seized, midbreath. *No, not Benje.* Though the boy didn't have similar features, he somehow had the look of his son—a seven-year-old with red hair and freckles, and the same earnest expression.

"Can I have your autograph?"

JB reached for the program with shaking fingers. "Sure, son." Scrawling a jerky rendition of his signature, JB thrust it back at the kid and turned to his work. He was drained. It had been a long day.

"Hey, JB!" He turned as Mitzi bounced up, excitement shimmering off her. "Everyone's going to dinner, then to this great bar Angie's sister told her about. I thought you could squeeze probably five in your truck. What do you think?"

He thought being in a crowded bar all night was the last thing he wanted, but a night out after the event always helped him sleep. Besides, what else did he have to do? Sit and stare at the TV all night and catalog regrets? "Okay. Let me finish up here, and I'll meet you at the truck." He knew once he got to the bar, he'd have a good time.

"Daddy!"

Char's father ran for the fence, moving fast but hindered by the gimp in his arthritic knee. The bull thundered behind. He threw a look over his shoulder. Char put her hands over her eyes and looked from between her fingers. As the bull lowered his head to hook a foot-long horn into his back, her father dropped low and cut left. The bull tried to follow but slipped in the damp grass. Reaching the fence, her dad scooted between the barbed wire strands. Char's head pounded with adrenaline. When she jumped from the pickup bed her legs gave way, landing her on her hands and knees in mud churned up by the cattle's hooves. Up in a flash, she tore open the door, hopped into the cab, and cranked the engine.

She drove to the fence, then jumped out and ducked under the wire to where her father leaned, hands on knees, trying to catch his breath.

"Daddy, are you all right?" she said, panting, though she hadn't run anywhere.

Her father looked up, a twinkle in his eye. "Shoot, Honey, I've been doing that since before you were born." He straightened, puffing out his skeletal chest. "Ain't a bull alive gonna catch Benjamin Enwright, bad knee or no. I may be a bit slower now, but it doesn't matter; all I need to be is smarter'n him."

Char put a hand to her chest, to hold her heart inside. Dad seemed fine, but what if his mind hadn't been clear in that few seconds? What if he'd forgotten that cut-and-run move?

As she drove them back to the house, recriminations pecked at her like a roadrunner on a stinkbug.

What if I lost him too? The full ramifications of her edict to Jimmy bloomed in her mind as the weight of unwanted responsibility spread over her.

She pulled up next to the house, took the truck out of gear, and pulled the parking brake. "Daddy, I've got to go get my purse, then we'll head into town and buy feed, okay?" She opened the door and glanced over. Her father's blank profile told her he was gone again. "You stay here. I'll be right back." She cranked up the heater for him and slid out of the truck.

The orange prescription bottle on the window ledge called to her as she entered the kitchen. She strode to where her purse hung on a dining room chair. Glancing down as she slung it over her shoulder, she noticed her muddy knees. No time to change, but she could at least wash her hands.

Everything outside the house was now her responsibility, and she had no one to blame but herself. The siren call of the pills wailed as she sidled up to the sink. Surely after this morning she'd earned a break.

Char ground her teeth. "No. I committed to this only three hours ago." The words echoed hollow in her ears as the aching want rose, dwarfing every other thought. *Yeah, but that was before I almost got Daddy killed.*

A rumor without a leg to stand on will get around some other way.

—*John Tudor*

Squeezing the gas nozzle, Char turned her face to the sun. The cold metal stung her bare hand, but the feed store sheltered the gas pumps from the wind, creating the illusion of a warm summer day. Her mind meandered, content listening to the gurgle of fuel as the tank filled. *Jimmy doesn't know what he's talking about.* All the pills did was knock the sharp edges off life, allowing her to walk around in it without getting bruised. And she'd only taken a half dose. She was driving, after all.

Ignoring the crunch of gravel when another car pulled to the only other pump, she kept her eyes closed, hoping whoever it was would respect her reverie.

The engine died, and a car door opened and closed. "Oh, Char, dear, it's so good to see you."

Lately, she cursed living in a small town. She opened her eyes at a touch on her sleeve and yet another solicitous, assessing look. "Hello, Salina. How are you?"

"The question is how are you, Hon?" Salina's gaze flicked over Char, her delicate brows furrowed.

Char squirmed inside, blood rushing to her cheeks. "We're doing just fine, Sal." She sniffed the air, hoping mud was all that caked her jeans. *Dang it, how dressed up do you have to be for a trip to the feed store?* It figures she'd run into Salina; her obvious concern was worse for being heartfelt.

In a former life, Salina and her husband, Larry, had run in Char and Jimmy's circle, a part of the group of former schoolmates that played cards together, each couple taking turns hosting. Of course, they'd invited her, after. But the thought of sitting in the middle of all those prying eyes, alone, was part of the reason Char hadn't answered the phone for months. Thankfully, it didn't ring much anymore.

Jimmy was a pariah with their old crowd now; they'd circled the wagons, and he was Cochise. Her girlfriends had sniped about him, thinking commiseration would make her feel better. It didn't.

But what Jimmy hadn't destroyed of her good name, Char'd done herself.

Salina took a step to the driver's door, glancing into the dim interior. "Oh, hey, Mr. Enwright. How you gettin' on?" Char knew from her father's owlish stare that he didn't remember the girl who had practically lived at his house during Char's high school years.

Salina turned from the window. "You're going to need some help here soon, Sweetie. I know, from what my mother went through with my grandma." Her stage whisper could have been heard from the road. "I have the name of a good facility. You just let me know."

The pump clicked off, releasing Char. She hung the nozzle with jerky movements and stepped to the cab. "Well, it was nice seeing you, Sal. I've really got to get moving." Opening the door, she scooted inside before her friend could give her a hug. She started the engine and pulled out, not looking back at what she knew would be a hurt look.

Char pulled to the front of the store, hands shaking on the wheel. Maybe Salina could put her grandma in a facility, but if they came to take *her* daddy from his home, they'd better come with a gun. She parked, shut down the engine, and turned to her father. "Daddy, will you go in with me?" She patted his cold hand. "You can drink coffee with your buddies while I order feed, okay?" He nodded and fumbled with the seat belt.

They walked to the blond, brick-fronted building. The cowbell on the glass door clanked when she pushed it open. A blast of heat and the familiar smell of grain, cigarette smoke, and dust would have told her where she was with her eyes closed. Her father removed his cowboy hat as he stepped onto the dirty linoleum of the showroom. Sacks of goat chow, cartons of sheep dip, and bales of chicken wire lined the walls. Bulletin board flyers ruffled in the breeze from the open door.

"Well, look what the wind kicked up!" Ben was hailed by the gaggle of old men who lounged around a scarred linoleum-and-chrome table from the 1960s, smoking cigarettes and drinking coffee.

"Hey, Ben," the feed store owner, an obese, grizzled old-timer in overalls, called out. "Get yourself over here. I can't be the only voice of reason in this group of jackasses."

Her father broke into a huge grin. "Well, Junior, you should know not to socialize with polecats and Democrats." He ambled to the table and dropped into a rickety chair.

"I'll be in the back, okay, Daddy?" Her father waved her off, already sucked into the spirited argument of local politics. Funny how some faces clicked for him and others didn't. The doctors had warned her the disease would progress, in spite of the medicine.

She pushed open the swinging doors to the business side of the store, a cavernous pole barn. Pallets of feed for every domestic animal in East Texas towered in racks; parts and tools nestled along the walls. A fake wood-paneled counter faced her, covered in seed flyers and John Deere parts catalogs.

At the end stood a woman perusing a dog-eared catalog—a woman Char had never met but recognized from the gossip. This was that Yankee who'd moved in a few months back. *Just where do you go to get an outfit like that?* Red shortie cowgirl boots, a lacy black square-dance miniskirt puffed with petticoats, a white bustier cut down to *there*, and a black lace bolero jacket. Char swallowed, attempting to focus on the woman's features. A nimbus of black curls overwhelmed her deathly pale, sharp-boned foxy face. Huge dream-catcher earrings bobbed with her every move. *She looks like Dolly Parton gone Goth.*

Clannggg! Char jumped at a horrific crash from the back of the barn. It sounded like someone had dropped something heavy against a metal wall, and the tall ceiling amplified the sound. The woman looked up, glaring at the pallet racks. "Damn it, Travis!" The shrill New York accent echoed. "Will you quit fiddle-fucking around? You tear down the place, your uncle Junior's gonna eat your bony ass for lunch!"

She must have heard Char's sharp intake of breath, because she turned and leveled a stony look at her sole customer. "Nepotism is not a good idea when your family tree doesn't branch." She took a loose-hipped stroll behind the counter.

Char stood, open-mouthed. When the woman's eyes narrowed, Char scrabbled for something to say before she could get started on her. "I need food."

A raven eyebrow arched. "You may not have noticed; this isn't a restaurant."

"Not for me." Her face heated. "For my cattle." She clasped her hands behind her back to get rid of them. "Well, actually, they're not my cattle. I only collect the bulls' semen."

The eyebrow went higher and the woman stared as if Char were an odd bug.

The word in the coffee shop was that this Yankee was single and, since she'd taken a job with all-male clientele, was looking for action. Toni Bergstrom, the town's most reliable gossip, said the feed store job was only to recruit for her part-time job. A woman's *oldest* part-time job.

Who was this woman to judge her? "Oh, I don't think I need to explain to you."

The raven-haired harpy planted her fists on her hips. "Listen, honey, don't you get all snotty with me. I don't give a good goddamn if you get the semen the old-fashioned way. Just tell me what brand of feed you want, and how much."

The sound of a two-stroke engine fired up in the back and got louder at an alarming rate. They both turned to the warehouse as a four-wheeler loaded with feed sacks slid from around a corner, going too fast.

A lanky teenager in sunglasses and a backward baseball cap leaned almost horizontally over the handlebars, bony elbows waving as he barreled across the floor. When he hit a patch of spilled grain, he cut the handlebars to the left, and the four-wheeler spun in a series of donuts across the floor in front of the two women.

"Travis! You sap-headed Dumpster monkey! Get off that thing before you hurt something!" The woman rolled her eyes, turned back to Char, and, in a strident voice, said, "What can I get your majesty?"

Char opened her mouth to speak, then realized she hadn't written down the brand off the feed sack. *Come on, Char, focus*. Netting, covered in paper. What color? Her sluggish brain sorted facts with slothlike speed as the woman stood staring in pointed disinterest.

Silence spun out.

The heck with the brand, how much should she buy? The cattle seemed content with the two bags this morning, but if they're pregnant, maybe they needed more. *Who am I to know?* All she wanted was to get back to the sanctuary of her own kitchen. Instead, she'd fallen through a looking glass with a push of the warehouse's swinging doors. Off-kilter and overwhelmed, Char did the only thing that could embarrass herself further. She burst into tears.

Not just tears. Gulping, gut-wrenching, snot-inducing sobs. The Ugly Cry.

• • •

JB let the heavy door to the arena close behind him and tilted his hat to block the sliver of sundown that sliced his brain like a hot poker, his head throbbing to the beat of amplifier echo. His carryall brushed his leg as he walked to the parking lot, empty save a few cars, trash fluttering in the sporadic breeze. The silhouette of his Peterbilt towered over the sedans, and he sighed seeing the crowd that surrounded it.

He walked up, shaking his head. "There is no way all of you are going to fit in that cab. Y'all are going to have to call a taxi."

Mitzi stepped up and took the carryall from his hand. "We've got it all worked out, We can fit eight in the sleeper and, if we squeeze, four more in the cab." Beseeching eyes searched his face. "Oh, come on, JB. It's not very far. It'll be fun!" The crowd agreed, anxious to get the evening started.

JB remembered when this would have been a lark; now all he thought about was the legal ramifications. When had that shift happened? *What the hell.* "Okay." The couples high-fived each other and walked to the cab. JB reached into his pocket for the keys. "But." The kids turned to him. "If I get a ticket, ya'll are anteing up to pay it. You got that?" They nodded, and he caught the humor-the-old-man look that passed between Josh and Andy out of the corner of his eye.

It must be nice, not having responsibilities. JB was used to them. His parents had been killed by a drunk driver on their way home from a monthly movie date when he was just a toddler. He'd been raised in a loving home by his grandparents, but they were elderly even then. Luckily his shoulders had grown fast enough to handle the responsibilities of the family farm. He was in high school when his grandfather died, killing JB's dreams of community college. He took over, making sure that Grams had enough.

He smiled, watching the laughing couples pile into the truck. Maybe a lark was exactly what he needed.

JB did a triple step, hesitated, then turned. The band was on a break, and Billy Currington wailed "That's How Country Boys Roll" on the jukebox. JB cocked his hat, did a shuffle step, kicked, and turned. When the song ended, and he strolled off the dance floor, his bum hip shooting a hollow ache down the long bone of his leg. *Nothing another Bud won't fix.* He sank gratefully into his chair.

The mood in the bar was raucous. The bull riders celebrated their triumphant rides or, at least, surviving the dismount. No small feat in a sport when your turn wasn't over until you outran the wicked horns of an enraged one-ton animal.

The bar was packed to the walls with PBR riders, roadies, production people, and fans. "Hey, JB," Stony Brewer yelled above the crowd noise. "When I get to the championship round, I'm picking Mighty Mouse. If you make his first corner, you can win the round on him."

JB smiled at the fresh-faced farm kid from Wyoming. They got younger every year. "You'd best worry about your next bull first, son."

Cody Tanner leaned around the girlfriend in his lap. "Yeah, Stony. You won't get no mother's milk outta Bombadier. He's got bad timing to go with the attitude."

The riders argued about their draw in the next round as the band shuffled back in. With the crash of the first guitar riff, any attempt at conversation died. *Why do they have to crank the amps so hard? Jesus, we're sitting twenty feet away.* Judging by the happy faces around the table, JB figured his opinion was in the minority.

He looked around the room. When had he gotten to be the oldest one there?

The drum backbeat of Carrie Underwood's "Cowboy Casanova" reverberated in his chest as the girls around the table rose as one and strutted to the floor.

The female lead belted out the lyrics in a sultry, breathy voice, and the dancers added the bumps and grinds. Every male eye in the place lasered in on the dance floor.

JB watched breasts bounce and hips roll in skintight jeans, back pocket rhinestones flashing in the lights.

Char had loved to dance, back in the day. But she never would have danced like that. He felt his face heat. Call him old fashioned, but stuff like that should be saved for the bedroom.

He glanced around. Barely a thirty-year-old in the crowd. What was he doing here? A limping old lone wolf in a pack of paired-up pups. He'd never noticed the age difference when he'd been with Jess.

God, had he spent the past four months an oblivious poster child for midlife crisis?

"Oh, heck, shoot me and have it over with," Char blubbered. The woman had handed her a paper towel from behind the counter, and Char'd been too embarrassed to look up since. "I didn't mean to be snotty with you. I'm just not having a good day. I almost got my daddy killed, we're out of feed for our danged heifers, and I have no idea of what brand or how much we need—much less how I'll get it unloaded when we get home." Char took a breath. She honked into the damp paper towel to make herself stop babbling. "And I'm late getting my father home for his medicine."

A snort came from behind the counter. Char raised her head. The woman stood hands on hips, face expressionless. "That blows. What you need first is a cup of coffee." She strolled to the glass door, hips rolling. "Do not move. I'll be right back."

By the time Char caught her breath and finished mopping her face, the woman had returned, thrusting a Styrofoam cup of sludgy-looking gray liquid at her.

"This should buck you up, but don't drink the whole thing. The dregs could be lethal."

"Thanks." Char took a sip and winced. Junior's coffee was infamous. His patrons claimed the local mortuary used it as embalming fluid.

"Why don't you tell me your name, and I'll look up what brand you get from your past orders."

Jeez, why couldn't I have thought of that? "I'm Charla Rae Denny."

"JB Denny's wife? Well, hell, why didn't you say so to begin with?" The woman's face lit up. In spite of her front teeth being a bit crooked, she really was pretty when she smiled. "I've got a pallet of feed on the loading dock with your name on it. Emilio was supposed to pick it up two days ago."

Char winced again, but not from the coffee. The

clerk really was an outsider if she hadn't heard the juiciest gossip to hit this town since the justice of the peace and his male clerk were found snuggling on his office couch.

"By the way, I'm Bella Donovan." She turned, cupped her hands around her mouth, and yelled, "Travis! Get your furry butt up here. You've got a customer!"

An hour later, Char turned into the long drive to the house, grateful to be home at last. The crying jag seemed to have wrung the last bit of starch from her; even holding the steering wheel took effort. She drove the truck to the back of the house, grateful for the evening shadows that cloaked the yard. Even so, she couldn't help seeing the tree stump as the truck rounded the corner.

She pulled to the barn and cut the engine. "Let's go in, Daddy. I'll put some dinner on." What, exactly, she had no idea. She glanced in the rearview mirror at the feed bags stacked against the back window. *I'll worry about that tomorrow.*

Her father came around, opened her door, and handed her out. He wrapped her hand over his arm and, patting it, said, "It was a good day, Charla Rae."

She looked up at his smiling face. There was no telling; he could be remembering a day from twenty years ago. They called it sundowner's syndrome because his memory got worse with nightfall. She sighed and squeezed his arm. "Yes, Daddy, a good day."

They'd only gone a few steps when the sound of another vehicle coming up the drive silenced the evening birdsong. Headlights swept as a stakebed truck rounded the turn, blinding them. Pulling abreast, the tinted window unrolled. Char recognized Travis, the kid from the feed store.

"Bella sent me to unload. Where should I put it?"

Char's shoulders slumped in relief. *Thank you, Jesus.* And Bella-Goth Dolly-Donovan.

CHAPTER 4

The reward for work well done is the opportunity to do more.

—Jonas Salk

CJ Denny Bucking Bulls, Charla speaking." Her new job nixed the luxury of ignoring the phone. It could mean business. She'd learned at least that much in the past week.

"Missus Denny? I am Rosa Castillo, from Pedernales County Senior Services," a melodic, Hispanic-accented voice said. "Reverend Mike asked me to call. He said you may need some help with your father."

Char jerked to attention so fast her vertebrae clicked. *The county?* "We don't need the government's help. We're doing fine." Dang it, why wouldn't do-gooders just leave her be? She hadn't been to church since...well, it had been awhile. The voice coming out of the handset on the way to the cradle caught her attention.

"—free nursing help."

She returned the receiver to her ear. "You're a nurse?"

"A nurse assistant. I give in-home care to Alzheimer and dementia patients."

Char looked at her father sitting on his bed, shirt buttoned cockeyed. She'd been helping him dress when the phone rang. He studied the boot in his hand as if he had no idea what it was used for. She could hear the bawl of hungry cattle from here, and she hadn't even put the coffee on yet. "I'm sorry, I don't have time to talk right now."

"I could make an appointment to come out and tell you about it. You'd want to meet me, and I'd like to meet your father."

The idea of government help rankled. Her family had always taken care of their own. But her family was now down to her and her father. Char knew she couldn't ignore the reality of her dad's condition any longer. Not after yesterday's fiasco. "Hang on, Daddy. I'll help you with that." He tugged at the boot that he'd put on the wrong foot. "Listen, I really have to go. But I probably need to hear more about this. When can you come out?"

Two hours later, she waved to her father as he and Junior strolled up the Double D ranch's drive. As much as it stung her pride to ask for help, she'd forced herself to call over to Junior's and see if he'd mind a visit from his old sidekick. Luckily, he'd been elated.

Char didn't pretend to understand the odd friendship. She had to smile at Junior's massive backside in overalls, waddling beside her tall, lean father. Their personalities were the flip sides of a coin as well; her dad's Atticus Finch to Junior's Vinnie Gambini. Local legend had it that the two had torn up the countryside when they were in high school. Hard to imagine.

She sighed and backed the truck down the drive. A long day of work waited at home. She gritted her teeth. "*Without* a pill."

Char eyed the massive white thunderheads piled on the horizon, hoping they didn't mean what they probably did. At the bottom of the drive, she pulled out her cell phone and dialed the number on the grimy business card paper-clipped to the sun visor. Her mother had taught her to do the job she dreaded most first. She hit *send* and pulled out onto the deserted farm road.

"Junior's Feed & Seed." The harsh Yankee accent barked from the speakerphone.

"Hello, Ms. Donovan. This is Charla Rae Denny." Her words came out in a rush. "I wanted to call and thank you for sending your boy out to unload for me the other night."

Silence, then a throaty chuckle. "Hey, looked to me like you got a weasel deal. Fuggedaboudit."

"Um. Yes. Well, thank you again."

"Hey, Charla Rae. You wanna have coffee sometime?"

"Oh." She pictured herself sitting in a booth at the coffee shop, every eye in the place glued to the two of them. "I'm sorry. That would be nice, but I'm so busy. I have the cattle to care for, and my father..."

Bella's voice could freeze meat. "Yeah. Whatever." *Click.*

Char's conscience pricked as she closed the phone and tucked it into her shirt pocket. The woman was brash and dressed like a floozy. But...Char recalled the rush of relief she'd felt when Travis pulled up in the yard. Her mother had taught her better.

Topping a hill a quarter mile from their land, Char slammed on the brakes. In the middle of the road, not twenty feet from her bumper, stood a cow. It turned. Not just any cow. *Her* cow.

She didn't know many of the stock on sight. Mighty

Mouse, of course, and Kid Charlemagne, their best buckers. Most of the heifers didn't even have names, just numbers. But not this one. Tricks chewed her cud, staring at the truck as if wondering what it was doing on her road. Jimmy had spent too much money to buy this granddaughter of the legendary Houdini. So far, all she'd lived up to was her granddaddy's name, escaping from an intact fence.

"Dadburn it!" Char actually reached for the phone in her breast pocket to call Jimmy, then let her hand fall to the door handle. She stepped from the truck, keeping the door between her and the massively pregnant black-and-white spotted cow.

"Shoo!" She waved her arms. "You get home now, y'hear?" When the curious cow walked over, Char scooted into the cab, slammed the door, and yelled out the rolled-up window, "Get off the road, you dumb broad!" She beeped the horn, but Tricks just sniffed the windshield, smearing green drool. She strutted like a bovine diva to the opposite side of the road to partake of the high grass in the bar ditch.

"I do *not* have time for this." Char put the truck in gear and hit the gas. She had to saddle a horse and get back here ASAP. Jimmy had artificially inseminated Tricks with semen straws from Dillinger, the two-time PBR Bull of the Year. Just as the heart to run was passed down in Thoroughbred horses, the urge to buck could be passed down in bulls. She knew they'd be able to sell the calf for big dollars, even before it was old enough to be bucked. But Jimmy had no intention of selling. He had visions of standing in the arena, accepting the Bull of the Year award at the finals in Las Vegas. Char's wants were smaller. They revolved around an orange bottle on the kitchen windowsill and the oblivion of bed.

When she got home, she jumped out of the truck, ran for the barn and horse bait. She jogged to the yard, eyeing the shaggy horses grazing in the field. Standing outside the fence, she banged the bucket of oats on the slats to get their attention. Char gulped as they trotted over. Jimmy had always teased her about it; she'd grown up on a ranch, the daughter of a champion barrel racer and an all-around champion cowboy, yet she was afraid of horses. She forced her shoulders back. She knew how to ride. She wasn't afraid, exactly. They were just so—large.

Jimmy had even bought her a horse as a Christmas present a few years ago, figuring the petite palomino would help her get over her aversion. Char had gotten on Buttermilk a few times, but her house chores and Benje had come first, so her mare mostly languished in the pasture, getting fat. That blond head was the first through the fence to grab the oats, and Char slapped a hackamore on before she could bolt. "Come on, Pork Chop, we're on a mission." Jimmy's nickname had stuck to the rotund, pint-size mare.

Char cross-tied her horse in the barn aisle, gave her a quick brush, picked out her hooves, then went in search of her saddle. She found it, in a dark corner of the tack room, dusty as an antique in the back of a curio shop. One more thing to put on the list of things to be done, a list that would surely be as long as her arm by now, if only she had time to write it down.

"Oomph." Dang, why did these things have to be so heavy? Her arms shook, holding Western saddle high enough that the stirrups wouldn't drag in the dirt. It took her two tries to throw it over Pork Chop's broad back.

"Now, you're going to be a lady, right?" Char lectured while tying the cinch. "Ladies have good manners, mince their steps, and never, ever run."

The horse's ears pricked when Char unsnapped the tethers. "There's a sweet girl. You and I are going to get on famously, I have no doubt." None she wanted to express, anyway.

Char squashed the bugs flying around in her stomach, gathered the reins, and put her foot in the stirrup. The palomino sidestepped, swinging her hips away. Char took a startled hop, clutching the saddle like a lifeline. The mare stepped away again. Char hopped after her until she could wrestle her boot out of the stirrup. They now faced the back of the barn. Char put a hand to her chest to slow her galloping heart. If something bad happened, there'd be no one looking for her for hours. Visions of being dragged through the brush, one foot caught in the stirrup, did nothing good for her courage quotient.

I could call over to the Sweeneys'. They said if I needed anything...She imagined word getting around town, people *tsking* and shaking their heads. Poor Charla Rae. The banked fire flared.

"Now listen, you." She grabbed both sides of the hackamore, pulling the mare's face to hers. "I don't want to do this either. But it has to be done, and by God we're going to do it, if I have to drag your fat butt at the end of the reins the whole way." She tugged the mare by the head to stand alongside the stalls and, gathering the reins once more, crammed her foot in the stirrup and swung aboard before the nag could escape.

"Now *move*, Pork Chop." After a not-so-gentle nudge in the ribs, the mare clopped out of the barn. Char neck-reined her to the right at the bottom of the driveway, and they ambled along the side of the road.

A breeze brushed Char's face, bringing a rich scent of tilled earth from the field across the road. She closed her eyes and breathed deep the pungent perfume. "Now, this isn't so bad." The horse's ears swiveled, listening. The rhythmic clopping lulled Char's tense muscles. She'd forgotten how much you could see from horseback. The gentle hills dressed in early spring green, dotted with towering oaks, rolled away. Looking down, she spotted her first bluebonnet of the year, bravely flowering all alone at the fence line. Her mouth twisted. *That counselor was right about one thing. Life* does *go on. Whether you want it to or not.*

Before she'd gotten pregnant with Benje, Jimmy would push her to ride the herd with him as the sun went down. She sighed. Those days seemed a different lifetime now. The sun on her body melted the tautness, freeing some unnamed emotion to well in her, rising painful and glorious. A single tear spilled over, running to her smile.

The horse's head came up and her ears pricked. Tricks stood in the bar ditch, not fifty yards ahead, making good inroads into the deep grass.

"Yippie ki-yay, Pork Chop." Char nudged the mare to a faster walk. Tricks eyed them warily when they ambled past, ignoring her. Once by, Char reined the horse around. Pork Chop snapped from somnolence. Char felt muscles cord under her. The mare strained at the bit, taking mincing steps. "Easy now." Char tightened the reins, alarmed at her lazy horse turned charger.

Tricks took one look at them and bolted straight across the road. Pork Chop galloped after her. Char panicked, lost a stirrup, and grabbed for the horn, sawing at the reins with the other hand. She whipped her head in both directions. The road lay blessedly empty.

Tricks turned left, away from the ranch. Ears laid back, Pork Chop gained on the lumbering mama cow. Char, a frightened, flopping observer, clung to the horn with both hands, scrabbling for her lost stirrup, heart beating in her ears louder than the horse's hooves.

Pork Chop galloped alongside the straining cow and, leaning in, turned her neatly toward the ranch. About the time Char gained her stirrup and gathered the reins, the cow gave up and dropped to a walk, sides heaving. In the onslaught of adrenaline pouring into her bloodstream, Char's giddyup got up and went. Her mount slowed, and within a few steps morphed once more to her pudgy, staid horse. "Wow, Pork Chop, who knew?" Char relaxed a bit but kept a tight hold on the reins and the saddle horn, just in case.

When the ranch drive came up on their left, Char touched her heels to the horse's sides and Pork Chop broke into a trot. Char actually helped this time, reining the horse to show her where to lead the now-docile cow. They clattered once more across the road and up the drive. Tricks's ears perked when she spied her compatriots in the field, and she trotted to the gate as if she'd been lost all this time, trying to find her way home.

Char reined the horse to the gate, leaned over, and opened it. Tricks sauntered in with a swish of her tail, ignoring the peon who held the door for her regal highness. Char shook her head. Another hour gone, and not one chore on her list checked off.

"Why couldn't we have owned a hardware store, where the inventory sits on a shelf, not running around trying to commit suicide?" She checked twice to be sure the gate latched.

Reins tight, in case the palomino got a mind to wander, Char kicked her feet out of the stirrups and slid from the saddle. As her feet hit the ground, the long muscle in the right thigh seized, a bolus of agony shooting to her groin.

"Arrghh!" She clung to the saddle, frozen, until the knot loosened. She waited another few minutes to be sure it was gone. Running a light hand down her thigh, she assessed the damage. It felt like a half-thawed chicken: nasty mushy on top, rock hard underneath.

She leaned her forehead against the saddle, kneading her thigh, the fear of another cramp all that kept her from running to the cocoon of her kitchen and the little orange bottle that called to her.

Scenes of what could have been flashed in her mind: a car on the road, Pork Chop slipping on the pavement and going down, Tricks going into labor from all the running. Char raised her head and pushed herself upright. "Thank you, Lord for watching over this poor fool."

A docile Pork Chop followed as Char limped to the barn.

Jimmy would never believe she'd attempt this, let alone get it done. She patted the blond mane bobbing beside her. "Stallions. We don't need them, do we girl?"

JB smacked a palm to his head and reached for the cell phone in his breast pocket. He hit speed dial, ignoring Wylie's raised eyebrows across a table littered with dirty breakfast dishes. JB put a finger in his other ear to block the babble from the busy restaurant. "Come on, some-body answer."

"Junior's Feed & Seed," the Yank-slang voice barked.

"This is JB Denny. You've got a pallet of feed on the dock for me. Can I get it delivered?" He checked his watch. "Today?"

"No."

"Oh, hell. Come on, New York. Help me out here."

"What kinda man leaves his wife alone, no help, no feed?"

Too late. JB felt the back of his neck heat. How could he have forgotten? Busy with recriminations, his automatic answer of the past months slipped out. "Not my wife any longer."

"Oh. Well then, why didn't you say so?" *Click*.

The heat spread up his neck. He deserved that. "Shit." He flipped the phone closed.

"You ready to talk about it, JB?" Wylie shot a knowing look over his coffee cup.

"Nope." He took a mouthful of coffee, more to have something to do than for the caffeine.

Wylie seemed to consider his words before he spoke. "Look. Everybody knows what happened. On the outside." His friend leaned in. "But I've known you for ten years. Leaving his wife, then messing around on her, is not something the JB Denny I know would do." Wylie's eyes bored into his. "Either I don't know you as well as I thought, or there's more to this story. So I'm asking you: Are you ready to talk about it?"

JB remembered the warm nights, moonlight turning the room into a stark negative photo. The two of them lying in bed, neither sleeping, but pretending to, the long white strip of sheet between them an impenetrable wall. JB knew, because he'd beaten himself bloody against it so many nights. *There's more than one way to leave a marriage.*

"Nope." JB put his cup down and grabbed his hat. "But thanks."

Later that afternoon, JB shot the last bolt to the trailer and turned to sign the release form held by a coliseum employee. He patted the side of the trailer on his way to the cab. His bulls had brought the goods this weekend. Even the youngsters bucked well.

Futurity events gave stock contractors the chance to see how their youngsters compared to the competition by attempting to buck a small robot off their backs. A bull might be born to buck, but they all needed training. These competitions also helped them get used to traveling, disruption of their routines, and crowd noise.

JB reached for the door handle of the cab, his glance falling to the stickered logo on the door. He could still see the shadow of "& Son" in an outline of glue between "Denny" and "Bucking Bulls." He tried to ignore the surgical stab of guilt between his ribs and climbed up into the rumbling cab, then cranked the A/C and put the truck in gear. The adrenaline of the event had burned off, leaving the dregs of exhaustion pulling at the last of his energy. He wasn't sleeping well.

It was always the same dream. It started out good, in the beginning. He'd actually put the chores off and built Benje the tree fort he'd pestered for. He let the boy help, and the memory of his earnest face, red hair falling in his eyes, tongue caught in his teeth as he pounded a nail tightened JB's chest. Then the dream spiraled into the nightmare of reality. It had been a day like many before it but none after. He'd been in the barn, repairing tack, when he'd heard her scream. He knew then. Not what had happened, but that life had just irreparably been altered.

It was *his* job to keep his family safe—to keep the wolf from the door. The lancet of blame cut deeper. While he'd been on guard at the front, that goddamn wolf snuck in the back, stealing his most precious possession.

He pressed on the gas and headed for whatever awaited at home.

CHAPTER 5

*If we could sell our experiences for what they cost us,
we'd all be millionaires.*

—*Abigail Van Buren*

Charla leaned on the shopping cart, hobbling a bit
as she cruised the cereal aisle. Her groin muscles pro-
tested. Pork Chop's wide back had pushed them past their
limit, and now she couldn't quite hold her legs together.
She'd almost skipped Walmart this afternoon, but she
was out of everything. Her lower back gave an alarming
tweak, threatening spasm. She stopped in the main aisle,
straightened, and put a fist to the muscles of her lower
back.

Delighted laughter came from behind. Though carefree was a distant memory for Charla, happiness was still
an irresistible force. She turned.

The blonde she'd last seen perched on the seat of Jimmy's truck stood laughing, hanging on the considerable
bicep of a young man in a T-shirt and cowboy hat. Their
faces glowed with enchantment for each other. They stood

in the center of the aisle, oblivious to the shoppers who veered around them.

She knew that feeling. Char hurtled back in time, to when she and Jimmy had existed in a shiny bubble of new love and the rest of the world seemed separate, extraneous. Her hand stole to her chest, to rub the ache that spread like a bruise.

There was no way a woman could feel like that with more than one man at a time.

Jimmy had told the truth. This time.

Guilt-tipped talons pinched her heart.

She turned away, pushing her cart into the next aisle. Dropping a box of generic shredded wheat into the basket, Char punched the price into her calculator. The cookie aisle was out. She still had to buy her father's prescription, and she was not putting all this on a credit card. Especially since she hadn't yet checked out the business finances.

Scanning the boxes of cereal, her gaze snagged on Benje's favorite brand. Her fingers tightened on the cart handle. How dare it still be here when he wasn't?

She'd gotten pretty good at steeling herself against these little jabs to the heart, small wounds that drained her if she didn't avoid minefields like the toy section or the kid's clothing department. *But how do you shield your heart from Count Chocula?* Her finger traced the cartoon vampire on the box, then she made herself move on. If someone found her sobbing over a box of cereal, they'd probably haul her away. *Cleanup on aisle six!* Lord, she wanted a pill so badly her skin crawled. Surely she'd earned it today.

After chasing down that fool cow, she'd put out hay.

Jimmy always made it look easy, manhandling the bales. Lifting her palm, she tested a blister she'd gotten in spite of the gloves. Char had discovered that in a wrestling match with a hundred-pound bale against her one-twenty, she could hold her own—barely. Sighing, she dropped her hands back to the cart handle and pushed. Standing here licking her wounds wasn't getting it done.

She took a left at the end of the aisle while checking out the line at the prescription counter. *Krssh!* The impact of the cart collision traveled up her forearms. "Oh, I'm sor—" Bella Donovan looked as startled as Char felt. A hopeful look flashed across Bella's face before the usual mask of jaded indifference fell.

That quick glimpse was the last push Char needed. "Bella! I've been thinking about you." Char glanced down at her cart, noting it held nothing that wouldn't stand a ten-minute break. "Do you have time for that cup of coffee?"

The woman looked down her sharp nose and snorted. "Here?"

Bella's outfit today was as unfortunate as yesterday's— white fringed boots, a white lacy cowgirl hat, and, in between, a micro denim skirt and a long-sleeved leopard leotard with a plummeting neckline.

"Hey, if you can drink Junior's sludge, Walmart coffee should be ambrosia. I'm buying."

"Oh, all right," Bella said with wary look. "But I've only got a few minutes." She did an about-face and led the way to the fast food area.

Char couldn't look away from Bella's heart-shape rear. *At least she has the body to carry off the getups she wears.*

They parked their partially loaded baskets in the Kart Korral, with its ridiculous Western theme, and were served coffee in Styrofoam cups with running horses on the sides. A small, guilty part of her made Char sit with her back to the store. She hated to give the local women any more fat to chew on. Bella slid her long legs into the other side of the orange plastic booth.

Now that she was here, Char didn't know what to say. She hadn't imagined this scene that far ahead. "Well. How do you like our little town so far?"

"I think the place needs a good mechanic."

Char cocked her head. "What do you mean?"

"I have to think the Welcome Wagon is just busted. I've lived here three months, and you're the first woman I've had a halfway friendly conversation with."

Bella wasn't quite wrong about the women in town. Char felt her face flush. "Where did you live before?"

"New York." Bella rolled heavily mascaraed eyes. "I know, the accent *is* subtle." She smiled, taking the sting out of the words. "Russ got transferred down here, and he's traveling a lot."

She must have seen surprise on Char's face. Bella reached up and tugged on a gold chain around her neck. A diamond wedding band strung at the end of it popped out of the band of spandex. "Yeah, yeah, I know. I'm the whore home-wrecker all you ladies are afraid of. I overheard all the gossip from under the dryer at Macie's Clip 'n Curl.

"I guess you're not afraid to talk to me because you have no man for me to steal, right?"

Char's hand jerked, and coffee slopped onto the table. She jumped up. "Now, that was mean, Bella Donovan."

She grabbed napkins with one hand to mop up the mess, reaching for her purse with the other. "I can vouch for almost every person in this town, and for the most part, they're good, honest people." As she glared across the table, her groping hand finally found the strap of her purse on the back of the chair, and she tugged it over her shoulder. "And I'm the woman who was trying to have a friendly conversation with you."

"Don't get your thong in a twist, East Texas. I didn't mean anything by it."

Char finished mopping up the mess and shoved the sodden napkins in the cup.

Bella sat back. "Look, I'm sorry to take it out on you. I have a feeling that you can relate to how it feels to be the source of gossip." She stood and put her hand on Char's arm, stopping her. "And I'm sorry for your boy too, Char."

There was no pity in Bella's gaze. Concern, yes, and regret. But no pity. Maybe Bella had a point. Maybe they did have something in common, after all. The anger receded as quickly as it had advanced. Char sniffed. "I accept your apology."

Bella's dark, canny eyes searched hers. "You know, Char, sometimes it's easier to talk to someone you didn't get sand in your diaper with in the neighborhood park." Bella reached for her purse. "I have to get going too. Russ is coming home tonight for the first time in three weeks, and I have to get sexy for him." She wriggled, tugging the hem of her skirt down.

Char lifted an eyebrow. "I think you're done already."

Bella looked up and barked a surprised laugh. "You know, Charla Rae, you may be a little odd, but you're okay."

Char eyed Bella's getup. *I'm odd?*

They threw away their trash and walked to the shopping carts. Bella was right about one thing. It *would* be easier to talk to someone who didn't know the old Char—the little ranch wife who went about her charmed life, unaware that it could vaporize in a moment. She dropped her purse in her cart and turned to Bella. "Have you ever seen a working cattle ranch?"

"Hon, I'm from the Bronx." Bella's dark curls swung as she shook her head. "The only cow I've come close to came on a bun."

JB set the glass of iced tea on the battered coffee table and sat, automatically avoiding the lump in his butt-sprung couch. He crossed his stocking feet next to the two-inch pile of bills on the table and balanced the laptop on his legs. The spreadsheet didn't look any better than it had five minutes ago.

Might as well face facts. As crappy as this apartment was, he couldn't afford it. The business couldn't support two households. Not without more bulls.

Buckers that he didn't have the cash to buy.

He glanced around the depressing, battle-scarred equivalent to a college dorm. He'd stayed when Jess moved out, not wanting the hassle of moving. That had been a mistake. Only the last in a long string of mistakes.

He could see now that Jess had just been a distraction. A Band-Aid, slapped on the shark-bite hole Benje's loss had made in him. He was an idiot. It wasn't bad enough that everyone in town knew it. But the truth was that a twenty-year-old coed figured it out before he had.

Jess had broken up with *him*. He snorted. She'd tried to let him down easy. There was apparently no limit to humiliation.

He remembered Char's expression, when she'd thought he'd now taken up with Mitzi. The sour twist of distaste on her lips, the look in her eye—like he was a toothless bum, stumbling out of a Dumpster into her path.

Why is it I seem to spend my life disappointing the people who matter to me?

Char carefully placed the glass of water and a pill on the edge of the computer table. It would be her reward after finishing her last chore of the day. The padded office chair squeaked as she sank into it, the seat so worn it retained the imprint of Jimmy's backside.

She felt bad, feeding her dad a quick dinner, dispensing his medicine, and hustling him off to bed. They'd fallen into the habit of spending evenings in the great room, her reading to him from a book by McMurtry, Zane Grey, or Elmer Kelton. Tonight, though, she was flat tuckered.

Yawning, she started the computer. Sleep wouldn't come until she had some idea of their finances. One more job of Jimmy's that had fallen to her the day she booted him off the property. How did he ever keep up with it all?

"Practice, I guess." She muttered, staring at the login screen for their accounting software. Password? She tapped in the first number that occurred to her, the date of their anniversary. The program popped open to the business checking account. A single, sparkly bubble rose from the depth of her mind. "Nobody changes those things once they set them." The bubble popped.

The balance wasn't as bad as she feared or as good as she'd hoped. Char did the math. Even a high school kid wouldn't work for what profit remained.

She visualized days like today, one after another, marching into the foreseeable future. The figures on the screen blurred. "I cannot do this. I'm not equipped to do this." Hearing it aloud made it real. This was impossible.

She stripped off her reading glasses, put her head on the desk, and let the tears come. It wasn't fair. Every woman she knew had time to go to the beauty shop, garden, read. She glanced at the clock on the screen. Here she was doing bookwork at midnight. Heck, even Bella Donovan had a husband to go home to.

Whoa up here, Charla Rae. The last thing she needed to add to this mess was another man. She'd barely survived the first one. Lifting her head, she grabbed a tissue and honked into it. "All right, dang it, this is the end of the pity party." Sitting up straight, she put her glasses on and stared at the screen.

Short of going hungry or cutting off the heat, there was no way to reduce expenses in any way that mattered. That left only the other side of the equation. She opened her Internet browser.

The judge had offered her alimony in the divorce settlement, but the thought of standing with her hand out, waiting for Jimmy to dole out money, stuck in her craw. After what he'd done, she wanted him as far out of her life as possible.

Not long after their separation, she'd heard the rumors.

Jimmy had taken up with a girl half his age. Char had even seen them together, eating lunch at the diner in town. Jimmy'd sworn the gossips had it wrong, that she was only a vet student he was mentoring. Char didn't think anything of it because he'd done that before, helping college students gain experience while he got a cut rate on vet bills. But in the past the students had always been men.

Separated or not, she and Jimmy were still married in the eyes of God. Jimmy said he wasn't dating the girl and she'd believed him. JB Denny didn't lie.

Char put her elbows on the desk and dropped her hot cheeks in her hands. Her head couldn't fathom it, but the brass-knuckled lies had battered that fact into her heart. This man wasn't the one she'd married. That Jimmy Denny was as dead to her as her son.

Now Jimmy owned the bulls, and she owned the ranch. The judge finally ruled that any proceeds from the business would be considered a combination of alimony and lease payment for pastureland. Money Jimmy earned as announcer for the PBR, or any other job he took, was his.

A bolt of insight jarred her shell-shocked brain. What had really changed? She'd left the finances to Jimmy, same as she always had. He'd been keeping the books, tapping into the home computer from his laptop. She was still standing in front of Jimmy with her hand out.

"Jeez, Char. Where have you been all these months?" She shuddered. Nowhere she wanted to think about. Or go back to.

The revenue split sounded great in theory, yet with the increased expenses...

She cruised the Internet, pricing semen from other PBR bulls. This was the risky side of investment. A bull could be an amazing bucker but not pass that ability to the next generation. Proven sires were few and far between, and their semen straws fetched a pretty penny. Well, Mighty Mouse's son had been a top futurity bull last year, and that should count for something. She checked out Yosemite Sam's straw price. He'd retired a two-time Bull of the Year four years ago. The Mouse was his son, so...she compared the price of a straw of Mighty Mouse's semen to the market. It was too low. She was sure of it.

Char went to their bucking bull website. How much should the price be? Too high, and she'd price herself out of the market. But if the price was too low, the buyer would assume that it wasn't worth much. She learned, from sales at the mall, that you never wanted a sweater as badly as the one the woman next to you picked up.

She increased the price by twenty-five percent and took most of the inventory off the website. As she clicked "save," she had a moment of self-doubt. Jimmy was going to throw a fit.

"Well, tough titty. He can throw his own pity party." Char tossed the pill back and drained the glass. "The semen belongs to me."

JB dropped the nurse's resume on the kitchen table and looked around the apartment. If this was a normal day, he'd be out feeding cattle. Pulling the phone from the pocket of his shirt, he dialed Char's cell.

It rang and rang. Before it switched to voice mail, he hit speed dial for the house.

"Denny Bucking Bulls." She sounded out of breath, sharp, and professional. "Hello?"

"I tried your cell, but you left it plugged in the charger in the bathroom again, didn't you?"

"Listen, Jimmy. If you've called to lecture me, you'll have to call back later. I've got a million things to do." He heard the rustle as she moved the phone to the other shoulder. "No, Daddy, it's not Junior, it's JB."

His ex-father-in-law's gravel voice barked, "Hurry up and get home, son." Char covered the mouthpiece.

JB closed his eyes and rubbed them. The old man's voice took him back to the days when he'd call from the road after a long day. He'd stand in some diner somewhere, picturing the cozy kitchen, Ben helping Benje do homework at the table, Char cooking something on the stove. It had only been a year, but it seemed he lived in some alternate universe now.

The hitch in Little Bit's voice told him she remembered too. "What do you need, Jimmy?"

"Char, let me bring the bulls home from the vet. You have a hard time driving the Peterbilt. Who's going to spot for you?"

"Don't you dare." The steel was back in her voice. "I've got it under control. Don't worry yourself about that."

"But Char, you can't—"

"Oh yes, I can. Just watch me." *Click.*

JB hung up and leaned back in the chair, sipping coffee, trying to ignore the pang of nostalgia. He'd never had much family. After Gramps died his senior year, Grams went downhill, suffering a massive stroke less than a year later. He wouldn't leave his dog in the nursing homes that would accept her Medicare. So he'd sold the farm, using the proceeds to place her in the best facility in three counties. Though he wasn't sure she was aware of him, he'd visited her several times a week, on his way home from work.

Char's family sustained him through those hard times. They took him in as their own, her mom having him over for dinner most nights. Char's dad had quietly mentored him, teaching him something he'd shown a knack for: training young bulls.

Char had wanted to get married right after graduation, but JB wanted a nest egg first, to convince himself as well as her family that he could provide for her. He took on a second job, working at Junior's feedlot. He hadn't slept much, but he was young and proud to be building for their future.

When Grams passed away two years after the stroke, there wasn't a lot of money left, but he'd added his savings to it and went to Ben, asking for two things: his daughter's hand in marriage and a partnership in the business.

Now Char's friends acted like he was diseased, crossing the street to avoid him. He'd lost his son. His actions afterward cost him the only family he had left.

He stared at the apartment furnishings: the buttsprung sofa, scarred coffee table, and two-by-four-and-cinder-block bookshelves. He took up most of the tiny kitchen, leaving scant room for the two-person table. Now he couldn't even afford this.

He stood and dumped the rest of his coffee in the sink. *Crap, I haven't moved on. I regressed. No real home, and for the first time in twenty years, I'm out of a full-time job.* He rinsed the cup and set it on the drain board.

The expenses would pile up even quicker now. He had to find something else. Maybe Junior would give him his old job at the feedlot. He lifted his jacket from the back of the chair and shrugged it on. It wouldn't hurt to ask.

CHAPTER
6

Friendship is born at that moment when one person says to another: "What! You, too? Thought I was the only one."

—*C. S. Lewis*

Char practically threw the enchiladas in the oven. Grabbing a dust rag from under the sink, she listened to the clock in her head tick the seconds away.

The chores outside had taken longer than she'd planned. A cow had calved, and she had to saddle Pork Chop and herd the pair to the adjacent pasture, to keep the valuable calf from getting trampled in the crowd. She longed for the spare cash to buy a four-wheeler. It would be faster, and less...intimidating.

Now she smelled like a horse, the house wasn't fit for company, and she was afraid to even peek in a mirror. *Maybe just a half a pill. That's all I need.* She hurried to the living room to get away from the orange plastic bottle on the sill.

She viewed the room with an outsider's eye as she snapped the rag over the furniture. Her gaze was drawn to the window and Mother's drab brown damask curtains. Ice trickled into her stomach and formed at the edges, like a pond in winter. *They still need to be replaced.* She saw herself pulling them down, the sewing machine perched on the coffee table. Her brain cut the memory midscene, like an old projector when the film strip snapped in two. She wrapped her arms around her midsection, to warm the block of ice there. Her eyes skittered away.

Was that a cobweb in the corner? She snatched a vase of dead flowers from the table in front of the window. She trotted to the kitchen, threw the flowers in the trash, dropped the vase in the dishwasher, then sprinted to the bedroom.

Standing in front of the closet after a spit bath and a gruesome encounter with the mirror, she chose an over-size button-down poplin shirt with pastel flowers that matched the periwinkle shell she tucked into her jeans.

Junior had picked her father up early this morning for a trip to Luckenbach, to look at a lot of cattle for an upcoming auction. They wouldn't return for hours.

When the oven buzzer went off, she jogged to the kitchen. She tossed on her apron and used the oven mitts to remove the bubbling dish, setting it on her mother's iron trivets.

The doorbell rang.

"Dang." She remembered that cobweb in the living room as she bustled to the front door. She unlocked it and pulled. Nothing. Using both hands, she braced a foot against the jam and tugged. The door didn't budge. It had swelled shut with the humidity . . . again. Jimmy never had taken the time to fix it.

She shouted through the door, "Bella, come around

back." On her way through the kitchen, she straightened a placemat on the dining room table.

Out of breath, she opened the back door. Bella stood on the back stoop in what Char supposed was, for her, casual clothes. Skintight jeans tucked into black stiletto boots, a fitted black suede vest with gold studs over a frilly plunging blouse with puffy sleeves.

She'd taken it easy on the makeup today as well. With an understated glossy lipstick and natural-toned eye shadow, her skin appeared delicate porcelain rather than a pallid death mask. The black riot of curls still overwhelmed her small, pointed face, but the huge gold hoop gypsy earrings were the right touch: exotic-foreign rather than *Night of the Living Dead* foreign.

"Well, do I pass inspection? Or do I need a password?"

"Oh, I beg your pardon." Char flushed to the roots of her hair. "Come in!" She led her through the mudroom into the kitchen. "Please excuse my messy house. I've been in the pasture all morning, and I didn't get the chance to...what?"

Bella stood in the middle of the kitchen, sniffing and looking around. "You're kidding, right?" She surveyed Char from head to foot.

Char frowned and cocked her head.

"I didn't know anyone still wore an apron. And what is that heavenly smell?"

"Enchiladas." Char looked at the frilly gingham that had been her mother's favorite. "What's wrong with an apron? It keeps my clothes clean."

Bella inspected the flowered placemats and dark green ceramic plates. "You set a mean table, East Texas. Show me the rest of the house?"

"Sure." Char led the way through the living room with pine floors, comfortable overstuffed couches, and rag rugs she'd braided herself. The oversized stone fireplace took up one wall. The tall hearth with tapestry cushions made a great place to enjoy a fire on cold winter days. She hoped the cobweb would go unnoticed.

As they retraced their steps, Bella lingered at the family photos in what Char had always called the Rogue's Gallery to tease her mother. "Six generations of Enwrights. A bit much, huh?"

Bella squinted at a hundred-year-old studio photo of a unsmiling couple, the woman seated, man standing behind her, hand on his pistol. "This guy looks like a bandit."

Char chuckled. "Rumor is that Great-Great Uncle Pete was a horse thief."

"Oh, cool." Bella faced her with a smile. "My uncle was in the mob."

Char gulped. "Yes. Well..." She moved on to the office, Daddy's bedroom, and the master bedroom, before leading Bella back to the kitchen, turning her head from the last closed door in the hall.

Bella pulled one of the barstools from under the kitchen counter and sat, while Char heated oil in a small cast iron frying pan to heat the tortillas.

"This is a great house, Char." She dipped a black corn chip in the homemade salsa Char pushed across the counter.

"Thanks, but I can't take the credit. I grew up in this house. Mom did most of the decorating."

"Where is your mom?" Bella said around a mouthful of chip.

Char snagged a tortilla with her tongs and dropped it in the hot oil. "She died a year after Jimmy and I married. We were living in an apartment on the other side of town. Daddy hated living alone and asked us to move in within a couple of months."

"Did that seem weird to you?"

Remembering, Char absently flipped the tortilla, watching to be sure it didn't spatter. "It was a mixed blessing. On one hand, it made me miss my mom more. I felt for the longest time that I'd turn a corner and see her. Especially here, in the kitchen.

"On the other hand, I was glad to come home. It was fun, in the beginning, setting up a new home for Jimmy and me at the apartment. But after a while, it was hard to find enough to fill my days."

"You didn't work?' Bella looked at her like an entomologist studies a new species of bug. "Damn, I thought June Cleaver died. Or at least retired."

"Why is it, in this modern age, when women are free to choose any career, I get grief for wanting to be a housewife?" Char bit back an apology for her snippy tone and dropped another warm tortilla to the pile in the ceramic container and replaced the lid.

"Old bruise, huh?" Bella picked up the bowl of chips and salsa and carried them to the table.

"A bit. Girls in high school were the worst. They thought I was crazy for not wanting to go to college." She took the tortilla cache to the table and returned for the enchilada platter. "All I wanted since I was little was to have a home of my own to take care of, a husband, and lots of kids. What good is liberation if I don't get to do what I want?"

"Hey, I think you should do what makes you tingle, Honey." Bella carried the small crock of refried beans to the table, then sat across from Char. "Besides, you're good at it. Your house is one of those places where people feel at home the minute they walk in, you know?" She scanned the mother lode on the table. "And if this is as good as it smells, your name changes to Betty Crocker anyway."

Char shot her a mock stern look before bowing her head briefly over her plate, then pulled the red checked cloth napkin from beside her plate and set it in her lap. "I'd rather be Charla Rae Denny, thanks all the same."

Bella dug in. When the first forkful hit her mouth, she closed her eyes and moaned. "This is fabulous."

Char colored. "It's not even homemade. I had to use chicken strips and canned enchilada sauce. I haven't had the time—"

Bella chewed a tortilla. "Oh, bull. These are from scratch. I've never eaten a homemade tortilla, and even *I* know that."

Char snorted. "Well, of course. My mother's spirit wouldn't let me through the door with a store-bought tortilla."

Bella ate small bites with relish.

Char lifted a forkful of enchilada and chewed. *Mediocre. It's better with Mom's sauce.*

"What did you want to be when you grew up, Bella?"

"Thin." She spoke quickly, her sharp tone revealing an exposed nerve. She nibbled at a tortilla but couldn't quite avoid Char's look.

Char raised an eyebrow.

Bella put down her fork and, lifting her arm, skimmed

her sleeve up to the shoulder. A fine pencil line of white scar tissue ran along the underside, armpit to elbow.

"Oh, my gosh. What happened?"

"I had bariatric surgery two years ago." Bella pulled her sleeve down. "When you lose two hundred pounds, the skin can't keep up. Had to have the seams taken in."

Char's jaw dropped. She pictured the perfect heart-shape butt swiveling in front of her in Walmart.

"I was the fat girl in school. I was born at fifteen pounds and never stopped gaining." Bella patted her mouth with her napkin, then dropped it beside her plate and leaned back in the chair. "You finish eating. I'll tell you the story."

Char put a tortilla in her open mouth to cover her shock and forced herself to chew.

Bella continued, "I'm Italian. I've got the typical huge family back in New York, and God, can they cook. When Momma and Nonna get in the kitchen, you wouldn't believe what they create: *bucatini*, *tagliatelle ai carciofi*, *osso buco*—mmmm." She kissed her fingers. "And the desserts!" She threw up her hands. "Don't get me started.

"Anyway, I blimped up. By the time I was in junior high, I was wearing a size eighteen, and the kids in the neighborhood called me *porcellino*—piglet. It stuck." She winced, remembering. "I became a full-blown food junkie, and Nonna was my pusher. She came from the old country, see, and didn't understand. She loved me fat."

Char surveyed Bella's prominent collarbones and delicate wrists. "It's just so hard to believe..."

"Well, believe it. I tried every diet known to woman. I ate carrots until my skin turned orange, and I still can't look at a grapefruit without my stomach hurting. I did diet pills. For a while it worked. I'd lose a few pounds here and there.

"But the smells from that kitchen." She closed her eyes and pulled a deep breath through her nose. "I swear I heard the leftovers call me at night, through the refrigerator door, all the way to my room. I'd lay there, determined, for hours. Eventually, though, I'd wear down, and I'd end up sitting at the kitchen table, shoving food in my mouth. I'd even eat it cold. I couldn't wait long enough for the microwave." Her eyes snapped open. "Did you ever want anything that bad?"

Char's gaze sought the bottle on the windowsill before she could stop herself. "No."

Bella didn't seem to notice. "I didn't have a single date in high school. I went on to college, resigned to becoming the spinster aunt to my brother and sister's kids."

Char reached for the tin of cookies on the counter, guilt picking at the edges of her conscience. She'd judged this woman. The whole town had.

Bella gazed through the window, a Mona Lisa smile softening the sharp angles of her face. "Then I met Russ."

"And?"

"Another day." Bella took a cookie and studied it a moment. "I haven't blabbed on like this since I left New York." She took a bite. "Hmmm. What is this decadent thing?"

"They're my creation. I call them my Chocolate Hunk PMS Specials, though not in mixed company."

Bella snorted a laugh, popped the last bite in her mouth, and dusted her hands. "I thought you were going to show me this hamburger-on-the-hoof thing."

• • •

Ten minutes later, Char led the way to the corral. Bella followed with mincing steps, trying to keep her spike heels from sinking in the dirt.

"And this"—Char strolled along the fence to where a small, stocky gray-and-black spotted bull stood, chewing cud—"is Jimmy's star bucker, Mighty Mouse."

"He's a little punk, isn't he?"

"Maybe, but you wouldn't believe what his semen's worth." As Char recalled hitting the button that would increase the price of a straw, a muscle in her stomach jumped. "At least, what I hope it's worth."

Bella faced her, hand on hip. "Just *what* is the deal with you and cow jism? Here you are, Little Ms. Housewife, wouldn't say crap if you had a mouthful and somebody asked you what you were eating. Yet you talk like this is acceptable dinner conversation."

Char waved away Bella's comments as if they were gnats circling her head. "It's business. Think of it like widgets."

Bella rolled her eyes, hand on the fence to help her balance on her toes. "Yeah, right. So how did you get in the 'widget' business?"

Char looked at the horizon, remembering. "When it came time to split the assets, neither attorney could decide how to divide the business. If they split it in half, it wouldn't be viable.

"I lived in a fog back then. I would have signed away everything, just to be left alone. But the judge wouldn't allow it. He was afraid Jimmy would take advantage of me.

"The solution he came up with was pretty clever. He gave Jimmy the bulls, and I get the semen."

Bella made a face. "Isn't that messy?"

Char let out a surprised bark of laughter. "You are such a city girl." She shook her head. "We take the bulls to the vet, to have them 'collected.' When someone buys it, the office ships it to them, to artificially inseminate a cow.

"Jimmy earns a fee, taking the bulls to PBR events, and makes even more if they win. What's more important is them bucking well and gaining a reputation. If they're a desirable sire, it drives up the price of semen and the value of their calves."

Bella held her nose as the bulls paraded by, a safe distance away. "Wow, they are ripe."

Char smiled. "My daddy says that's the smell of money."

Bella cocked her head, watching the bulls. "How do they, you know, 'collect' it?"

Char colored. "Trust me, New York, you don't want to know."

Junior stood at a back corral of the feedlot, watching a trailer of cattle being unloaded. JB took off his hat and strode to the fence. The hammered sun on Junior's features highlighted the years that had passed since JB'd last worked here. Crow's-feet furrowed the fat around his small eyes, and his jowls swung when his head turned.

"Well, if it isn't the big man."

Oh, this is going to be fun. "Junior." JB leaned his forearms on the fence, fingering the brim of his hat. "Could I talk to you?"

Junior perused the cattle. "Air's free, last I checked."

JB's stomach muscles tightened. "You need any help out here?"

"*You* looking for a job?"

"Yeah, part time. I've got two households to support now and—"

"That tends to happen when you hang your wash on someone else's line." Junior glanced over his shoulder.

"Okay, I get it." JB straightened from the fence. "And I deserve that. But goddamn it, Junior, I lost a lot too." When he didn't answer, JB followed Junior's gaze, to see his ex-father-in-law disappear into the shade of the barn. Shame burned in the blood that rushed to his face. "And I lost him too."

"Yeah. You did." The porcine little man stared him down.

"Never mind about the job, Junior. I should know by now that you can't go back." JB wanted to pound something. Instead, he slammed his hat on his head and walked away.

Maybe they needed help down at the Stop-n-Go off the interstate.

"Hey, Big Man."

JB spun back. "What?" It came out as a snarl, and he didn't care. He was done getting whipped. He stood his ground, jaw tight, shoulders tense.

"I may have something," Junior's canny eyes roamed over him. "In fact, it's right up your alley."

An hour later, JB whistled as he drove home, one arm draped over the wheel. The wind from the open window messed his hair, but it felt so sweet and fresh, he didn't mind. Junior had come through with a better job than he'd hoped for: part-time manager of the feedlot and sale barn. Seems he'd been thinking about partial retirement but hadn't found anyone he trusted with his operation.

Junior even agreed to let JB serve as auctioneer on the Saturdays he was in town. Oh, sure, he'd warned that the job wasn't all glamour, but that didn't bother JB. He'd been working since he was big enough to tote a water bucket, and sweat never drowned anybody.

The sun shone warm on the arm he draped on the window ledge. Maybe the dark days of last winter were finally behind him.

He smiled. His new beginning would break with tomorrow's sunrise.

CHAPTER 7

The Stage 5 Alzheimer's Patient: Will require an assistant to complete daily tasks: dressing, cooking, reading. At this stage, personal information may be forgotten, such as address or phone number. A major gap in memory can be detected. The names of children or spouse can still be recalled, but less frequent visitors may not.

—Your Loved One and Alzheimer's,
Gillespie County Board of Health

Daddy, just relax. How about sitting in the rocker? You always liked—ouch!" Char ignored the sting on her forearm from her father's flailing hand. He'd been fine through dinner, but since then he'd gotten agitated. Now he stood in the living room, yelling gibberish at his own reflection in the patio door. Wanting the nurse to meet him, Char had held off giving him the pill that would relax him to sleep.

She stepped in front of him to distract his focus. "How about if I read to you?"

He roared and shoved her aside. Her shins smacked

the edge of the coffee table, and after a teetering moment, she grabbed the corner, caught her balance and her breath. Rubbing her shin, she gaped at him. A memory flashed of the man from her childhood. Daddy, arms akimbo and knees bent, squeezed into her kid-sized chair, an invited guest to her teddy bear tea party. Her heart ached more than her bruised shin. How could this be the same person?

The doorbell rang. Char limped to the door, keeping a wary eye on Dad as he continued berating the window. She unlocked it and tugged. It didn't budge. *Jimmy. Dancripity! He should have taken care of this.* The doorbell rang again.

I'm not asking the nurse to go to the back door. Char wrapped her fingers around the doorknob, mad enough to rip the devil right off the hinges. Bracing her foot against the jamb, she gave a mighty jerk. Something pulled in her shoulder, but the door let loose all at once, and she just caught herself from tumbling backward.

A round-faced, mahogany-skinned woman stood in the pool of light on the porch.

"Missus Denny? I'm Rosa Castillo, from Health Services."

"Please come in." Char smoothed her hair with one hand, opening the screen door with the other. "I'm afraid we're—" When her father hollered from the other room, Char's welcoming smile wobbled.

The nurse stepped in and looked around Char to the living room, then shrugged out of her wool coat. She held it out and let go, not caring if Char caught it or it ended up on the floor, then bustled down the hall.

A cauldron of emotion churning in her chest, Char opened the coat closet door with a shaking hand. She was mortified, for her father and for herself, for being embarrassed. Char only hoped the nurse wouldn't get the wrong impression after stepping into this melee. Suddenly aware of the silence, she closed the closet door and stalked to the living room.

Her daddy sat, eyes closed, in her mother's rocker. Rosa Castillo knelt beside it, singing. Amazed at the transformation, Char rested her butt on the back of the couch and listened. More a chant than singing, the tonal notes rose and fell, and her dad rocked gently in cadence. There weren't words, just guttural sounds in the rhythmic repetition. Char felt her own muscles loosening.

The woman seemed unaware of Char's presence but, after a few minutes, whispered without turning, "Would you bring his medication? I'm sure he's tired."

Her words broke the spell. Char rose and walked to the kitchen for his pill.

A half hour later, her dad settled in bed, Char and the nurse sat in the kitchen, sipping from steaming cups of tea. While Char had taken care of her father, Rosa had made herself at home in the kitchen, brewing chamomile tea that Char didn't know she owned.

She studied the little woman over the lip of her mom's china cup. Rosa's round, lined face reminded Char of dolls in the tourist shops, their heads made from dried apples. In blue surgical scrubs with cartoon cows on them, she looked like a grandma in pajamas. "That was amazing. I had no idea that singing would calm him like that."

"There have been studies done on the effect of music therapy with Alzheimer's patients."

"Well, it sure worked. Was that a Native American chant?"

Rosa's obsidian button eyes flashed. "Navajo. I was raised by my mother's people in New Mexico."

Char cocked her head. "You're obviously qualified, and my father must trust you to react like that. Though I'm curious, how did you hear about us?"

Rosa's glance flitted around the room. "I ran into Reverend Mike at Saint Luke's one day, and he told me that you could use some help."

"Oh." The blood rushed to Char's head and pounded at the back of her knees. "We're fine at night." She recalled the pandemonium the woman had walked into and rushed on. "We are. I need help most in the mornings. If I leave him alone for more than ten minutes, I start worrying. Daddy really is fine most of the time. He recognizes his friends, and if you didn't know him well, you might not even guess—"

"No need to explain." Rosa put her hand over Char's. The skin felt smooth and cool. "I can see how much you love him. I'm sure your father is a wonderful man. It's my job to be sure he is allowed dignity and is safe."

The woman's touch delivered comfort and something like peace. Char's heavy burden of responsibility shifted a bit. She cleared her throat, but the words still came out a choked whisper. "I'm so glad you came."

An hour later, Char smoothed cold cream onto her face as she walked from the bathroom. *What a day.* She'd been saying that a lot lately. She stretched, her tired muscles protesting the labor of the past weeks. On the upside, she'd been too busy to mope, and the siren song of Valium was easier to resist out of doors. She still struggled every day, but had weaned herself down to one pill, before bed.

She turned off the overhead light on her way by the door and clicked on the lamp on the nightstand. Its yellow aura formed a warm oasis in the shadowed room. Her flannel nightie billowed as she sank onto the bed, the dregs of the day bitter at the back of her throat. She'd be wide awake until the pill took hold. The past crept out of the dark room in her mind to attack with slashing claws.

Casting about for something to distract the beast, her glance fell on a paperback on the nightstand. *Healing Wisdom: Easing a Path through Grief*. A parting gift when she'd been asked to leave the grief group.

She'd put the book down and forgotten all about it. *It's probably some pompous load of cow pie.* Now she brushed the dust off, turned it over, and read the back cover. It appeared to be a collection of quotes, meant to soothe mourners. Char opened it and the first line her eyes focused on:

> *There are as many nights as days, and the one is just as long as the other in the year's course. Even a happy life cannot be without a measure of darkness, and the word "happy" would lose its meaning if it were not balanced by sadness.* —Carl Jung

It sounded like her well-meaning friends' advice— time healed all wounds. What a load of crippy-crap! As if hearts and flowers sprinkled on blunt-force loss would help. Before she could stop herself, she read the next entry:

> *Parting is all we know of heaven and all we need of hell.* —Emily Dickinson

Char snapped the book closed. Now, there was some wisdom she could get behind. She dropped the book on the nightstand, turned off the light, and slid into bed. The shiver that snaked up her body was only partially due to cold sheets. Maybe the pill would take hold faster tonight.

The cold white light of a flashlight moon spilled in the window as she lay huddled on her side of the bed, staring at nothing. Would she ever get used to sleeping alone? She scooted to the middle of the bed and spread-eagled her arms and legs. It felt wrong, so she rolled back to her side of the bed. She ached for her charmed life, when her son dreamt little-boy dreams down the hall.

Jimmy would slide in beside her and pull her into his arms. They'd lie like spoons in a drawer and talk about the day. Well, Jimmy would talk. She would listen to the deep rumble of his voice, as she slid seamlessly to sleep. Cradled, sheltered, safe.

A tear slipped to the pillow. Only time's veil separated her from that glittering dream, and if wanting was enough, she'd be there right now. Instead, she lay here, her heart as cold as the sheets. God was a cruel jailor, taking both her precious possessions, one after the other.

The tailwind of regret hit, and Char shifted, restless.

It's not really fair to blame God for what you had a hand in, Charla Rae.

Was that her mother's voice in her head?

Jimmy had tried. For months. On a night much darker than this, he'd lain facing the wall, on the far side of the bed. Not because he wanted it that way but because she couldn't stand to have him touch her, have anything touch her.

After all, that's what the pills were for, weren't they, Missy?

Go away, Mom.

Then one night Jimmy's deep voice had shattered her dark refuge: telling her he'd reached his limit. He had tried everything, but she'd gone somewhere he couldn't follow. He had to let go.

She understood then, saw clearly the fork in the river, but in the churning current, sinuous shapes slid past, baring teeth. Hungry, guilt-tipped teeth. Petrified to numb cowardice, she let him leave and floated away on her life raft of Valium.

Face it, Charla Rae, he didn't leave the marriage first. You did. The voice in her head wasn't her mother's. It was hers.

If only I had it to do over again...The cold, damp spot under her cheek had spread, so she shifted to a fresh spot on the pillow. No. Given the meager resources she had left at the time, she'd done all she'd been capable of: survive.

The past's veil was inviolate. All she could do was get up tomorrow and begin with what she had left. She rolled over, punched the pillow, and willed herself to sleep.

Two hours later, she snatched the phone from the charging cradle in the bathroom, then stalked back to bed. "You happy now, Mother?" She almost snapped on the bedside light but flopped onto the tossed sheets instead. This would be easier done in the dark. She hit speed dial.

"Charla? What's wrong?" His deep rumbly voice held no sleepy edges.

"Nothing that an exorcism wouldn't fix, Jimmy." Realizing she lay facing his pristine pillow, she rolled to her other side, to the accusatory glowing numbers on the alarm: 2:30.

"I'm sorry to call you so late. But I had to. I saw that little girl in the store the other day. The one you had out here the day you came to pick up the bulls? I know she's not your girlfriend."

"Char, I—"

"No, let me get it all out before I lose my nerve, Jimmy." Rev. Mike said confession was good for the soul. But stripping naked in church would have been easier than this. She swallowed. "I'm sorry too, for pushing you away. After B—" She took a shaky breath. "You know, after. I couldn't have done anything else. But I want you to know. I know what I did was wrong."

"Oh, Charla—"

"I can't do anymore tonight, Jimmy. I'm sorry for this too." She hit the "end" button.

CHAPTER 8

Good judgment comes from experience, and often experience comes from bad judgment.

—*Rita Mae Brown*

A spot above JB's right eye beat to the rhythm of the throbbing engine as he hit the lever to drop the bucket on the skip loader. "This job's not all glamour, he says." Since he'd taken the job as manager of the feedlot a week ago, Junior assigned him nothing but work like this—clearing a month's worth of manure from corrals.

"Right up my alley, huh? When I finish, I'm putting this job right up *his* alley." JB adjusted the bandanna tied around his face that did little to block the stench. The sun seared his shoulders and the humid air clung like a damp wool blanket. This job sucked now. By summer it would be excruciating. They'd find him passed out, facedown in a foot of cow brownies. At the end of the row, JB raised the bucket and drove to the railcar-size Dumpster to drop his load. Pulling upwind of the mess, he shut down the Bobcat and yanked off his hat. A stray breeze tickled his sweaty scalp, and he raised an arm to wipe his face on the sleeve at the crook of his elbow.

It wasn't just this job eating him. Benje came to him in dreams most nights now. Waking to the breath-stealing guilt seemed a fair trade to see his son's face. He yearned for the ranch and working with his bulls. He wanted the soul-feeding routine of *home*.

Home? Hell, he didn't even have a place to lay his head.

This month's expenses had devoured the rent money. Come Monday, he had to either be out of the apartment or face eviction.

His knees cracked like pistol shots as he jumped from the tractor. Once he told Junior where to put this job, he'd run down to the 7-Eleven off the interstate to see if they needed help. Crappy pay, but spending the summer in air conditioning looked pretty good about now. He swiped his sweaty neck with his bandanna and started the long walk to the office.

A wall of air conditioning hit him like a slap as he opened the door. He stood savoring it as he wiped his feet. Gilda, Junior's big-haired Jabba the Hut receptionist eyed him over her glasses to make sure he made a good job of it. She had the temperament of a harpy and struck fear into the heart of more than one hombre. Junior hired her decades ago to keep order and collect his receivables. Needless to say, no one owed Junior money.

"Hey, gorgeous. Junior in?" Spying his boss through an office window, JB walked back and knocked on the door, ignoring Gilda's exaggerated sniff as he passed. As he stepped in and closed the door behind him, Junior looked up from his computer screen.

"Beef futures are up at the close of the bell, JB. That's good for us."

"I can see how that affects the quality of manure dropped in the south corral." Ignoring the chair, he stood across the table from his boss.

Junior's button eyes sharpened and his lips pursed. "You got something you want to say to me, JB?"

"Yeah, I do." He leaned his knuckles on the desk. "If you wanted payback for what happened between Char and me, you've done it. Can we stop playing this little game now?" The exasperation of the past two weeks rang in his voice. "You hired me to be your manager, then gave me every scut job on the place." He ticked off the offenses on his fingers. "First, you had me castrating and cleaning out feed troughs that hadn't been scraped in months. Then you wait for the first hot day, and I'm skip-loading manure." He shook his head. "This isn't a job, it's hell. I quit." He strode to the door.

"Got your attention, did I?"

Hand on the knob, JB spun and glared.

Junior opened his hand, gesturing to the chair. "Sit down, JB. Now that you're listening, I've got a story to tell you."

He hesitated, hand on the door. Ten more minutes wouldn't matter. Curious in spite of himself, JB strode to the chair and sat.

"You know that Charla Rae's dad, Ben, and I go back a good ways." Junior leaned back in his oversize executive chair and steepled his fingers. "No one knows this but him and me, so I'll trust you to keep my confidence."

At JB's nod, he continued. "He and I ran with the same crowd but didn't know each other well. We were all farm kids, full of beans and ourselves, wanting something to happen."

His unfocused gaze strayed to the window. "Ten or so of us were out to the fairgrounds for the rodeo, and we ended up at the racetrack. You know they race the quarter horses there every night during the county fair." He sounded wistful. "We watched for a while, and couple of us decided to bet our date money for the week." He smiled, but it looked sad. "I bet on a gray filly. Still remember the name, Silver Dollar. The guys thought I was throwing away money but all I could see were the odds. At twenty to one, if she won, I'd turn a twenty into four hundred twenty."

JB leaned forward, elbows on his knees. "You won, didn't you?"

Junior nodded. "I won. Big time." His smile broadened and his face lit up. "I tell you, I was legendary. Four hundred bucks in the sixties was a lot of money, especially in these parts. I strutted the halls at school for a week. The girls noticed me. Hell, I even took Gilda out."

Junior laughed at JB's horrified expression. "Hey, she was a looker back then."

He sobered. "I'da been better off losing those twenty bucks. See, I found I liked being the big man. But it's like trying to balance on a ball: When you step up, the view is great, and everyone looks up to you. Then you start slipping off, and you scrabble to get back on top again.

"I took the money I hadn't blown and went down to Austin on the weekends. They used to have a dog track there." He shook his head. "I was hooked. On the excitement, the money, and most of all on how people looked at me. Like I was somebody, you know?" He shot a pointed look across the table.

"I couldn't make the trip to the track every weekend, so I discovered the world of bookies. I could bet over the phone! Problem was, I was lucky. I was on top of that ball, and I loved it. I got way too good for this little burg.

"Right up till I woke up one morning into the bookie for two grand. If four hundred bucks was a lot of money back then, two thousand was unthinkable. Turns out, my buddy the bookie had connections, and he wasn't a patient man."

JB rested his chin in his hand, a bit irritated as he grasped the moral of the story but captivated just the same.

"Ben Enwright did some snooping around and found out. When he came to me, I thought it was over, thought he'd tell everyone. That was the only thing I could think of worse than the bookie's threats." Junior reached over and snapped off the computer monitor. "How stupid was that? A man had threatened to drown me in the Pedernales, but I thought it would be worse if everyone knew how dumb I was." He shook his head.

"Ben didn't, though. He said he'd help me. Told me that if I'd give him my solemn oath to never gamble again, he and I could work all summer and fall, and we'd have the money to pay off the debt.

"I was stunned. Why would he do that? I asked him, but he just smiled and told me that, underneath all the bullshit, I was a good person. Besides, he said, it was an investment; I'd have to agree to pay him back." Junior smiled, looking out the window. "With interest."

JB resented lectures. He resented preaching. More than anything, he resented condescension. "I'm a little old for bedtime stories, don't you think?"

Junior raised a sausage-fingered hand. "Hey, you're the one who asked me why you got all the crap jobs. I want you to understand why I'm protective of the best man I've ever had the privilege to know." His eyes were small but piercing. "And that includes his family."

JB pushed the chair back and strode to the door. Junior had been manipulating him all this time. And here he'd been sweating his butt off, trying to prove something to the shifty little turd.

"JB?" If it had been a demand, he'd have walked out. The quiet request made him turn to the fat little man in the big chair. "Ben taught me that everybody deserves a second chance."

He jerked the door open.

"You coming back after the weekend?"

JB didn't turn. "You'll know if you see me coming." He walked out.

JB had hoped to work a deal with the landlord, to pay this month's rent in installments. That would be tough to do now that he was out of a job. Again. He leaned back and put his stocking feet on the coffee table, put the laptop on his thighs, and fired it up.

Why are people in this town so damned comfortable wandering around in my business?

Junior's story had stirred dust he thought long settled. He missed Ben. Junior was right about one thing: His father-in-law was a good man. Ben had given his time, his knowledge, himself, with his patient explanations when JB was learning the bull business.

But Charla had slammed that door and locked it. It felt like for the second time in his life, JB's family had been killed in a car crash.

Only this time he'd been driving.

He signed onto the Denny Bucking Bull website. He'd always liked the photo of Mighty Mouse on the home page, bucking almost vertical on his front feet.

"Now, there's one damn fine bull." He smiled, reading the Mouse's stats, then clicked to the semen order page. "Goddamn!" He grabbed for his phone and hit speed dial for the house. What the heck was Charla Rae thinking, raising the price?

She was laughing as she picked up the call. "I'm not going to let anything happen to you, just relax. Hello?"

He hadn't heard that delighted, tinkling laugh in over a year. It slammed into his chest like a fist. He sat up and dropped his feet to the floor. *Who made her laugh again?* "Char?"

"Oh, hi, Jimmy. We're about to head out."

She sounded like a carefree teen, off for a day of partying. Something in him tore open, unleashing a flash of fury. "Why the hell did you change the price of Mighty Mouse's straws? Don't you realize that you're gonna price us out of the market? You shouldn't be messing in something you don't know anyth—"

"Sales are up." Her voice bristled with ice. "Way up. Check out the income statement. Oh, and Jimmy?" She hesitated. "Keep your opinion out of my side of the business."

Click.

His fingers flew, signing onto their accounting software. He pulled up a current income statement. Damn. Little Bit was right. The semen *had* been undervalued. She'd made a good business decision, and she could use the money. So why did it feel like someone had taken a torque wrench to his innards?

• • •

"Bad news?" Bella stood, hand on the back door.

Char shook her head to rid it of Jimmy's angry voice. "Old news." She picked up her pocket knife, slipped it in her jeans pocket, and strode to the door. "Are you ready for a day in the life of a rancher?"

Bella laughed. "I get a day off at the feed store, and I'm spending it playing cowgirl. If my friends in New York saw me, they'd have me committed."

Char looked her friend over, from hair to boot tips. This time, at least, Bella wore jeans, but Char insisted she wear a denim work shirt over the tube top so she wouldn't burn to a crisp. "Hang on a minute." She snagged a battered straw cowboy hat from the rack that hung next to the door and slapped it on Bella's head. "Now you look the part."

Bella settled the hat at a jaunty angle and winked. "Let's go rustle us some cattle, pardner." She spun and strutted out the door, hips rolling.

"Rosa, we'll be out back!" Char yelled.

"We're fine." The nurse's muffled voice came from the living room. She'd gotten out the old albums, and Ben was telling her stories behind the photos. Char's step was light as she crossed the yard. Rosa was a godsend, literally. She had to remember to call Reverend Mike and thank him for the referral.

That afternoon, with Bella's help, Char got ahead of the chores for the first time. They mucked stalls, tossed bales of hay from the loft, and fed the cattle.

Now Char reclined on a hay bale, instructing Bella on the finer points of currying a horse. Her new friend worked her way down to the hindquarters when the stocky bay whisked her tail, slapping her across the cheek. Bella ignored it, gave the shiny flank one more swipe, and walked to the horse's head to give her a pat.

"Well? How do we look?"

"Bar B looks super." Char grinned. "You, on the other hand, could use some work." Bella's pretty boots were covered in manure and her two-hundred-dollar jeans were grass-stained at the knees. Straw dangled from the sleeve of her filthy work shirt, and the white tube top looked like a ragbag escapee. The tail swish had left brown stripes, like war paint, across Bella's sunburned cheek. But her blue eyes sparkled over a self-satisfied grin. With thumbs hooked in her front pockets, she stood hipshot like a saucy teenage tomboy.

"It's not fair. You look as cute in dirt as I do dressed for church." Char heaved herself to her feet and crossed the aisle. Lifting her shirttail, she licked it, then scrubbed it across Bella's cheek.

Bella ducked away. "Yuk."

Char felt blood pound to her cheeks. "Sorry. Habit." She glanced to where afternoon sun stood centered in the barn doorway. "Should we save the horseback riding lesson for another day? There *will* be another time, won't there?" She felt guilty about putting Bella to slave labor, but she'd insisted, and Char was learning that this woman didn't do anything by halves.

Smiling, Bella trailed ragged fingernails down the horse's smooth flank. "Can I ride Bar B?"

"I take back most of what I've thought about city girls. They're tougher than they look." Char shook her head. "Just remember, you asked for it. Next lesson, how to tack up a horse."

Twenty minutes later, Char backed Pork Chop into a corner, put her foot in the stirrup, and swung her leg over. The past weeks had given her a tentative pride in her improving riding skills but not much confidence in the vagaries of equine behavior.

Bella sat aboard Bar B, a white-knuckled grip on the saddle horn, beaming as if she'd just been crowned Gillespie County Rodeo Queen. Char gathered the bay's reins with her own—no reason to take chances with a greenhorn.

Once her toes found the stirrups, Char squeezed with her thighs. The mare's ears twitched. She gave a gentle nudge with her heel, and the horse stomped a hoof. "Dang it, Pork Chop, you're lazier than a hound dog in the sun." Char gave her a good kick. The mare snorted, then stepped out. As they clopped down the breezeway of the barn into the hammered sun of the yard, she looked over at Bella. "I'll be glad when I can afford a four-wheeler. So much more efficient."

"Those loud, nasty things? Besides, you'd miss this gorgeous view." Bella's head swiveled, trying to see everything at once. Char had been too busy lately to see the homestead as much more than a job to be done.

The yard drowsed in the searing afternoon sun. Swallows darted from the hayloft of the barn, dipping and diving, chasing bugs. Bees droned in her mom's neglected rose bushes where they grew against the house, stems akimbo.

The old bathtub that served as a watering trough was a white block against the tall grass that had flourished in its splashes, bluebonnets hiding in the shade of the lip. Char inhaled the first scents of summer in the dust stirred by the horse's hooves as they ambled across the yard.

"Oooh, aren't they adorable!" Bella nodded toward

the pasture they used as a nursery, where young calves cavorted at their mother's sides.

Char snorted. "This is a business, city girl. Those calves are revenue, whether they grow up buckers, brood stock, or bound for the sale barn."

"You can't see this, can you?" Bella spread her arms. "I get to work with Junior, sacks of manure, and a Dumpster monkey."

Still holding both sets of reins, Char led the way down the path to the pond where bullrushes crowded the shore. A chevron of mallards cruised the mirrored surface, leaving scarcely a ripple. When she and Bella reached the shoreline, the horses nickered and lowered their heads to drink. The sun's heat on Char's back relaxed her sore muscles. She soaked up the serenity of the scene. She recalled the lazy days of her youth, when the vacation months stretched before her like the best kind of dream. A sigh escaped before she could stop it.

"Tell me about your life, Char, before the accident."

Her diaphragm hitched as her breath caught. Thoughts of Benje leached the warmth from the day.

Bella held up a hand. "Only the parts you feel comfortable talking about. I don't mean for it to hurt. I only want to know you better."

Bella's worried glance told Char she meant well, so she considered. Bella had bared her soul at the kitchen table. Weighing how she felt about baring her own scars, the Valium called to Char for the first time today. Want zinged beneath her skin like a poison ivy itch. She scrubbed her palms over her forearms in a fruitless attempt to soothe.

Maybe if she said it…

Bella sat patiently watching. Char focused on the

peace of the placid pond and her happy memories, hoping to calm the jitters.

"A fairy tale." She said. "That's what it was like. Before." She crossed her arms over the saddle horn as Pork Chop lowered her head to graze.

"Once we'd settled into marriage and moved back here, Jimmy and I about wore ourselves out trying for a baby. We planned to have a house overflowing with kids." She chuckled, remembering. "Poor Jimmy. I'd call him when my temperature spiked, and he'd come running, wherever he was. I started to feel like one of our cows, getting serviced. The doctors said there was no reason we couldn't conceive, but for years, we didn't."

She felt the corners of her mouth lift. "Until we did. After ten years, we'd given up and decided we'd have a good life, just the two of us. But having Benje was like going from watching black-and-white TV to color; you don't realize how dull it was until after."

She searched for a way to explain. "June Cleaver. You called me that once, and you were right. I had the house, Jimmy, and Benje. We lived in this charmed bubble. I'd found my exact perfect place in the world. It never occurred to me that, for all its beauty, a bubble is by nature a fragile thing.

"Benje's accident, Jimmy taking up with that cup-cake, and my—" She swallowed the ball in her throat so she could spit out the word, "*addiction* finished off the marriage, but there were problems building, even before. Somewhere along the line, Jimmy changed. Real slow, at first, so I hardly noticed."

"What do you mean?"

Char struggled to put the feelings into words. "In the

beginning, Jimmy was so grateful. For me, for the ranch, for my family. His parents died when he was young, and his grandma too, right after high school. He had nobody. And family meant everything to Jimmy." She glanced over to Bella's rapt attention. "After Benje was born, and Jimmy got the PBR announcing gig, it was like he got bigger, and we got smaller. We took up less and less space in his life."

"Did you talk to him about it?"

"No. I knew something wasn't right, but it happened so slowly, I couldn't put my finger on what was wrong. We didn't fight. It wasn't awful. It was like some wasting disease took over our relationship, bit by tiny bit.

"Then the accident." Flashes of The Day, under the tree, exploded in her brain, and she jerked upright, her body rigid. Pork Chop threw her head up, uneasy. Char's mind skittered away from the memory. Some things were unspeakable.

A cool touch on the back of her hand pulled her from the trance. She looked down to where Bella's hand covered hers, fisted tight in the reins. Bella's cool fingers laced with hers in wordless comfort. An itinerant breeze brushed her face as Pork Chop lowered her head again to graze.

"Jimmy made all the arrangements, after. My brain worked slow, like a computer with a virus. I'd start to speak, but I'd hear a static hiss of white noise in my head, so I'd stop to listen. I could almost decipher a voice in the babble. Next thing I know, Jimmy's shaking me, and his panicked look scared me more than the fact that I lost several minutes."

She waited, trying to squeeze the words past frozen

vocal cords. "I didn't want to go." Acid splashed like a sheet of ice water in her gut. "To the funeral. It was as if the accident walled me off behind a barrier that only I could see. I didn't know these people. Not anymore."

And that wasn't the worst of it. "I sat there drugged, in the packed, too-hot church, hundreds of eyes crawling on my back. Jimmy sat beside me, holding my hand, tears sheeting down his face. I sat like a small rabbit, frozen in the knowledge that I'd have to face the yawning black hole that would swallow my baby."

Bella's fingers spasmed in hers. But now that Char had started, she couldn't seem to stop the truth gushing from her mouth.

"I imagined myself breaking away from Jimmy, running to the flower-draped casket, tearing it open, and rescuing my Benje. After all, isn't it a mother's job to protect her child?" She turned her head away. She didn't want to know Bella's reaction. "I had to wait. The right time would present itself. I had to be ready.

"My eyes jittered over the white roses covering the casket. The reverend's monotone became a drone—like summer bees."

Her lungs had labored against the cloying smell of roses and smothering heat. A single white rose blurred, then came into perfect focus. A slight tinge of tan marred the edge of one petal, a glistening drop of moisture on another. She watched, rapt, as a small bee climbed from the center, its drone combining with the others, swelling, filling her head with a manic, reverberating hum. She'd clapped her hands over her ears and watched with horror as the bee crawled to the edge of the rose. Teetering on the edge, it looked right at her with an obscene, leering grin.

"I woke up in my own bed twelve hours after the funeral." Char dropped Bella's hand and lifted her hair off her sticky neck, hoping for a breeze. "I'd passed out in the church."

Two shiny tracks ran down Bella's smudged face. "You missed the graveside service. I'm so sorry."

Char shuddered. "I'm not."

CHAPTER 9

If you're going through hell, keep going.
                                    —*Winston Churchill*

Char closed the mudroom door behind her. A chilly wind lifted her hair. She hesitated, hand on the knob. The setting sun spotlighted spectacular yellow-white thunderheads to the north. Purple-black ones roiled behind them, like a portent of evil. She considered exchanging her denim vest for something more substantial, but the remainder of the sky showed a vivid cerulean blue, and she didn't smell rain in the air. Yet.

Fumbling with the zipper, she trotted to the battered white ranch truck. It would only take a few minutes to drive to the pasture and dump the evening feed. It better not take longer; she'd left a pressure cooker full of red beans hissing on the stove. She opened the truck door and settled in, smiling, remembering Rosa and her father at the kitchen table, working a jigsaw puzzle.

These past weeks, Rosa taught him to navigate the widening gaps in his memory and calmed him through his frustration. He looked forward to the nurse's visits and accepted her help without protest. He quoted Rosa to Char daily, and every time, it bit with a ridiculous wasp-sting of jealousy. Char couldn't dislike the nurse. Her gentle ways eased her into the current of their lives with barely a ripple. Char could now work outside, knowing her dad was safe and happy. But it came at a price; she missed being the only woman in her daddy's life.

"You are one pathetic creature, Charla."

She drove to the pasture gate and opened it. Pulling in, she repeated the gate exercise in reverse, scuttling into the cab as the herd converged. The truck bumped over the uneven ground, trailing cows like the Pied Piper. A few hundred feet into the meadow, she shut off the ignition.

Putting on canvas gloves, she looked down and lifted the door handle, jumping when a wet nose appeared in the crack of the door. "No, no!" She swatted at the invader, then slammed the door shut. The startled cow gave her an indignant stare, and Char yelled through the closed window, "Humans inside. Cows outside." The cow lowed and continued the stare-down. Char waved at the interior of the truck. "Cow-free zone!" The heifer licked the window, her huge tongue smearing drool over half of it. Char grimaced. "Oh, yuk."

"First, I'm jealous of my father's nurse, and now I'm arguing with a cow. I've got to get a life."

The cab darkened as the cattle surrounded the truck, their huge bodies filling the windows. After thinking a moment, Char twisted in the seat to slide open the back window. Crouching, she wriggled through the narrow opening. After a dicey moment when her hips hung up, she squirmed until she fell in a contorted ball into the truck bed.

Not a graceful entrance, but only cows witnessed it. Pulling a pocket knife from her jeans, Char slit a bag of feed on the tailgate. "Such demanding broads." She waited for the flow to stem to a trickle before upending the rest onto the ground.

Char noted a few new calves in the herd. What she didn't see was a black-and-white spotted hide. "Dang that Tricks. If she's out again, I swear, the minute she drops that calf—"

As she straightened, a tail of wind, harbinger of the front, hit her like a slap. She glanced up. The advancing army of black, bruised clouds obscured fully half the sky. Brushing wind-blown hair out of her eyes, she scanned the rolling pasture and caught a flash of white out of the corner of her eye. That suspicious white bulge under an oak, on the distant rise; were those black spots?

Char slit the second bag and dumped it on the ground. Eyeing the crowd surrounding the truck bed, she decided on the prudent exit, squeezing through the back window once more. It was harder this way; she ended up between the seats, parking brake poking her kidney, one leg stuck in the window. "Danged useless animals." She squirmed, tugging at her leg. "If they're not running away, they're drooling on you or trying to die.

Finally settled in the driver's seat, she fired the engine and left the herd behind. Nearing the hill, the white spot coalesced into a downed cow. Tricks, in labor. Had been for some time by the look; her flanks were slick with sweat. Char pulled up, shut down the engine, and stepped out. Tricks seemed unaware of her approach, head flat on the ground, eyes unfocused. The massive side shuddered, and the cow strained, eyes rolling. Something was wrong.

Char reached into the pocket for her phone. Nothing. She slapped her chest, looking for pockets. Hands over boobs, the truth sank in. The cell phone sat in the charger, plugged into the bathroom socket.

"Rats! Of all the gol-durned, brainless—" She shot a hopeful glance to the house, then back to the cow. By the time she drove there, phoned the vet, and he got out here, it would be too late.

Whoa up, Charla Rae. What are you considering here? You know zip about animal husbandry. Even if you were strong enough, which you aren't.

Tricks lowed as another contraction hit, but nothing was happening at the business end.

Heart jackhammering her ribs, Char wrenched her gaze away, taking one hopeful scan of the darkened meadow for the cavalry. Only a golden laser of sun remained at the horizon, ominous smoky-black clouds loomed overhead. Another gust of wind whipped through the trees, new leaves rattling in wild protest. Tension permeated the ozone-scented air. She felt the hair on her arms rising.

The death of this calf would be devastating financially. A heavy blanket of dread bowed her shoulders. A tremor began in Tricks's back leg. Not to mention the loss of their best bloodline cow. How much more calamity could one family stand?

She threw her head back and yelled at the scuttling clouds. "Who am I to do this? I'm a *housewife*!" Tricks lifted her head, and her eyes reflected the light like a cat's. Spooked, Charla shuddered, rubbing the gooseflesh on her upper arms.

She shot one last hopeful glance to the house in the distance. The kitchen light had come on. Leaning into the truck, she pulled the headlight switch. If Rosa or her dad looked out the window, surely they'd recognize the stationary headlights as odd and come investigate. Hopefully, with a cell phone. She searched the truck for anything that could help. Grabbing a hank of rope from behind the seat, she backed out, slammed the door, then retrieved the two empty feed sacks from the truck bed.

After laying the sacks at the end of the cow, she knelt, trying to remember everything she'd ever heard about cow birthing. A calf should be born with its head nestled between the two front feet. Obviously that wasn't the case here.

She glanced to the black clouds, almost close enough to touch. "Watch over me, Lord—I'm going in."

After removing the canvas gloves, she skinned her right sleeve to her shoulder. Bracing her left hand on the cow's hip, she paused, swallowing the acid at the back of her throat. No time for the luxury of getting sick.

Tricks flinched at Char's intimate touch. "Relax, sister. At least you're not in stirrups, freezing your tail off in a paper gown."

Closing her eyes, Char envisioned the picture her fingers relayed. The calf's neck was bent back, head facing its back feet. She could only feel one hoof, the other was folded back as well. "Double crap." Withdrawing her hand, she sat back on her heels.

This is hopeless. Her heart sank. This valuable cow and calf, the brightest spot of hope for their future, were going to die. She should be in the house, cooking dinner. Where she belonged.

Lightning zipped across the black sky. A boom of thunder followed on its heels. Damp, rain-scented wind slammed into her, rocking her on her knees, blowing her hair straight back. She ought to be perfecting her pecan pie recipe for the county fair, not up to her shoulder in the back end of a cow.

"*Damn* you, James Benton Denny!" she yelled into the wind. "This isn't my problem!"

Tricks groaned as another spasm ripped through her. Her hind legs shook and her hide rippled in a shiver. *Good lord, is she going into shock from the long labor? I've got nothing to lose. I might as well try.*

Lying on the feed bags, she flinched when the first fat raindrop spattered her face.

An hour later, Char lay shivering, soaked to the skin, every speck of energy gone. She knew she should be using the lull between contractions to try once more, but she had to rest. The bones in her arm ached from the crushing. The feed sacks had sunk into the mud during the wrestling match.

She had managed to slip the hank of rope over the tiny hoof and, between contractions, to pull it alongside the other. But the head was wedged tight—and she wasn't strong enough to straighten it. The cow seemed to be weakening, and Char wasn't even sure the calf was alive; it hadn't shown any signs of life since she'd begun.

How long had she been at this? An hour? Two? Felt like eons. Why hadn't anyone come looking for her? She'd never felt so sapped. So raw. So *alone*.

The closest she'd felt to this was in her twenty-hour labor with Benje. Near the end, disheartened and exhausted, she'd given up. The doctor took pity, offering the oblivion of anesthesia and a cesarean section.

She'd have taken it too—but Jimmy got in her face. He cajoled, shouted, coaxed. He did everything but push that baby out by sheer force of will. Jimmy convinced her she could do it, and a half hour and five mighty heaves later, Benje was delivered into their lives: healthy, beautiful, perfect.

Jimmy's the strong one. I like following. It's not like I'm some diva, eating bonbons and expecting to be waited on. I work hard. In fact—

But I don't see anyone around to lead. Do you, Charla Rae?

She groaned. Oh great, Mom, thanks. Your gentle, wise words are just what I need right now. She sat up and pulled her foot from the mud. It let go with a gross sucking sound.

At her movement, the cow lifted her head. Her brown eyes shone with acceptance—of whatever would come next. Tricks let go, and her head fell to the ground, so hard it bounced off the grass.

Something clicked in Char's sluggish brain. Tricks may be a cow, but she was a mother. And she was giving up, just as Char had, all those years ago.

Her body jerked, anger flaring. "I am *not* losing

another baby." Scorching heat surged in the blood pounding in her ears. Resolve barreled down her nerve endings, melting the shivers as effectively as a flame thrower. She threw her eyes heavenward. "Do you hear me, God? You are not getting this one."

Dragging mud-laden legs, she twisted to her knees. She slapped Tricks's hip, and the sound snapped like a pistol shot in the night-quiet meadow. "If *I* can do this, then, by God, you can." The cow barely flinched.

Char pushed her hand down the calf's bowed neck once more, to the head. Still an inch short—even with her armpit snugged against the cow, her fingertips barely grazed the chin. Straining every muscle fiber, she pushed those fingers forward.

"Come on, God, a little help here..."

There! The toe of her sneaker hit something solid, in the mud. A tree root. "Thank you, Lord."

Ten minutes later, the motionless calf slid into Char's lap so fast she sprawled on her back in the mud. She lay stunned a moment, staring up at the few stars winking between the blackness of clouds. The calf's legs jerked under her hands. Joy rose like a fountain of sparks in her chest as a sobbing laugh burst from her throat.

Tricks lowed. Probably as relieved as Charla.

She struggled to sit up, tears streaming. In the weakening truck lights she looked down at her lapful of bull calf—gray, with black spots, gummy and wet—the most beautiful thing she'd ever seen. As it struggled to right itself, she pushed it out of the mud pit, onto the grass. Lifting its head on a wobbly neck, it bawled.

Char crawled away on her hands and knees and, once clear of the mud, pushed herself to her feet. She stood, swaying, breathing heavily. The cow lowed once more, and the afterbirth was delivered where Char had been sitting a moment before.

She stepped to the cow's head. "You did it, Mama! A strong baby boy."

The cow lay still, eyes closed. Char frowned. "You rest. I'll take care of him."

She walked on needle-prickling legs to the truck. A laser of light flashed in her eyes and danced over her. Headlights bounced through the field toward her.

"Now the cavalry shows up," she grumbled, opening the truck door. In the dome light, she dug in the mess behind the seat until she came up with a grease-stained towel. She carried it to where the calf lay shivering, struggling to collect its long legs beneath it. Her back creaked as she leaned over to clean out the nostrils, then scrubbed the towel over the calf's body to dry and warm it.

Rosa's ancient El Camino truck pulled up, the headlights spotlighting the tableau. She started babbling before she got out. "Oh, Charla, I'm so sorry!" Her pale scrubs flashed in the light as she trotted over. "I was teaching Ben to make bread, and you know how you can get wrapped up in that—"

"This woman could talk gum off a wall, I swear." Her dad walked up. "Well, whadya got here, Charla Rae?" They watched the calf struggle to its feet. It stood, tottering on wobbly legs, turned its face to them, closed its eyes, and bawled. Rosa laughed, took the rag from Char, walked over, and rubbed down the calf.

"He had his head and one leg turned back, but he seems okay now, Daddy. But I'm worried about Tricks."

Char took his hand and led him to the cow, lying still, right where she'd left her. "Shouldn't she be up, so the calf can suckle?" Her father leaned over, lifted the cow's eyelid, then straightened and strode to the truck.

She followed. "Will she be okay?"

"She's plumb tuckered, hon." He rummaged in the area behind the seat. "I always kept sorghum in here, just in case..." He extracted an aluminum gallon can, set it on the grass, then dug some more. He straightened, a baseball cap in his hand. "This'll do for a trough."

"Oh, but Daddy—" That wasn't any baseball cap. That was Jimmy's state championship senior league softball cap. She wished she had a nickel for every time he'd told the story of his base-clearing homer in the bottom of the ninth inning. She knew that wherever he was right now, he was missing that cap. She rubbed her aching, blood-spattered, bone-crushed forearm and glanced down at the rag that used to be her favorite turtleneck. "I think that'll do nicely."

He filled the hat with molasses, carried it to the cow, and put it under her nose. Tricks lifted her head, sniffed it, and took a tentative lick. Then another. Soon all that remained was a gooey, tongue-smeared brown stain.

Her father squatted beside the cow's head. "Bring the calf, Little Bit. He'll do the rest."

Rosa relinquished the baby with one last swipe of the filthy rag. "At first I tried to rub the spots off. I thought he was dirty!"

Char half lifted, half pushed the calf the few steps to its mother. When she saw the calf, Tricks lowed and slowly heaved herself to her feet. The baby squalled, and the cow nudged him to her udder. Once he located dinner, the calf drank with gusto, approval apparent down to his flicking tail.

Char looked up, blinded by the lights of another vehicle bumping across the field toward them, too fast.

She raised a hand to block the glare. "Who could that—" The truck had almost slid to a stop when the engine died. The door flew open, and Jimmy leapt from the cab.

Char shot a glare at Rosa, who lifted a shoulder. "You left to feed over two hours ago. I was worried. If there's trouble here, who else am I going to call?"

Realizing she held the gooey evidence, Char whipped the cap behind her back.

Jimmy ran up, his eyes flashing wild in the car's lights. "Are you all right?"

She took a step back. "Sure."

He bent over, hands on knees, sides heaving, way more out of breath than he should have been running ten steps.

Her dad said, "Dang it, JB, you're always on the road when something big happens. Glad you're home, son. Come look at what a ranch wife can do in a night's work." He stepped aside.

"Oh, wow." Jimmy breathed out the words like a little boy who just got his heart's desire for Christmas.

While her dad explained the problem birth, Char backed to the ranch truck and tossed the evidence onto the shadowed floorboard, and slammed the truck door.

Jimmy turned to her, head cocked, eyebrows scrunched. "*You* did this."

She walked the few steps back, puffing out her chest. "Didn't see anyone else available."

She remembered that look. From back in high school, when Jimmy thought she was all that.

"You're amazing."

At his boyish smile, her heart took that tiny familiar pinch. She wiped her sticky hands together. "Rosa gave me an idea for a name. But it's your calf, so . . ."

"He wouldn't be here if it weren't for you, so you get to name him. What is it?"

"Dirty Tricks."

Her dad barked a laugh and pushed the straw cowboy hat to the back of his head. "I can just hear JB announcing that at the PBR finals."

"Your mouth to God's ears, Ben. I think it's a great name." Jimmy stepped over the mud pit to Tricks, patting and murmuring to her. He bent and lifted her lip, examining her gums. "She's dehydrated. We need to get her back to the barn and some water."

Now that the drama was over, Char felt as limp as raw bacon. She turned to walk to the truck and stumbled on the uneven ground.

Her dad was there, his arm around her waist. She leaned on his bony shoulder. "I'm so tired, Daddy."

"You did a good thing here tonight, Charla Rae. I couldn'a done better. Now let's get you home."

Char bent and lifted the hank of rope from the mud. "In a minute, Daddy." She walked to Tricks, looped the rope around her neck, and rubbed the broad forehead. "Come on, girl, let's take your son to the nursery."

"Do you mind if I tag along?"

If Jimmy wouldn't have asked in that voice—that polite, assume-nothing voice—she'd have said no. "Okay."

It was his stock, after all.

Rosa took her dad's elbow. "Let's go, Ben. We left dinner on the table. Will you help me heat it up?"

"I'll turn off all the lights, Charla Rae." Ben walked to the ranch truck. "This battery is about gone. JB, you give her a jump if she needs it, hear?"

"Yessir, I will." Jimmy shrugged out of his fancy PBR letterman-style jacket and settled it over her shoulders.

Char had been cold so long she'd forgotten what warm felt like. The jacket still held the heat of Jimmy's body, and she shivered. It held his smell too, and, God, how she'd always loved that.

When the El Camino pulled away, the darkness, held at bay by headlights, took over. Char tugged on the rope, and Tricks followed, Jimmy walking on the other side of her head. Char kept the pace slow, so the spindle-legged calf could keep up. The going got easier when they left the muddy, tromped-down area.

The sky had cleared. The moon painted the wet meadow in brushstrokes of silver: the edges of grass blades, the shine off a hunk of quartz, the branches of a dead tree they passed. The storm had shushed the night birds and crickets. The only sound was the wet grass brushing their jeans.

His deep voice came from the dark but somehow was a part of it. "You sure you don't want me to carry you?"

She remembered. A hot, humid night, shortly after they'd moved back to the ranch. Neither of them could sleep on the sticky sheets, so they'd snuck out of the house, Char in her nightgown, Jimmy in sweats, giggling like kids. Jimmy'd stopped to pull on boots, but she was barefoot. He'd scooped her up and carried her all the way to the edge of the pond.

She shook her head, to break off the rest of the memory—the skinny-dipping part. She glanced up to see the moonlight flashing off his smile.

You can accuse James Benton Denny of a lot of things, but a lack of courage isn't one of them. Before she could clamp down on it, a giggle slipped out. She ducked her head and slowed, dropping back to check on the calf. "I remember." She'd almost whispered it, but knew he'd heard when his chuckle drifted back to her.

By the time they'd gotten Tricks and her calf settled in the pasture, the adrenaline Char had been running on ran out. She stood in the circle of the security light on the barn, looking across the field, not knowing where she'd get the energy to make the trip back.

"Why don't you sit down, Charla?"

Jimmy's worried expression told her she must have looked as bad as she felt. She tucked her hair behind her ear. "I've got to get the truck."

"I'll go fetch my truck and drive you to the house. Tomorrow I'll pick up a battery in town and bring it out."

"Jimmy, I'll be fine. I can do this." She took a deep breath and started walking.

In two of his long strides, he'd caught up to her. "I know you can, Charla Rae. After tonight, I wouldn't wager there's anything you can't do." He took her elbow to help her navigate the uneven ground. "The thing is, you shouldn't have to."

They walked across the moonlit field.

She knew she should step away from his touch, but his hand was warm and comforting. This kind of endearment reminded her of how close they once were, how much he'd cared.

He felt solid, like she could lean on him, depend on him. He felt like *her* Jimmy.

Lord, how she missed him.

CHAPTER 10

The art of living is more like wrestling than dancing.
—Marcus Aurelius

JB had left the coat closet packing for last. Dropping to his knees, he dug through the flotsam on the floor: a bowling ball, worn-out shoes, and dust bunnies as prolific as their breathing namesakes. When sweat blurred his vision, he sat back on his heels, scrubbing a hand over his beard stubble. "Where is the danged thing?"

He'd spent all morning packing. He'd promised the landlord he'd be out by noon. But he couldn't leave without his championship cap. He stood and felt blindly on the top shelf. Winter gloves, stocking caps. "Ah, finally!" He tugged a navy baseball cap from under an umbrella. "How the heck did it get—" He read the familiar logo emblazoned across the front:

JUNIOR'S FEED & SEED
IF WE DON'T HAVE IT, YOU DON'T NEED IT.

"Crap." The kitchen clock, ticking loud in the silence,

chimed twelve times. He crammed the contents of the closet into the last two boxes. The cap wasn't in the apartment. At least that narrowed the choices.

Thank God for Wiley. Good to know he had at least one friend. After hearing about JB losing the apartment, Wiley invited JB to come live with him, his wife, Dana, and the baby.

Saved my bacon, that's for sure.

He took a last tour of the apartment to be sure he hadn't left anything else. Funny, the place didn't look much different with his stuff gone. A bit less cluttered maybe.

His life, on the other hand, looked more like the Grand Canyon. At night.

Traveling alone to events had become strange. Sure, he had traveled alone when he and Char were married, but that was different. He'd gone straight to the hotel after the events. Everyone knew he had a wife at home.

When he was with Jess, they were the center of the social scene. He'd tried to keep that up after they broke up, but everyone at the bar looked past him, as if he no longer belonged.

How could he not have known? Those kids weren't his friends, they were Jess's.

Being alone with Little Bit last night brought it all back. How much he missed being her husband, the man by her side looking out for her, taking care of her. How much he missed the love and trust in her eyes. Touching her made him miss her, like a piece of him was gone.

He shook his head, snugged Junior's gimmie cap over his hair, balanced the last two boxes in his arms, and jerked the door open.

He was going to have to get used to being alone,

somehow. Char made it very clear she didn't need him anymore, and that cut him deep. He reckoned she had a right to feel the way she did, but it didn't make things any better.

When he walked out of the apartment for the last time, the *snick* of the latch echoed in the empty hallway.

"We've missed you in church, Charla Rae." Reverend Mike's deep voice wasn't accusatory, but she felt caught, just the same. That would teach her to pick up the phone without checking the caller I.D.

"It's been crazy here lately, Rev. There's Dad to care for, and I've taken on more responsibilities around the ranch." She switched the phone to her other hand, scrubbing her sweaty palm on the leg of her jeans. "You know, to stay busy."

"I'm glad, Charla Rae. Busy hands can soothe a troubled heart. I want you to know that the congregation and I are praying for you."

"Thank you, Rev. It's been nice talking to you."

"You know that it's natural for a person to be angry after what you've endured, don't you, Charla?"

Her fingers tapped a drumbeat on the kitchen counter. She didn't need this right now. "Rev., I appreciate your guidance, but Jimmy—"

"I wasn't speaking of Jimmy, Charla Rae. I'm referring to anger at God."

The soothing voice did nothing to stop the tremor in her fingers as she reached for her coffee cup. "Oh. Well." She gulped cold coffee to give her time to come up with something to say.

"I was at Saint Luke's last week, visiting Ms.

Gansvoort. Her diabetes is progressing, but, thank the Lord, they've managed to stabilize her."

"Rev., that's wonderful. But I need to get out and feed—"

"I ran into Toby, the grief counselor of their community outreach."

Her mother's china cup chattered to the saucer and overturned. Char's mouth opened, but no words came out. The fact that she hadn't been prepared for the punch made it worse, though she should have been.

She was sure the whole town knew about her meltdown at the grief group by now. She couldn't believe she'd screamed in the face of another human being, much less a grief-stricken old woman. One more shame on her long list.

Coffee spread on the counter.

"Charla, won't you tell me what happened? Talking about it may help."

The phone chirped in her ear. She pounced on the excuse. "Rev., I'm so sorry. I've got to take this call. It's business." She didn't know why God would take her side over the reverend's, but she wasn't about to question the reprieve.

"All right, Charla Rae. I'll call some other time—"

The joyful beep interrupted once more.

"—just know that there are many who care for you, and that you are in our hearts and our thoughts."

"Thank you for the call. I'll talk to you soon." She blew out a breath, then clicked to the next call. "Denny Bucking Bulls, Charla speaking. Can I help you?" *Oh poop.* She'd been so flustered she'd forgotten to thank the reverend for referring the nurse!

"Hi, Little Bit." Jimmy's upbeat voice reminded her, once more, that God was not kind. "How's Tricks?"

The hot flash of anger felt good. Anger she could deal with. "James B. Denny, just because you chose to hang out with foul-mouthed children doesn't mean you can talk to me that way."

His wry chuckle burbled on the line. "Char, I meant the *cow*."

"Oh. Sorry." Grabbing a sponge from the sink, she mopped up the coffee. A shadow stain remained. "She and Dirty Tricks are both fine." She pulled Bon Ami from under the sink and tapped it onto the stain.

"Well, you did a great job, Char. With those bloodlines, he's going to be a winner. I'll see about getting him registered with the ABBI."

"Okay, good. Listen, Jimmy, I've got to get ready, so I'll talk to you later." She reached for the "off" button.

"Wait! Char. Char?" Jimmy's tiny tinny voice drifted up from the receiver. Sighing, she put the phone back to her ear.

"Yes?"

"Look, Char. I don't want to make you mad. But we have to talk about the business. The young bulls are in the pasture eating their fool heads off. If I don't start getting them used to the bucking chutes and the trailer, we're going to lose a whole season with them. Kid Charlemagne and the Mouse aren't going to buck forever, and—"

She sighed. Eight a.m., and she already had more to worry about than she had brain cells. "I know, Jimmy, I know. I need some time to think about it, okay?" And she sure couldn't sort out her feelings with him on the other end of the line.

"Yeah, Charla, sure." He hesitated, a sure sign he was marshalling arguments to launch an attack of reason.

Yet reason had nothing to do with the boiling in her gut. "I am running seriously late, Jimmy. I'll call you later. Bye." She mashed the "off" button before he could get a word in and dropped the phone on the counter.

Jimmy was right. She knew it. The business couldn't survive without good buckers to advance the ranch's reputation. Not to mention the price of their semen. The thought of having him on the property again...

Don't forget, for all his salesman's arguments, he lied to you about the bimbo. He's got an agenda you don't know about. You can't trust a liar.

But what if the Jimmy she'd sensed in his touch the other night had been real? What if her Jimmy was still in there somewhere? She remembered his hand on her elbow, remembered his hands other places on countless moonlit nights.

She shook the whimsy out of her head. What would people say? Poor Charla Rae, bless her heart, sucked in again.

Besides, if he came back, you'd lose your job; go back in this memory-stuffed house, full time. She heard the whisper of Valium from the box in the garage where she'd hidden it from herself.

If she fell in that hole again, she'd never have the guts to climb back out.

Nope, she couldn't risk it.

Are you sure there isn't one more reason, Charla? Are you afraid if he was around all the time you'd forget you're mad at him? He's a good-looking man, and he's single agai—

"Mom. Cut me some slack. I'm doing my best here. Besides, even if I was worried about that, which I am not, it would be another reason not to let him back on the place, wouldn't it?"

She straightened her shoulders. "Besides, I've done well, taking on the ranching chores, birthing the calf, handling things."

Her shoulders slumped under with the familiar weight of worry. She didn't have the physical strength to train the bulls, even if she had the knowledge, which she didn't.

"There's got to be another way." Leaning her forearms on the counter, Char stared at the dining room wall. If she could only lay her hands on some cash, she'd be okay. All she needed was enough to hire a trainer for one season. By next year, maybe Jimmy's betrayal wouldn't burn like the exposed meat of a raw wound. Surely it couldn't. Could it?

Her glance lingered on the dusty china hutch. One more thing to put on the li—"Wait." She sidestepped the counter and the table, to stand before the glass-fronted cabinet housing her great-grandmother's china. She squinted at the busy brown-and-cream pattern. Horses pulled sleighs through muddy-looking snow, saltbox-style houses set off in brown curlicue frames, men in tricorns escorted big-skirted women. Her mother had dubbed the collection "the patriotic burden." They'd laughed about the hideous stuff. In her memory, it had never been out of the hutch save for an obligatory annual wash. "Could I really?"

She could. It was ugly, but what did she expect from something over a hundred and fifty years old? It had to be worth a pretty penny. Putting an Internet search at the top of the to-do list in her mind, she whistled on her way down the hall to wake her dad.

Women. JB dropped the cell phone on the truck seat. God, he was sick to death of them: their judgmental attitudes and their uneven tempers.

He'd been married to Charla for twenty-two years and still couldn't figure her out. He pulled the toothpick from his mouth and tossed it out the window. Time to quit sniffing around women and focus on the important stuff. Of his three jobs, only the PBR event announcer remained. Reaching down, he loosened the buckle digging in his gut.

Time to get his feet under him again.

There's no way he could afford another apartment, given his job uncertainty as well as the expenses for Ben's nurse. If Charla knew he'd done that, she'd have thrown a wall-eyed fit. But it was obvious she needed help with Ben. Help she was too proud to ask for. He smiled to himself. He admired the hell out of that plucky woman, even if her claws could shred him. Divorce or no, Ben was family. And JB intended to take care of his own.

It was the "how" part he wasn't sure of.

He still had no access to train his own bulls. Hell, he'd sleep in a barn, if he could lease pasture space somewhere for them, but he couldn't afford that either. The Galts lived outside Kerrville, a quaint town about twenty miles from Fredericksburg. The commute wouldn't be too bad.

He turned off the county asphalt to the dirt road that led to Wiley's house. When dust blew in, he raised the windows and swerved to miss the worst of the washboard ruts.

I should've pushed harder with Little Bit to let me back on the ranch.

"Oh yeah, you're a real gentleman." Guilt settled on him like the grit billowing onto the uncovered boxes of belongings in the truck bed. "Lean on the grieving mother, with an old man who's losing it, who's trying to run the ranch by herself."

He could only blame himself for the situation. If he hadn't lied about his relationship with Jess, things may not have been so bad with Little Bit.

He snorted. He'd lived here all his life. Had he really thought that a juicy secret like his affair with a coed wouldn't hit the street like cars at the start of an Indy race? But Char's question that day had caught him flat-footed, and denial was the first thing that fell out of his mouth. He'd meant to go back later, to explain. But explain what, exactly? He knew Char. To her, a separation wouldn't negate their marriage vows.

Hell, it wouldn't to him either if he'd been in his right mind.

Shit. Good thing he was swearing off women.

He turned at the white aluminum sign announcing "Galt's Goats" onto the dirt track that served as Wiley's driveway, pulled up to the tiny aluminum-sided house, and shut off the engine. He gathered his gifts from the floorboard: a bouquet of spring flowers for Dana, a garish pink stuffed pig for the baby, and a six-pack for Wiley.

Grabbing his cowboy hat from the gun rack behind him, he settled it on his head. "Last stop, JB. You can't blow this one."

Bella wore the black faux leather like chain mail. It hugged every curve, bend, and hollow. As the woman crossed the sidewalk to the car, Char let her eyes slide to the knee-high stiletto slouch boots with silver chains across the instep, jingling like a cowboy's spurs with every step.

She leaned across the seat and clicked open the passenger side door. "I didn't think to tell you, but women hereabouts don't generally dress up for a trip to the Clip 'n Curl."

Bella slinked in and slammed the door, her sea of black curls taking up almost as much space as her body. Her earrings matched the silver chains on her boots, and one strand stretched to a diamond stud in her nostril. She noticed Char's stare. "Don't worry, it's a magnet, not a piercing." She reached for the seat belt. "I figure I've got a closetful of New York badass black, and if there was ever a day for it, it's today." The buckle snapped with a decisive *click*.

Char glanced down at her own outfit. An old-lady seersucker blue-and-white-striped blouse with embroidered daisies, pedal pushers, and slip-on tennis shoes. "How about I drop you off and I'll go shopping? I owe you a manicure for working on the ranch, but I don't need to go."

Bella stared through the windshield, a muscle working in her jaw. "If you think I'm going into that wolf's den alone, you'd better think again."

Char chuckled and put the car in gear. "Don't tell me a tough city girl like you is afraid of a bunch of good ol' country gals. I don't believe it." She wheeled out of the apartment complex into the traffic on North Washington.

"You're kidding, right? Those women would eat their own young, then gossip while they picked their teeth with the bones." Bella fingered the rings on her necklace as if they were prayer beads.

"Why don't you have your rings resized? I know a great jeweler. In fact, we'll be going right by there."

"No, way. Russ gave them to me, and they're not coming off my body." Bella's hand fisted over the rings. "Not for anything."

Char turned at the Nimitz Home and Museum at East Main and headed downtown. "When am I going to meet this mystery man, anyway?"

"Right now he's only home for two days at a time." Bella dropped a wink. "I'm not letting him out of bed longer than it takes to pay for a pizza."

An ancient memory broke the surface of Char's brain. She and Jimmy, just married, living in the apartment. Sex, no longer illicit, became their favorite hobby. They'd whiled away the weekends playing in bed. She'd imprinted his long body lines into her brain, the taste of his skin onto her tongue. And he . . . he had made her scream.

A small puff of nostalgia escaped her lips before she could catch it. "You sound so happy. What's he like?"

Bella's tense features relaxed. "He's one of the original computer geeks. You know, one of those chess club, D&D, gamer guys from high school?" She turned to Char with a wicked smile. "He's now the chief information officer of a multinational credit firm." She sat back with a sigh. "And he loves me. He loved me when I met him my first year of college, when I was fat and pretty darned unlovable."

"Do you really believe your weight—"

"No, I don't mean my weight. You may find this hard to believe, but at one time in my life, I had a Rock of Gibraltar–sized chip on my shoulder."

"No!"

Bella chuckled and fluffed her hair. "I haven't always been the model of deportment you see before you today."

Char wheeled into the parking lot and slid into one of the few remaining spots. She turned off the car and grabbed her purse from the floorboard.

Bella sat assessing her. "Have you ever thought of getting some highlights?"

Char shook her head.

"Nothing crazy. I'm talking about a lighter shade of blond on the top layer and around your face." Bella cocked her head. "It would brighten your skin and set off those cornflower blue eyes."

Char looked in the rearview mirror at herself. Same blond, shoulder-length hair she'd had since high school, caught up in the usual ponytail. But the light through the sunroof shone off the silver. When had that happened? Char ducked her head. *Yeah, and then comes a touch-up every six weeks at forty bucks a pop.* "Nah, maybe just a cut." Char pulled herself out of the car. Bella unfurled from it like a starlet on the red carpet. She looked from herself to Bella. "We look like a joke about the grandma and the dominatrix."

Bella let out a startled bark of laughter. Then her face sobered as she looked toward the Clip 'n Curl. "I'm regretting the decision to leave my leather whip home."

As they approached the salon, Bella's steps shortened, and her chin got higher.

She balked at the door, a little girl's uncertainty on her face. Char leaned over, pulled the door open, and held it for her friend. "Come on, sista. I'll show you round the 'hood."

They walked in laughing.

Saturday was the busiest day at the salon. Every station was occupied, with several women perched on floral couches rifling through magazines in the waiting area. One by one, the women fell silent. Char could almost hear the necks creak as faces swiveled toward the door. The women on dryer row eyed them from under their clear plastic helmets. Char waved to Penny, her hairdresser, who pretended to have her hands full of electric curlers for Ms. Richardson's steel-gray hair. She gave a tiny shake of her head.

Well, Bella's outfits did tend to smack the eye. The girls would settle once they got used to it. She took her friend's elbow, led her to the manicurist, and put her in the chair. "Now, Denise, I owe this lady a lot, so you give her the works, y'hear?" Her voice rang in the quiet room. She turned and, cocking an eyebrow, stared them down. Glances sidled away, and the interrupted conversations started up once more. Though she felt sure the subject had changed.

She patted Bella's shoulder, then strode to Penny's now-vacant chair. "Penny, I do believe it's officially summer. That calls for a change." She plopped down and looked at her tired face in the lighted mirror. "I need highlights." She tilted her head. "And maybe some bangs. What do you think?"

Two hours later, Char tilted her chin to see the back of her head in the mirror Penny held.

"You look fabulous." Bella stood behind her chair, beaming at her in the lighted mirror. "Five years younger, at least."

Char swallowed. She looked so different. The highlighted blond bangs and wispy sides framed her thin face, softening the hard lines, setting off her eyes. She didn't dislike the woman who stared back at her; it's just that she wasn't sure who she was. *Well, given the past year, maybe that's not a bad thing.* She reached for her checkbook. "I think I like it."

Bella chimed in. "Well, good, because we're going for ice cream to celebrate. My treat."

As Char scribbled the check, her ears picked up threads of the beauty shop babble around her.

"So I told him, I am *not* leaving my mother—"

"...right in the PTA board meeting. Can you believe it?"

Char tore the check out of the book and handed it to Penny.

"You heard she was thrown out of that grief group over at Saint Luke's, right?"

Penny's eyes skittered to Char's, then away. She took the check, a red stain flooding her face.

"After all she's been through, we shouldn't be surprised, bless her heart."

"Betty told me that hussy solicited her husband at the feed store. Something's got to be done."

No mistaking Toni Bergstrom's strident whisper. Char felt Bella snap to attention at her side.

She flicked her glance to the mirror. Bella's delicate eyebrows gathered over the storm in her eyes. *Now that's enough.* Char reached in her purse and pulled out the car keys. "Hon, would you mind starting the car for me? I've got one thing to take care of, and I'll be right there."

Bella shot her a rebellious look.

Char returned it, saying under her breath "My 'hood, remember? I'll handle it."

Bella snatched the keys, turned, and put an extra roll in her hips as she strolled slowly to the door, holding the eye of every woman brave enough to stare.

The door closed behind her.

Righteous anger pounded in the pulse banging through the veins of Char's neck. "Hey!" Char's strident voice silenced the room. "*Ladies.*" She inhaled a deep breath, then recited the Pledge of Allegiance in her head to calm down. Yelling would only give the biddies more gossip fodder. Besides, it wasn't needed. You could hear a hair-pin drop in the salon.

"I am not going to stand here and preach to you. I'll leave that to the church y'all will visit tomorrow." She shot a meaningful look around the room. Several women had the grace to look away. "I've known most of you my entire life, and there are way too many glass houses here for all the rocks flying around." She shot a pointed glance at Toni Bergstrom, who flushed but held her stare. Char's brave tone faltered. "God knows, I've got way too much glass of my own to be throwing them.

"When I first met Bella, I judged her like ya'll are doing right now: the outrageous too-young clothes, her loud Yankee accent..." She smiled and shook her head. "That hot body."

Toni Bergstrom opened her mouth but closed it when Char pointed at her.

"Bella Donovan is a *married*, caring woman who moved to our town four months ago. In all that time, not one of us deigned to speak with her. In spite of that, she helped me when I didn't know how to ask for help." She put her purse strap over her shoulder. "I'm proud to call her my friend." She held her chin up as she strode the gauntlet of chairs to the exit.

A bell tinkled as she pulled the glass door open. "So if you need somebody to talk about, you can talk about me. There's enough meat on that bone for you to chew on for weeks, I'm sure. But give her a rest."

CHAPTER
11

Courage is going from failure to failure without losing enthusiasm.

—*Winston Churchill*

And this is your room." Wiley walked through the open doorway to the screened-in porch.

JB looked around the box in his arms, careful that he didn't trip over the step down. Added as a pleasant haven from bugs on warm summer evenings, the porch did double duty as a storage room. Bicycles leaned against the house, mud boots and discarded outdoor shoes lined up next to the step. Opaque storage containers marched along the knee-high outside perimeter, screens stretched above them to the sloping ceiling. Two plastic webbed lawn chairs faced the yard, a scarred white table between them. Tucked against the wall to his right sat a narrow fold-down cot, made up neatly with a faded patchwork quilt.

Wiley set his box in a corner and dusted his hands. "It's not much, I know, but we used the spare bedroom for the baby."

JB dropped his box of clothes on the bed. "Are you kidding? With the pretty summer we've got, you're going to want to trade rooms with me." He crossed the patio bricks, hand extended. "I'm sorry as hell to barge in on you like this, partner. It happened so fast." He let the lame excuse dangle.

"You're welcome for as long as you want to stay, JB. We're proud to have you." Wiley's firm grip underscored the welcome. He turned his head at a muffled infant's cry from the back of the house. "Well, there's the dinner bell. Why don't you wash up? We'll bring in the rest of the boxes after we eat."

Ten minutes later, JB stood beside a chair at the plastic-tablecloth-clad dining room table.

When Dana bustled in, put a plate of biscuits on the table, and sat, JB pulled out his chair and did the same.

"Sorry for the informality, but here lately, if it's not easy to clean up, it's put up." Dana smiled. Her husband deftly avoided his son's grasping hands to fasten a bib around his neck.

JB had met Dana before but had always found her a bit different: an owl in a henhouse. A tiny thing, with short spiked hair and an athlete's body, she owned the local gym and training center in town. The gym made good money, so when they decided to start a family, Wiley offered to be Mr. Mom, staying home with the baby during the day, traveling weekends to PBR events. It seemed odd to JB, but Wiley appeared content.

Dana filled two bowls with steaming stew, then passed the dish to him. Wiley waved a spoonful of orange goop in front of the baby. "Come on, Monty, you know you love this repulsive stuff."

JB passed the biscuits to Dana. "He may need to do some growing into that name. Where did you come up with it?"

"Dana's family name is Lamont. We named him after her side." Monty decided he did like the mush his dad put in his mouth and smacked his fat hands on the high chair, demanding more. Dana set Wiley's plate at his elbow.

JB took a spoonful of stew. He'd been expecting beef, but the heavy, rich taste of goat filled his mouth instead. "This is wonderful." The stew tasted spicy and exotic. "The goat I've had in the past was kind of tough and didn't have much flavor."

Wiley looked up from the baby. "That's because you haven't eaten *my* goats before, bubba. I raise them on corn; that's the difference."

Monty took advantage of his father's inattention and slapped his hand in the baby food bowl, upending it and spattering squash-colored mush on the table, himself, and Wiley.

At Wiley's horrified look, Monty broke into a gale of giggles. Dana joined in the laugh at Wiley's expense.

Wiley mopped the baby's face. "Oh, little man, little man, what to do with you?"

JB now understood the roll of paper towels perched on the end of the table.

Dana pulled off several sheets, walked behind the baby, and began the cleanup. Dana knelt beside Wiley's chair. "Now you." She caught his chin in her hand and pulled his head around. She studied his face, then swiped at a few spatters. "You're good."

She was halfway to her feet when Wiley hooked his arm around her waist and pulled her into his lap. "Only good, am I?" He leaned her back over his arm. "I'll show you good." He growled and lowered his head to kiss her. Her arms came around his neck as she opened to him.

JB knew they had forgotten they weren't alone. Want fired in his chest. Not lust, but an aching, empty *want*. Everything JB had lost lay before him: a warm kitchen, a good meal, a tight family. Memories superimposed over his vision. This could have been Char and him, back when Benje was a baby.

After the wave-break of memory, the emotions crashed: the smug satisfaction with life, pride in his home and family, the peace that came from reaching his dreams. As he watched the baby, the wanting tightened his chest until only shallow breaths could fit around it. Benje's coloring was lighter, and he was longer, less chubby. But the goofy all-in grin was the same. JB's vision blurred. He blinked to clear it.

Monty, suddenly realizing a target was within reach, twined his fingers in Dana's short hair and pulled. "Unnngh!" Dana broke the kiss, laughing. "Ow, Monty, stop!" Wiley pulled the baby's hands away, laughing down into her face.

They both looked up, across the table at JB. Had he made a noise? Must have. Mortification spread heat to his face. He ducked his head to wipe his mouth, then scooted his chair back and stood. "I'm going to get after the rest of those boxes in the truck."

Dana's brow took on a mother's concerned furrow. "You don't want more dinner, JB? You hardly ate." She stood.

"No, ma'am, thank you. The dinner was great."

Wiley's face flashed a mixture of guilt and pity. When

Dana would have taken a step toward JB, he caught her hand, twining his fingers in hers. "We'll be right here, JB."

He cleared his throat, spun on his heel, and escaped.

It was full dark by the time JB carried in the last of his stuff. He dropped the box and locked the door behind him. In the silence of the kitchen, he could hear the tick of the clock on the mantel in the living room. The Galts had retired early to the bedrooms at the rear of the house. JB hefted his burden one last time and walked to his room, hearing the lilt of a muffled radio and a low chuckle from the hallway he passed.

He stepped down onto the porch, stacked the box on top of the pile sprawling over half the room, and closed the door to the house. He stretched, vertebrae popping. Bugs ticked on the screens, trying to reach the small yellow light of the Tinkerbell lamp on a box at the head of his bed.

God, he was tired. He sat on the edge of the bed and worked at pulling his boots off. This was not the kind of tired that a night's sleep could fix. It felt more like a lead blanket of weariness weighted his soul.

Work. The first order of business tomorrow would be to stop by the feedlot and see if Junior was still willing to take him back. He couldn't even afford pride lately. He shucked out of his shirt and jeans, laying them on the plastic chair. Twenty-one years of work, and all he had to show was a porch full of boxes and a championship belt buckle.

He clicked off the light, shoved the blanket to the end of the bed, and crawled under the sheet. A metal bar under the mattress pressed into his back. He stretched his arm up to rest his head on it.

The night poured through the black screens, reclaiming its rightful territory. Homing beacon gone, the bugs stopped worrying the screen, and crickets in the yard tuned up a night song.

The fresh smell of damp grass in the dark reminded him of walking with Charla the other night. They hadn't spoken, just walked along together. Charla had never felt the need to fill up a pretty moment with words; it was one of the things that had drawn him to her, way back in high school. She wasn't one of those chatty, giggly girls; if Charla spoke, it was because she had something to say.

He'd almost forgotten how rare and wonderful they'd been together. Or maybe his own guilt made him shove it all to the back of his mind, so he could live with himself.

JB stared into the dark, his thoughts a projection screen for his memories. Char, dressed prim and proper for church after a night of hot loving. Mighty Mouse, bucking hard, tossed a rider over his head. His gut twisted. Benje. Sun glinting off his copper hair, squinted up at him, hero worship clear as the freckles on his nose.

He whispered to the dark, "Lord, I know you don't throw more at a person than they can bear, but you do get close to the line sometimes."

JB knew from experience that when he got a headache from ramming his head into a problem, it was because he'd stopped listening. As he rolled to his side, the support bar dug into his ribs. "You got my attention, Lord. I'm all ears."

No reply.

The cricket concert slowly released the day's tension from his body, but sleep didn't come as easily.

• • •

Bella cleared her throat. "I just stumbled across it online."

"Don't you hate how you can't surf the web nowadays without hitting pop-up ads for bull trainers?" Char chuckled. "It's okay, Bella. I'm not going to call New York and tell them you've taken an interest in ranching."

"Look, do you want it, or do I chuck it?"

"Oh no, I want it. I appreciate you thinking about me." Char jotted the number on the pad at her elbow and hung up. Clever Bella. It would have never occurred to Char to search online for a trainer.

It felt so darned good to take her life in her own hands and do something instead of cowering, waiting for the next disaster to hit. *Maybe I'm finally beating my way out of the weeds and onto the road to recovery that the grief counselor talked about.* She hadn't had a pill in four weeks, two days, twelve hours. The chores, formerly an unending series of pratfalls, were becoming routine. The cattle were fat and sleek, grazing on the spring grass.

Thank you, Great-Grandma. The china had sold for more than she'd dreamed. She'd banked enough money to fund a trainer for a year, at least. Char glanced to the china hutch, filled now with her mother's colorful collection of floral patterns. Smiling, she whispered, "Good to have you back in the kitchen, Mom."

She ripped the trainer's number off the pad. There was more than one bull trainer in Texas. She tucked the scrap of paper in the back pocket of her jeans as she walked to the living room.

Her dad napped in the rocker, and Rosa stood at the sliding back door, speaking into her cell phone. "I'd say it's going very well. His condition is advancing, of course, but he's adapting and seems calmer." She turned and started, seeing Char. "I have to go now. I'll call you later with a full progress report, all right?" She snapped the phone closed and slid it into her pocket. "That was a relative, calling about another patient." Still watching Char, she reached for her purse, perched on the edge of the table. The back of her hand hit it, knocking it to the floor. She grumbled and bent to retrieve the scattered contents.

"Rosa, you're allowed to get a phone call now and again. Don't worry about it." Char knelt beside the rocker. "Daddy? Rosa's leaving. Do you want to say good-bye?" As she rubbed his forearm, he jerked awake.

"Wha?" He frowned down at her. "Peggy. Did you get the liniment from Junior's?"

Her heart gave a painful pinch. He'd mistaken her for her mother. Would she ever get used to this?

Rosa touched her shoulder. "This disease can be harder on the caregiver than the patient. You should try to get away sometime, Charla. Take a vacation."

Yeah, maybe the family villa in the South of France...

"You are my vacation, Rosa. I'm so grateful that you ran into Rev. Mike that day."

"Lot Number twenty-three: sold, to bidder number five forty-six."

JB tuned out the auctioneer's drone. He should load the calves he'd bought and hit the road. It was an hour and a half ride from Austin back home. But it felt good to relax in the anonymity of a crowd of strangers. No frowns aimed his way, no behind-the-hand whispers.

As the stands cleared, he put a boot on the riser in

front of him, rested his arm on his knee, and watched the workers prep the ring for the next lot.

When he'd shown up for work at the feedlot on Monday, Junior had seemed relieved. And he must have at least partially forgiven JB, because buying calves beat shoveling shit any day.

He had a job now. That was one problem off the plate. *As to the rest—*

"'Scuse me."

A big man slid into the open seat next to JB. A light gray Stetson covered black hair, cut short, and there was a bronze cast to his high cheekbones.

Some Indian blood there, I'll warrant. Whipcord tough, weather-beaten, and tired, he looked like the Marlboro Man, from those cigarette commercials in the sixties. JB touched the brim of his hat. "Howdy."

The man nodded, studying the auction catalog in front of him. "Is the Kobe lot next?"

"Not sure. I'm done buyin'." He stuck out a hand. "JB Denny."

The man's grip was as hard as his face. "Max Jameson, High Heather Ranch."

"Well, you sure aren't from around here. Nothin' 'high' in East Texas."

"My ranch is outside Steamboat. Colorado."

JB whistled softly through his teeth. "A long way to come, for a cattle auction."

The man watched the activity in the ring, rolling the catalog in his hands. "I came to check out the Kobe calves. I'm thinking about running them on my place. Price is three times my steers, and they dress out heavier."

JB snorted. "No offense, but you don't look like the

type to be massaging cow flesh." Kobe beef come from a genetic strain in Japan, where ten head was considered a large herd, due to the labor involved in raising them. "Ranchers" brushed their cattle and massaged sake into their coats. He'd heard a real Kobe steak was worth every penny of the two-hundred-dollar price tag.

Not that he'd ever eaten any. He even couldn't afford to pay attention, lately.

"I misspoke. I'm looking to run Kobe-*style* beef." Max let out a dry cough that might have been a chuckle—except he didn't look happy. "Anything gets massaged on my spread, it's gonna be me."

"I hear that."

He turned. "How's the beef business in Texas?"

Seeing Max's expression, JB realized he wouldn't want to be the one who put that pissed look there. "I manage a feedlot, part-time. The owner doesn't look like he's going hungry." The man would have no way of knowing what an understatement that was.

"Well, I'll tell you, no ranchers are fat and happy where I come from." Max swore under his breath. "That's reserved for the rich tourists and ski-resort owners, who can afford it."

"I read that y'all are having a time of it. Property taxes killing you?"

"Between that, the beef prices, and the BLM threatening to shut down grazing on Federal land, my damn ranch is close to failing."

JB grimaced. "Shoot I got you beat—my whole damn life is failing."

"Tell me about it." Max stared at the arena that JB was sure he didn't see. "My girl just left me for the rancher down the road who's in bed with the developers." His lip curled, but it looked more like a wolf's leer than a smile.

"That's going to make for a crowded honeymoon," JB said, then immediately regretted, as Max's glare smoked a hole in him.

Wrong move. JB straightened, lightly fisting his hands.

Max studied him for a long few seconds. Then he chuckled, and held out his fist for a knuckle-bump. "I like you."

Glad not to be feeling those hard knuckles anywhere else on his body, JB bumped. "Once this lot is done, you want to grab a cup of coffee? I'd like to hear more about your spread."

Dinner over and the kitchen cleaned, Char and her dad sat on the couch before a crackling fire. She closed the McMurtry novel she'd been reading aloud. Usually the solitary, windswept descriptions of the Old West transported her, but tonight they left her restless and melancholy. "How about some hot chocolate, Daddy?" Uncurling her legs from beneath her, she looked over at her father.

He stared into the fire, silent tears glistening down the long furrows bracketing his mouth to his chin.

"Daddy, what's wrong?" The ravaged desolation in his eyes sent alarm racing down her nerves.

"I miss them, Little Bit."

"Who, Daddy?" She took his hand, running her thumb over the parchment-thin skin.

"Your mother. Benje. JB."

A startled sob burst from her. They hadn't talked about it, any of it. Ever. Her dad was a private man about his emotions. She didn't know if his silence was due to reticence, or if he'd lost those memories. For his sake, she'd wished the latter.

The naked pain on his face tore something open in her, something hot and festering.

Of course she'd cried when they'd lost Benje. Isolated in a bell jar of agony, she'd done nothing else for weeks afterward. But when the raging emotions finally ebbed, they left behind a desiccated husk. On the day Jimmy left, there wasn't enough moisture left for tears.

"Why did everyone leave, Charla Rae?"

Hot, acid tears flooded her as she choked out, "I don't know, Daddy. I wish I did."

Her father's arms came around her, and she fell into his chest, sobbing. The trauma from the last maelstrom of grief left scars. At the deepest part of her, Char lived in dread that another bout would shatter her so completely that the pieces would scatter, impossible to gather. Instead of a tornado, this felt like a soaking spring rain. Cradled in the safety of her daddy's arms, his chin on her head, they rocked together and let the tears have their way.

Mistakes are a part of being human. Appreciate your mistakes for what they are: precious life lessons that can only be learned the hard way. Unless it's a fatal mistake, which, at least, others can learn from.

—Al Franken

The office chair creaked when Char stretched, yawning. This morning she felt lighter, as if last night had washed something poisonous out of her system. She'd fallen into bed and slept like a child, sweet dreams and all.

Staring through the office window at the sun-baked yard, she longed to saddle Pork Chop and ride out to check on the calves in the nursery pasture. Instead, she swiveled toward the desk, whistling softly. The last office chore lay before her: the bull trainer's resume. Once Bella had given her the idea, she did a thorough online search. Every trainer she'd called was contracted elsewhere. The one who agreed to talk to her quoted a rate twice the one Bella had given her.

Reaching for the phone, she hesitated. *Maybe I'll*

check email first. Her fingers flew as she signed on to the Internet. No mail. *Maybe one game of solitaire.*

Dang it, why the procrastination? The answer popped to the front of her brain. The past months had been brutal. Life was just now feeing safe again, as if she'd spun a soft cocoon around the ranch and snuggled in. Bringing an outsider here would change that.

You sure you don't feel a little bit bad about cutting Jimmy out, Charla Rae?

She sighed. *Yeah, Mom, maybe just a little.*

Her old life now seemed a happy dream. She hadn't realized how much easier Jimmy had made her life. She'd taken it for granted. And lately he had been awfully sweet to her. He was trying, that much was plain. But then she remembered Jess and bitter poured over the sweet, smothering it. Jimmy sure hadn't looked back. Darned if she would. Reading the phone number at the top of the sheet in front of her, she dialed.

"Yeah." The smoke-rough voice at the other end of the phone sounded annoyed.

"Red Gandy?"

"Yeah."

"Mr. Gandy, my name is Charla Denny, of Denny Bucking Bulls. You sent me your resume?"

"Yeah."

"Yes, well, I was reviewing it. You're obviously experienced. Seven ranches over the past ten years. I recognize several breeders' names. I was wondering if you could send me a list of references?"

"Yeah. I'll email 'em to you."

"Providing they are in order, would you be willing to come out for an interview?"

"Sure. But if your husband likes me, will he make a decision that day? Laredo to Fredericksburg is a long way to drive for an interview."

She should have anticipated that. But she hadn't. "*I'll* be doing the hiring."

Silence. "Yes, ma'am. Is room and board included? I don't need much, just a stall and a cot."

"Oh no, that wouldn't be—" *Whoa.* No need to tell her circumstances to a stranger, not when she lived so far out of town. "I'm sorry, we don't have the room. I can recommend an inexpensive place downtown."

After scheduling a date and time, they hung up. She put a hand to her stomach to calm the butterflies. "Like Daddy says, worrying is as useless as setting a milk bucket under a bull."

JB leaned on the paddock fence of the feedlot's outside corral. Junior had been a member of the high school rodeo team back in the day. When he bought the business, he'd built a covered arena for the team to practice and for competitions. Grateful for the shade of the pole barn's roof, JB took off his Resistol and rubbed his forehead in the crook of his elbow. A breeze cooled his sweaty head.

Off work for the day, on his way to the truck, he'd stopped to watch. Besides, he was in no hurry. His next stop was the ranch, but he knew that Little Bit would be a harder sell than Junior had been. But he had to try one more time. Hopefully it would be harder for her to say no to a hat-in-hand, broken-down cowboy. Wouldn't take much acting on his part either.

"Now, focus this time. Loosen up and keep shifting your feet for the entire eight seconds!" The coach of the high school rodeo team yelled from the other side of the ring.

JB leaned his forearms on the fence as the gate swung open. The practice bull crow-hopped out of it, landing with jarring thumps. From the rear of the chute, kids shouted encouragement. The rider stuck through the first few jumps, but when the bull twisted and kicked out to the side, the rider overbalanced. He hung suspended at an impossible angle off the side of the bull until his hand popped out of the rope and he landed in a heap in the middle of the paddock. A young boy on a stocky chestnut hazed the bull to the gate as the rider picked himself out of the dirt and dusted himself off.

"That was better. Anyone can get caught out by a wicked belly roll like that." The coach walked to the center of the ring. "Do you see how you had more control when you shifted your feet? I know it seems counterintuitive, but the minute you clamp down, you're as good as off." He gave the boy a pat on the back, sending him limping off to retrieve his hat, ten feet away.

"Bubba Wanksta gorillas."

JB hadn't realized he had company. He did a double take. The lanky teen slouched on the fence beside him seemed to have dropped from some alternate universe. Skater shorts, crotch to the knees, black T-shirt, and backward-facing baseball cap. The nose and lip studs hurt to look at. As the boy turned his head to watch the next rider, JB eyed the tattoo on the back of his neck—a fish skeleton with a smile bristling wicked-sharp teeth.

"Say what?" JB asked.

The boy turned to him. "Very large assholes."

JB snorted. "Big words from someone riding a fence."

He pointed to the young cowboys. "It takes stones to get on an animal that wants to rip your guts out and stomp them full of dirt."

The kid puffed out his skinny chest. "I got the stones. Just don't have the interest."

JB glimpsed peroxide-white hair under the cap, a quick memory flashed. He'd seen this kid. Last week, when he'd been leaving the feedlot, splashing through puddles and sheeting rain on the way to his truck. The teen stood against the fence watching the bull riders, his back soaked by the rain the wind pushed under the roof.

No interest. Right. "I've seen you around, haven't I?"

"Probably. I work in the feed store. Name's Travis."

JB stuck out his hand. "JB Denny."

The kid looked him down, then back up. "I know who you are. I deliver feed out to your wife's ranch."

JB covered a wince with what he hoped passed for a rueful smile. "Well, you may have some stones after all."

The kid finally shook his hand.

"Where are you from?" JB asked.

The kid just looked at him.

"Come on. You're obviously not from around here."

"Hardly." His haughty tone made it obvious he thought that was a good thing. "Ohio. But my mom needed a job, and my Uncle Junior had one, so I got dragged to this—" He looked around. "—John Wayne movie set."

"You're wrong about them, you know." JB tipped his chin at the bucking chutes. "Bull riders have more in common with gymnasts or ballet dancers than gorillas."

Travis's turn to snort. "Ballet dancers?"

"Yeah. I know for a fact that all those guys tried out for

Swan Lake but couldn't fit their stones in a pair of tights, so they wound up here."

The pierced lips looked even more painful, smiling.

"If I followed your logic, the strongest guy would be the best. But watch this." JB pointed to a slight cowboy even smaller than Travis, who lowered himself onto the next bull. The kid ran his hand up and down the rope to activate the stickum on the glove.

Atop the slab-sided Brahma, the kid looked about ten years old. If he weighed more than a hundred pounds, JB would eat his missing cap. "That little guy is the best rider on the team." They watched as the rider wrapped the rope around his hand, effectively binding himself to the back of the plunging animal.

When he nodded, the tender opened the gate. The bull hung a horn in the fence, pulling his head around. When he freed it, he started spinning, bucking hard in a circle. Hand waving, the kid sat balanced in the middle, matching the bull's moves, making it look easy. When the timer blew the whistle, he jerked his hand out of the rope and was thrown off to land, catlike, on his feet. He hadn't even lost his hat. The cowboys on the chutes cheered.

"See what I mean? It doesn't matter if you've got massive biceps and can bench press eight hundred pounds, you're never going to be stronger than a bull." JB turned to a gaping Travis. "He found the sweet spot."

"Huh?"

"When you're in the right place, right behind the bull's shoulders, it's like the eye of the storm. Gentle. Easy.

"Done right, it looks simple. But it takes lots of skill and a butt-load of luck to get into the sweet spot and stay there." He settled his hat on his head. "See you around, kid."

Travis slouched against the fence to watch the next rider.

Char flicked the oiled dust rag over the coffee table, wiped her hands on her apron, and surveyed the great room as the cuckoo clock chimed the half hour. Dust motes danced in the light of her clean windows. She heaved a sigh. The minute she turned around, it would be dusty again. *And I still have to do something about those curtains.* Her neck spasmed and her head jerked as a flashback of green plaid skittered across her vision. Fleeing to the kitchen, she dropped the rag in the box under the sink and washed her hands, trying to calm their fine thrum with warm water.

A Crock-Pot full of braised short ribs bubbled on the counter. Crossing to the refrigerator, she opened it, glancing over the gleaming, orderly interior, the bowl of inviting fresh peaches front and center. *I could tweak that peach pie recipe for the fair.* When she noticed the sound of the clock ticking and her nails beating a counterpoint on the stainless steel, she let the door fall closed. Junior had picked up her dad this morning, and the empty house was giving her the heebie jeebies.

"Well then, go outside, Charla." She wanted to. But she'd made a deal with the new trainer when she'd hired him a week ago. He wasn't happy about doing the heavy chores around the ranch, yet he'd agreed, providing she wouldn't hover while he worked the bulls. He had a thing about that. Something about Red Gandy niggled at her during the interview. Nothing she could outright object to, but his language was a shade too familiar and his cold blue eyes a bit condescending. After he left, she convinced herself it was only a fit of nerves. After all, she'd never hired an employee.

She would have loved to have been able to call Jimmy. He'd know what to do. She remembered the days when Jimmy was home from the circuit and she'd look up and see him working the bulls through her kitchen window. She closed her eyes, savoring the feeling of comfort, knowing nothing would happen that Jimmy couldn't fix.

Until it did.

She sighed. Wanting Jimmy back on the place wouldn't make things right. However, she didn't like Gandy forcing her indoors. Trying to respect his request for not watching over his shoulder, she stayed out of his way but she missed the out of doors, the chores, and the cattle. Heck, she even missed Pork Chop.

I could finish that linoleum shelf paper project. The thought of dragging everything out of the pantry made her tired. No, not tired. An antsy, undone feeling set her fingers tapping again. *What did I used to do with my days?* Surely they hadn't always been as boring as this?

Well, not always. Her mind conjured Benje, running through the kitchen, dressed in his Cub Scout uniform. "Hurry, Mom, we're gonna be late!" She shook the echo out of her head.

What she really wanted was a nap, but the crawling antsiness precluded that. *All right, a pill, then a nap.* Her hand closed over the door to the garage before she realized she'd crossed the room.

"Gosh dang it, Charla, what is *wrong* with you?" She

untied the apron, and pulled it over her head. "You're not a prisoner, you're the owner, and his boss!" Tossing the apron on the counter, she strode through the mudroom to the back door.

Hope faded as she saw Pork Chop, in a halter and saddled, tied to the paddock fence. The trainer was nowhere to be seen. She understood the man needed a horse to work cattle, but why did he have to choose hers?

Probably because yours was the only horse in the barn, Charla.

She breathed in a lungful of fresh air. The day was too pretty for whining. She stepped off the porch and meandered around the corner of the house. White puffy clouds scudded fast, like sailboats in a regatta in the cerulean sky. Kicking stones, her glance fell on the strip of dirt between the graveled drive and the house that had been her and Benje's garden. Only the weeds and a few hardy perennials had survived a year's neglect.

For the first time since the accident, the garden didn't remind her of the funeral. The rose bushes were only plants, not the source of casket blankets. Longing hit. Her fingers suddenly itched to get into soil. She wanted the smell of dirt in her nose, to feel the stubborn weeds give under her tug, to see the rich brown of freshly turned dirt. Whistling, she headed for the shed and her garden tools.

Two hours later, Char straightened and put a fist to her cramped lower back. Leaning on the hoe, she swiped her gloved hand across her forehead and surveyed her progress. She'd worked her way halfway down the length of the house. The cultivated red-brown soil eased something in her.

Lemonade sure would taste good. She'd bet Gandy would appreciate some too. She leaned the hoe against the wall, tugged off her gloves, and walked around the house to the back door.

The trainer was busy in the large front paddock, working to separate the bulls from the rest of the herd. Char admired Gandy's easy seat as he darted in and out, cutting out the mama cows. A two-foot-long electric Hot-Shot dangled from a leather strap around his wrist, standard fare for a trainer working bulls.

Pork Chop seemed nervous. She fidgeted at the end of a short rein, her mouth working the bit. Char stopped, halfway to the door, realizing that Gandy had used a double curb bridle. Pork Chop had a tender mouth. The bit wasn't only unnecessary, it was counterproductive, distracting the horse rather than getting her attention. Char winced as he sawed the reins. The horse threw her head up, eyes rolling.

Char knew he wouldn't welcome her interference, but she couldn't stand by and watch him ruin her horse's mouth. She walked across the yard.

The herd milled uneasy in the paddock, stirring dust. Gandy ignored them, concentrating on the ten or so head remaining in the far corner. Char squinted through the cloud of dust. Only bulls remained, except Tricks and her calf. For some reason, the stubborn cow had gotten it in her head to stay with the bulls. She maneuvered to the middle of the pack to keep herself between her calf and the man on the horse. Gandy grabbed the cattle prod, Hot-Shot hanging at his wrist, and kicked Pork Chop in the ribs.

Oh, Tricks, you've gotten yourself in it this time. Dread

laced with the anger in her blood. She did not have a good feeling about this. She climbed on the fence, looking for a place to cross, but the milling herd made the paddock dangerous for someone afoot.

Char glanced at the trainer. His lips were set in a grim line, anger plain in his jerky movements. "Stop!" she yelled, knowing he wouldn't hear over the bawling cattle.

Gandy waded in, Hot-Shotting cattle out of his way. The horse stopped slightly crouched, facing the cow, ready to turn either way. Tricks feinted right, then left. Pork Chop shadowed her. But the calf wasn't as nimble. As a space opened, Pork Chop shot the gap. Tricks bawled as he jabbed the Hot-Shot into her over and over, but she refused to run. He stood between her and her calf.

Char looked over the churning mob of cattle. There had to be something she could do. *The gate to the pasture!* Before she had time to be afraid, she was down and running fast, darting between the huge bodies, yelling and waving her arms to shoo them out of her way. She cleared the herd and sprinted for the gate. Chest heaving with sobbing breaths, she threw the latch and swung the gate wide open.

The cattle, sensing freedom, plunged toward the opening. Gandy was so intent with Tricks, he didn't even notice the young bulls joining the fleeing herd. As the last cow went through, Char threw a look over her shoulder. Pork Chop, flinging lather from her mouth and steaming flanks, struggled to get her head and hold off the bawling cow. Gandy fought her and, leaning out of the saddle with the rod, Hot-Shotted the calf.

"No!" Anger shot through Char's limbs like spewing lava. She ran, waving her arms and screaming. "Stop it!"

The Hot-Shot delivered a high-voltage pulse. Used once on a full-grown cow's hindquarters, it got their attention. The shock was too much for a two-month-old calf. Dirty Tricks stumbled to his knees. Pork Chop reared and Gandy had his hands full, collecting the horse. Tricks took advantage of his distraction and darted around them to her calf, who struggled to its feet.

Char felt the earth vibrate as the cow and calf thundered by her to the gate. On shaky legs, she ran to her horse and grabbed the bridle.

"You get your *ass* off my horse this minute!" she screamed up at the man's florid face.

"What the hell do you think you're doing, Hot-Shotting a calf? There is no reason for that. Ever."

Gandy's face edged from florid to purple as he looked down at her. "You damn bleeding-heart owners, treating your livestock like they're pets." He kicked his feet out of the stirrups and jumped to the ground. "They're dumb animals. You treat them different, you're going to get hurt." He stood, too close, his rheumy eyes leering. "And what the hell would the little woman know about it anyway?" Thick lips twisted in a sneer. "Why don't you go back inside to your knitting and your vibrator?"

Shock hit Char like a slap across the face. She took a step back and stood for what seemed like forever, chest heaving, in stunned disbelief. "You're fired! Gather your things and get off my land," she ground from between her clenched teeth. "*Now.*"

He threw his head back and laughed. Then he raised his hand, the one that held the Hot-Shot.

The starch leached from Char. *What have I done?* Her knees threatened to buckle. This far out of town, her dad not due for hours, this man could do anything to her.

The deepest, most beautiful voice she'd ever heard came from behind her. "I think you'd better listen to the lady, Gandy. She's fully capable of throwing a full-grown man off her property."

CHAPTER 13

I believe we are solely responsible for our choices, and we have to accept the consequences of every deed, word, and thought throughout our lifetime.

—*Elizabeth Kübler-Ross*

Gandy gave her a disgusted look and brushed past her, grumbling under his breath. Char took a few moments to calm her lathered horse, and herself, before facing Jimmy. Crooning, she unbuckled the bridle and pulled the cruel roweled bit from Pork Chop's mouth, holding the reins for control until she could get a halter.

Her stomach hit 7.8 on the Richter scale. *How mad is Jimmy?* There was only one way to find out. She turned to him.

It was worse than she'd thought. He had his father face on.

"You." He pointed at her. "Don't go anywhere. I'll be back as soon as I get that trash cleared off the place." He spun on his heel and marched off.

Char clucked to the horse and they walked to the edge of the paddock and kept going, pacing the perimeter. Pork

Chop needed a cooldown, and so did she. She practiced the breathing technique from her grief group: pull air through her nose, hold it, then release it slowly through her mouth. *Picture all the tension going out with your breath...*

Okay, so Jimmy had a right to be mad. She saw it again. The Hot-Shot reaching out, touching Dirty Tricks on the ear. The calf convulsing, going down. If Jimmy hadn't shown up when he did, who knows what that man might have done to *her*. She shuddered, wishing she could use that thing to zap Gandy's private parts. *Take a deep breath, hold it...*

The trainer was a cruel, awful man. But that didn't absolve her. She'd brought him here. Why? *Plain stubborn pride.* An acid wave of shame washed over her. She wanted to show Jimmy that she could do it all. *Let out the breath, slow, through your lips...*

Pork Chop shuffled through the dust, calm now, walking at her shoulder. As they turned the corner, her heart stuttered. Jimmy stalked toward her. Over his shoulder, she glimpsed Gandy's truck, shooting gravel and a plume of dust as it fishtailed down the drive.

JB paced in the dirt. *If I'd have been an hour later...* He stopped in front of Char. His mouth worked, but nothing came out. He paced some more. *What if I hadn't come out today at all?* Scenarios swarmed in his brain like wasps, each one worse than the last. *Focus, JB, this isn't helping.* When he thought he could speak without yelling, he stopped in front of her again.

"What the heck were you thinking, Charla Rae? Every reputable owner in the business knows about Gandy. He's been fired from more jobs than we've got mice in the barn."

She stood all of five feet tall and stuck out her chin. "I checked his references first, Jimmy. I'm not stupid."

"Had you ever heard of any of them? Know any of them personally?"

"No."

He pushed his hat back on his head. "He gave you the phone numbers of his friends, and they vouched for him."

Her shoulders slumped. Her hat hid her face as she stared at her boots, but he heard the shake in her voice. "I'm sorry, Jimmy. I know it's my fault. I put the stock in danger. I just wanted so badly—"

He couldn't help it. He snapped, "Did it even occur to you that you were hiring a trainer for bulls that don't belong to you?" She cringed as if he'd raised his hand instead of his voice. Guilt bit into his stomach lining. *Jeez, Denny, kick a woman when she's down—you're not much better than Gandy.* He took a deep breath. "I'm sorry, Charla Rae."

When she looked up, the regret in her blue eyes pierced him.

"I was afraid. It just came out as mad, and I'm sorry." He pulled off his hat, to run his shaking hands through his hair. "It's just that I pulled up and saw that SOB coming at you with a Hot-Shot..." He blew out a breath. It was shaky too. "I'm going to have nightmares about what could have happened next for a long time."

Did she really hate him so much that she'd rather have a sleazebag like Gandy helping out around the place?

Looking down at the hurt in her eyes, he figured he knew the answer.

His words came out scratchy as sandpaper. "Charla, let me come back to work the bulls." Her eyes narrowed. "It's the only logical solution, Hon. Who has a more vested interest in them than me? Besides, my price is right, and you know I would never do anything to hurt you or the animals." He gave her his best smile.

He couldn't tell her that he missed her more than the ranch or his bulls. That all he wanted was to be close to her, to be a family again. She'd throw him off the property for sure if she knew. Instead, he had to go slow. Maybe if she trusted him to help out with the ranch, she'd trust him with other things, like her heart.

He noticed the minute she stopped listening. He recognized the look—that she'd heard it all, had been down every one of those roads.

Well, she probably had. He snapped his mouth closed. Pork Chop stomped a foot to dislodge a fly. A cow in the pasture lowed to her calf. He took a breath. "I know you have no reason to trust me, Charla Rae. And guess I don't deserve your trust." He stuffed his hands in his back pockets and looked her in the eye. "But when it comes to the ranch and the bulls, I don't fool around. I'll make you a deal, a business deal."

She watched him, wary as a rabbit without a hole in hawk country.

"Let me come back, to work the stock for a month. If, at the end of that month, you still don't want me here, I'll find you a trainer."

She cocked her head, looking for a trap.

"And I'll pay half his wages out of my pocket." He raised his hands slow, palm out. "Straight up."

She looked to the grazing herd in the pasture and thought on it.

"Well, the bulls have got to be trained." She shrugged. "And after what I did, I guess I owe you."

He relaxed for the first time since he'd driven up. A reprieve. A chance to try to make it up to her. Maybe she'd see that it was possible for them to be a team.

And who knew? Maybe having him around would remind her of the good times, and how they were together. God knows, he didn't need any reminders—nowadays, it seemed to be all he thought about.

"I want one thing clear between us, Jimmy." She squinted up at him. "Not one of your women is to step foot on the place. Ever."

"Not a problem. Don't have any." Before he could see how that registered, he turned and walked for the truck.

To still have her back up about other women after all this time, she had to care.

Didn't she?

Char retrieved the milk from the refrigerator, unscrewed the cap, and sniffed it. Satisfied it wasn't spoiled, she carried it to the counter.

What kind of idiot hires a trainer for bulls she doesn't own? Maybe I'm better off in the house, with what I know. The Valium itch crawled over her brain, stronger than it had been in days. *And do what? Rearrange closets? If that's all I can do, I might as well get the dang bottle and take them all.*

She couldn't believe she'd agreed to let Jimmy back on the property. Worry zinged under her skin, raising goose bumps. How could she work side by side with him, a constant reminder of her life before?

She'd known him over half of her life. Would that make it easier for her to fall back into the Jimmy habit?

She stared at the baking soda that she'd sifted into her bowl of baking powder biscuits. "Of all the bone-headed, stupid—focus, Charla."

Her dad looked up from the photo album on the kitchen table. "What's the matter, hon?"

She picked up the bowl and dumped the contents in the trash. "Oh, I'm just discombobulated tonight, Daddy." She snagged the bag of flour on her way back to the counter. "I'm as awkward as a high-schooler on the first day of home ec."

He patted the seat next to him. "Come set a minute. Dinner can wait."

She wiped her hands on her apron and rounded the counter. He'd lost the ability to read, but since Rosa had discovered the photo albums, her dad carried one with him most days. She sat next to him.

The page was open to a photo of her as a smiling teen, holding a blue ribbon from the county fair above her prize-winning pie. "Oh, Daddy, I remember that."

He turned the page. Photos of her and her mother, working in the garden. Her dad, standing next to a prize steer. Their life, frozen in sepia moments. He turned another page. Her heart stumbled as an eight-by-ten photo slapped her. A much younger Charla, in wedding white. A leaner, less careworn cowboy, his arm around her, grinning like he'd just won the lottery.

Her finger traced the edge of the picture. "God, we were so young."

"Charla?"

She glanced over. Her father looked tired. The lines on his face deepened to furrows as he gazed down at the album.

"When is JB coming home?"

She put a hand over his, on the table. "He's not, Daddy."

The weight of being a caregiver to her parent settled over her. She so missed leaning on his strength and wisdom.

"How much longer are you going to make JB pay, Charla Rae? You know the accident wasn't his fault." Sharp blue eyes studied her.

She jerked her head up. "I never blamed him for that, Daddy." At least, she didn't think she did.

"Then why isn't he here, washing up for dinner?"

No telling what facts had fallen out of the holes in his memory at any given time. "It's complicated."

He pulled his hand from under hers, putting it on top. "You know that little girl never meant squat to him, not really."

Another jolt shot through her. She jerked her hand from his and peered at him. "Have you been talking to Mom?"

His focus once more on the photo album, he turned another page. "I talk to your mother all the time. She's not real good about getting back to me though."

*You can clutch the past so tightly to your chest that it
leaves your arms too full to embrace the present.*
—*Jan Glidewell*

JB came awake with a snort. Something was different.
Opening his eyes, he glanced to the yard. The sun sparkled off the dew on the grass. Mockingbirds ran through
their morning repertoire. He hadn't slept until dawn in
weeks.

He threw back the covers, sat up, and took in a lungful
of cool, morning-fresh air. In spite of a sore back from
the cot's torture bar, he felt pretty good. After a satisfying
morning scratch, he limped to the box that held his clean
clothes.

The orderly kitchen supplied java, but not company to
go with it, so, coffee cup in hand, JB stepped out the back
door to find some. Wiley stood on the back porch, chor-
tling baby in arms, a canvas and aluminum contraption at
his feet.

"Mornin,' hoss. Guess I don't have to ask how you
slept."

During his weeks of residence, JB had always been on his third cup of coffee by the time the household awoke. "Where's Dana?"

"She left for work a few minutes ago." Monty, looking silly in his floppy blue sun hat, waved plump arms, appearing more than pleased with the day. Wiley looked around at his feet, then held the baby out. "Help me out here, will you?" Distracted, he plopped Monty into the crook of JB's arm. "This can be done solo, but it's awkward." He bent to adjust the contraption's nylon straps.

Steaming mug of coffee in one hand, armload of baby in the other, JB looked down. The baby stared back. JB smiled. Monty looked worried. When his little eyebrows scrunched up and lips pursed, JB knew he had to do something. Bouncing on the balls of his feet, he crossed his eyes and blew Monty a raspberry. Making up his mind, the baby's face cleared, and he giggled.

The baby butt fit snug in JB's arm; the soft weight leaned against his chest. A fierce longing fired in him, taking his breath. Lowering his head, he touched his lips to the baby's forehead. He closed his eyes and inhaled the scent of powder and warm baby.

God, I miss you, Benje.

"Oh, shit, JB, I'm sorry. I didn't think—"

He looked up to Wiley's stricken face. "It's all good. Me 'n Monty are just getting acquainted." Monty blew a raspberry back. JB chuckled past the tight wad in his throat. "World's full of kids, Wiley."

Wiley shrugged into the metal contraption, and JB realized it was a baby carrier. When he turned his back, JB set his coffee cup on the brick edge of the house and settled the baby into the backpack. Monty grabbed a hank of his father's hair and slapped his back with the other hand.

"Yeah, I know, giddyup. We're going." Wiley shrugged the carrier higher and snapped the buckle at his waist closed. "You want to check the herd with us?"

"A batch of smelly goats does not make a herd, partner." JB put down regret and picked up his coffee.

Wiley stepped off the porch. "Let's not start up a range war this early in the morning."

Once they left the mowed yard, the long grass left dark blue swipes of dew below the knees of their jeans. The fresh air held only a glimmer of the savage heat that would take over in an hour or so. The baby smacked the back of Wiley's head again, and he broke into a rocking gallop.

"Ride 'em, Monty! Let her buck!" JB trotted to keep up, then fell back into step with the pair. "You know, Wiley, I flat don't understand it. You're so ugly your momma gave you a meatball necklace to get the dog to play with you." He looked out at the rolling property, dotted with grazing goats. "Yet here you are, a spread, a wife, a baby. How'd you get so lucky?"

Wiley chuckled. "Hey, even a blind squirrel finds an acorn every once in a while."

They walked in silence for a bit.

"I didn't cheat on her, you know." JB watched a kid bounce around its mother, darting and butting her in play. "The marriage was over in everything but law before I fell into Jess's bed. I know that doesn't count for much, but—"

"Counts enough so you and I can stay friends, I'll tell you that." Wiley's nonchalant look didn't fool JB. He was dead serious.

"I tried everything I knew to pull Char out of it." The bleak mood of those awful days after the funeral settled over him again, and it seemed that gravity exerted a stronger pull on his shoulders than a few moments ago. "She went away, somewhere in her head, and she wouldn't let me follow. I tried being sweet. Tried to distract her. Tried settling into a routine. But none of it seemed to touch her."

JB rubbed the back of his neck. "I even booked a surprise trip for us to Hawaii. I figured that maybe, in a different place..." He remembered Char's panic when he surprised her with the tickets. Like a cornered she-bear, her savage attack had rocked him. She got in his face, screeching that she was not leaving home, and if he tried to take her, he'd be sorry. He'd actually been frightened, seeing the glittering malice in those eyes. "That didn't work either.

"I knew it was over." He looked at his friend. "Then I met Jess at an event. She was like a tropical island after nuclear winter. The attraction was like some force of nature." He snorted. "And now here I am, turned out and too worn out for stud."

"All that's past, JB. You've gotta focus on what comes next." Wiley strode forward, hands in the carrier straps at his shoulders. "Once your feet are back under you, you'll move on."

"Sure hope you're right, partner." JB put his fists to his sore back and stretched. "I'm too old for this."

Bella looked shaky as she pulled Pork Chop alongside Bar B. Char laughed. "Told you she could turn through the eye of a needle!"

"I think I wet my pants." Bella kicked out of the stirrups and slid to the ground, clutching the saddle when her knees refused to support her.

Char laughed. "That's how I felt the first time she and I cut cattle. Well, that's not exactly true. Pork Chop did all the cutting. I did the flopping-around part, just like you." She dismounted, and they walked the horses through the pasture to the gate.

"I wanted to learn to ride, but I don't know about this cutting business."

Char snorted. "Well, you sure look like a cowgirl, anyway." Bella's jeans were skin tight, but at least they were Wranglers, complete with iron-faded knife creases, workday boots, a counterpane white-and-blue-striped shirt, and a raffia cowboy hat. "I'd love to see your closet."

"Closet*s*." Bella led the horse through the gate Char held open.

"What is it with you and clothes?" Char led her horse through, then fastened the gate behind them.

Bella thought a moment before answering. "Two things. First, you can't imagine what it's like, being really large. If you go away for the weekend and forget your jeans or a bra, you stop at the nearest mall and buy it, right?"

They walked side by side along the fence line, horses shuffling behind them. Char nodded.

"Not me. They didn't stock my size. Have a seam blowout or wardrobe malfunction? You'd better carry a needle and thread. What shopping I did was mostly through catalogs. One of the best things about losing the weight is buying clothes off the rack.

"The second part is the real reason, though." Bella

stopped to watch the calves chase each other in the next pasture. "When I was young, I so envied the girls in the latest styles. They looked so together. I thought, if I only looked like them, I'd have it together too. As if you bought the lifestyle with the clothes." Her smile seemed sad. "When I finally got down to a size eight in college, I bought the store. Man, did I strut that campus!"

Char could imagine, having witnessed her exit from the Clip 'n Curl.

"When I found out popularity wasn't something you bought off the rack, I was pissed. The popular girls still treated me like I had two heads." Bella's smile turned wicked. "So I got even."

"I think I can guess how."

"I outdressed them. If tight skirts were in, I painted mine on. If heels got popular, I strapped on five-inch stilettos." She faced Pork Chop, stuck a foot in the stirrup, and swung aboard, Char did the same. "Lately, though, I've been thinking about crutches."

"In case you fall off your stilettos?" Char reined her horse closer.

"No, Charla Rae." Bella threw her an eye roll. "Have you ever had an ankle sprain? I did once, a bad one. The doctor handed me crutches and told me to stay on them for four weeks.

"Well, I stumped around on the damned things for three weeks, until one day it occurred to me: If I didn't try to walk without them, how did I know I still needed them?

"So I tried. Sure enough, my ankle was healed." Bella tilted her hat to block the late-afternoon sun. "I've been thinking, maybe I don't need the great clothes rebellion anymore. Then again, maybe I do. But if I don't try, I'll never know."

They ambled along the fence line, Pork Chop reaching to snatch mouthfuls of long grass. "Crutches are great things to lean on when you're hurting, but after that, they're a lot of work.

"I've got closets full of New York badass black and cool country clothes. Maybe it's time to find out who I am." She squinted at the horizon. "What I've been doing out here on your ranch may not be it for me, but it's close.

"Enough of my drama." Bella turned to her. "I'm sorry, Char. I feel responsible for that jerk of a trainer. And the fact that JB's back. How are you holding up?"

Char struggled not to shift in the saddle under Bella's canny gaze. Instead she studied the adjoining pasture where a mounted figure bunched cattle in the distance. "It takes some getting used to. I'm not giving up my outside chores, so it's . . . awkward. We're circling each other, trying to figure out how to do this." She sighed. "I'm exhausted."

"Yeah, but under that. Are there any, you know, feelings?"

"Like I said, I'm exhausted. Let's leave it at that for now."

As they trotted onto the packed dirt of the barn dooryard, the sun seemed to burn through a magnifying glass. The still air smelled of heat and dust. A runnel of sweat tickled down Char's neck as she kicked out of her stirrups and slid off her mount.

Bella scratched Pork Chop's head under her forelock, where she liked it. "It's always so blasted hot in this yard." She took off her hat and waved it at her heat-reddened face. "If I were you, I'd plant a shade tree."

Char's glance flicked across the yard, as if the stump were magnetic. A strangled sound finally brought her head around.

Bella stood, hand over her mouth, her face a study in horror. "Oh, hell, Char, I'm sorry," she whispered.

"You didn't know." She shook her head and tried to smile. "That tree stood over a hundred years. Mom and Dad planned the layout of the house and barn so that the tree would shade this yard."

She took the reins from Bella, her gaze straying once again to the stump. "I remember lying in bed, after, hearing the sound of chopping.

"Jimmy cut that tree down, then cut it up, with nothing but an ax. Got to where I heard it in my dreams. Then I'd wake up and someone would be there with a pill. The doctor said I'd get too 'worked up' if I didn't take them." She closed her eyes and lifted her face to the soft caress of a stray westerly breeze. "I thought I'd go mad with that sound. *Thunk. Thunk. Thunk.* It went on for days.

"Until it stopped." Char opened her eyes. "Then I thought I'd go mad in the silence." Something pricked her memory. She frowned. Something about the accident. Her brain could touch the edge of what bothered her, but she couldn't quite...

"Hey, Char." Bella held her elbow and waved a hand in front of her face. "Come on, Hon, let's put the horses up. We're gonna have a heat stroke if we stand here much longer."

After shooing Bella home, Char unsaddled Bar B first. She'd just finished currying and putting him up when Jimmy walked into the barn's breezeway. He sidled up to Pork Chop and loosened the cinch.

"What are you doing?" She pulled the sliding stall door shut behind her.

"Unsaddling the horse."

She strode over. "I've got it."

"This saddle's heavy. I'll—"

He released the leather strap when she swatted at his hand. "I've *got* it, Jimmy." She tugged at the stubborn knot.

He stepped back a pace. "Suit yourself."

Jittery from his scrutiny and a lack of personal space, she finally wrested the strap free. Now came the hard part. Pork Chop's back seemed ten feet tall, Char was short, and the saddle was heavy. On a good day, she barely managed without sprawling in the dirt beneath it.

Please, God, let this be a good day. She took a deep breath and pulled.

The saddle and blanket cooperated, sliding off the horse and onto her. Jimmy stepped closer but flinched at her glare.

Stifling a grunt, she got her arms around the sweaty, bulky weight and leaned back. The stirrups slid off the horse, thumping to the packed dirt.

Jimmy raised his hands in the universal sign of surrender and retreated to a straw bale outside the stall door to watch. Between the heavy strain and her embarrassment, Char imagined her face to be an attractive shade of eggplant.

Now all she had to do was haul the saddle to the tack room without dropping it or tripping over the dangling stirrups. She waddled away slowly, knowing that from the back, she must look like a bear humping a football. Despite the trouble, she managed it, with only one heart-stopping toe-stub at the door to the tack room.

She returned, snagging a bucket of brushes and her stool along the way. Keeping her back to Jimmy, she set the stool next to the horse, stepped up, and started brushing.

Jimmy's comment came from the cheap seats. "Well, now that you don't have to pay the trainer, I expect you'll be off to buy that four-wheeler Bella mentioned. You won't have to mess with Pork Chop anymore."

With a two-handed grip on the currycomb, she leaned in to penetrate the horse's coat. Pork Chop grunted with pleasure. "I'll have you know, this happens to be the best cutting horse in Fredericksburg." She pointed the brush at Jimmy. "She and I are a team, so show a little respect. And she's Buttermilk to you, Bucko."

Jimmy snorted a laugh. Charla turned back to the horse and smiled.

Silence spun out as she bent to her task, working up a sweat. This was one of her favorite times of the day. Grooming allowed her mind to wander, assess her progress, and cross completed items off her mental list. Yet today she couldn't focus.

His deep voice intruded on her stuttering thoughts. "You've changed."

She stepped off the stool and held it in front of her. "Not as much as you, I'll warrant."

She walked around Pork Chop's head, set the stool down, and began brushing the other side.

He colored. "No, I mean your hair. You've worn it the same since high school."

"Then I guess it was high time."

"Takes some getting used to, but I like it."

She glanced over the horse's back to see Jimmy, leaning

against the stall door, feet crossed at the ankle, head cocked, looking her over. She felt like a prime heifer. "You're assuming you still have a vote."

"A vote? Nope. Only an opinion."

She ducked her head and whispered into Pork Chop's side, "Yeah, after all, you're still breathing." Dropping the brush into the bucket, she hopped down and moved under the horse's head. "We need to talk, Jimmy. Things are different around here. *I'm* different."

"I noticed."

His tone gave no clue to how he meant that. "I'm not the little housewife anymore. I intend to stay involved, out here, in the business."

He thought a moment, squinting up at her. "You sure you wouldn't rather get a job in town?"

Her anger hit the end of its leash, biting and snapping. "I have as much right to the business as you do, Jimmy. I've worked my butt off these past months to keep this place running, and if you think I'm going to tuck tail for the kitchen because you're on the property, you can just—"

"You're off the pills, aren't you, Little Bit?"

She pulled a rag from her back pocket and wiped down Pork Chop's face. The concern in his voice and calm, assessing look had her nerves dancing like water drops on a hot skillet.

"Well, good on you." He stood, the shadows gathering in the hollows of his face. He looked old, gaunt, tired. "Look, Char, I'm not trying to chase you off. There's plenty enough work to go around. I just thought a job in town would bring you more money. Take some of the worry off you."

With a last look at her, he settled his hat and walked for the barn door, head down.

She stood in the middle of the aisle, left holding a squirming bag of emotion. *Damn you, Jimmy. How dare you make me feel bad for you?*

CHAPTER
15

You gain strength, courage, and confidence by every experience in which you really stop to look fear in the face. You must do the thing which you think you cannot do.

—*Eleanor Roosevelt*

People go to cemeteries every day." Char gritted her teeth as she reached for the car keys, hanging on a peg next to the back door. But saying it didn't make it happen. Resolve, so carefully gathered, dissolved. Dropping her hand, she glanced out the storm door to the few puffy clouds the dawn revealed. *There's nothing saying I have to go today.*

Besides, it would do her heart good to work in the garden—to finish the job she'd begun that awful day she'd fired Gandy. But she also knew the disappointment of letting herself down would bleed into whatever delicate peace she found in the garden.

She didn't even have her father as an excuse; he was at the feedlot with Junior.

Char glanced down at the pantsuit she'd so carefully

selected. *I'm already dressed. Might as well get it over with.* Her stomach did a roller-coaster drop and a shiver of longing ran through her as she pictured the box in the garage where she'd stashed the Valium.

Before her capricious mind could change again, she snatched the keys, opened the door, and marched for the car. *Remember what Bella said about crutches. If you never let go, you'll never know if you still need them.*

Rounding the corner of the house, the bedraggled flower beds caught her eye. In spite of her neglect, those trusty glads had managed to bloom again this year. The memory of planting them, with Benje, stopped her in her tracks.

He'd been five and had wanted to help. She'd dug the first hole, carefully explaining which end of the bulb went in first. Convinced he had the concept, she worked on the rose bushes. Returning a few minutes later, she caught him planting a bulb upside down. When she corrected him, he told her he'd done it on purpose; he wanted the people in China to have pretty flowers too.

Char brushed a tear that threatened to ruin her makeup and inspected the plants. The red flowers had some brown edges and looked a bit bug-eaten. She'd planned to stop at Walmart and pick up a bouquet on the way to the cemetery, but...Her stomach settled a bit. "These are Benje's flowers. He's not going to care about a few bugs." She headed for the tool shed to find her clippers.

Later, she drove past Saint Mark's, wondering why the church parking lot bristled with cars, parishioners trailing to the front door. Women flitted like pastel finches around their coat-and-tied husbands.

Oh my gosh, it's Sunday! How could she have forgotten?

Char hadn't set foot in church since the funeral. She hadn't planned on *not* going, but... She winced at a lancet stab of guilt. She still hadn't called Reverend Mike to thank him for referring Rosa. Her mama had taught her better.

She imagined sliding back into the social current of Fredericksburg—the questions from her neighbors, the pitying looks from her friends—the starting over. *I'm not strong enough for that yet.* She loosened her death grip on the steering wheel. *Let go of one crutch at a time.*

A mile down the road, on the outskirts of town, she forced her trembly hands to turn the car at the wrought-iron gates to Roseland. One good thing about coming on Sunday morning; the cemetery was deserted. Thank God. The gallop of her heart pounded in her ears as she rolled slowly past acres of dead people.

Although she'd never been to Benje's grave, she knew exactly where it lay. Generations of Enwrights rested in the farthest corner of the cemetery. She pulled up and shut off the engine, keeping her eyes straight ahead. Memories swirled in her mind like an out-of-control film, faster and faster, until everything blurred, a background to the roaring in her ears. She couldn't breathe. Char grabbed for the door handle and opened it, afraid she was about to be sick.

Resting her head on the elbow rest, she waited as gravity pulled blood back to her brain. Shaky, she straightened and shut the door. But in a scant few seconds, the pressure of silence and heat closed in. Damp, hot claustrophobia crawled over her skin. Not yet ready to face the marching row of headstones, she lowered the car window and fell back against the headrest. Slowly, sounds slipped into her jangled awareness: the ticking of the cooling engine, the sloughing breeze in the maples, sparrows twitter-ing. *It's just a plot of grass, Charla. Get over yourself.* She forced herself to pick up Benje's wilting flowers and exited the car.

Her dressy flats swished through the manicured, shade-dappled sod. Char focused her attention on the everyday sounds around her to quiet the panic welling in her stomach.

"Hi, Mom." She brushed her fingers across the rose marble of the headstone. Her father had his name carved on it too when he'd bought it for her mother. The blank space after his birth date dangled, reminding her that, someday, there would be a date etched there as well. She shook off the picture in her head of herself, growing old, alone on the ranch.

"Don't worry, Mom, I'm taking good care of Daddy." She patted the marker and moved on.

A low, crystal-white marble headstone stood next, the dates under Benje's name proclaiming God's travesty. Her knees let go, and she fell to all fours, half sprawled on the grave, the pain writhing like a large snake in her chest. Mouth contorted, she gasped for breath through the vio-lent, terrifying sobs.

She had no idea of how much time passed until pain's grip ebbed. Her chest felt hollow, her heart a papery husk.

The grass under her palms felt cool, and she leaned on one arm, to catch her breath. She pried her eyes from the headstone, noticing a small bouquet of wildflowers before it. Wild phlox, bluebonnets, and yellow primrose, so fresh that Char shot a quick glance around to be sure she was alone.

Small, dark objects dotted the top of the gravestone.

She crawled closer to inspect them. She lifted the first. Benje's Cub Scout Gold Arrow point. He'd been so proud to bring that home to her. She ran her finger over the tarnished brass, then put it back, before picking up the next bit, his attendance pin from Sunday school. The next in line was a circular pin, featuring an enameled bucking bull, foreground to the PBR logo. It looked familiar.

Jimmy. He'd always worn it on his hat band.

She carefully laid the pin on the cold marble, imagining Jimmy, hat in hand, placing it there. A guilt stiletto slipped through the tight muscles of her solar plexus. In all this time, she'd never thought about Jimmy's pain. Jimmy's grief.

Her vision blurred and she brushed a hand across her eyes. Those damn pills had blinded her to everything outside of her own skin. *Yes, but after the first week, when there was no one standing there to hand you one every few hours, you managed to take up that duty for yourself, didn't you?*

"Oh, stop it, Charla." Today wasn't for self-recrimination. Today was for Benje. A fresh breeze cooled her wet face, bringing the rich smell of life in the hayfield bordering the cemetery. She took a cleansing breath, letting the familiar scents and sounds settle her.

It's peaceful here.

"Benje? Are you all right, son?" The wind took her words. Birds cheeped in the tree overhead. As the restless, dappled shade slid over her, calm loosened her tight muscles.

After a few minutes, Charla gathered herself and stood. All this time, she'd dreaded this for nothing.

Her son wasn't here.

• • •

The pounding drum solo of Kenny Chesney's "Big Star" slammed into JB's brain. The stool in front of the damn jukebox had been the only one vacant, and now he knew why. Tipping back his Miller Lite, he attempted to squeeze his ears shut with the muscles of his face. Surely the band would be back from break soon.

I shoulda listened to Wiley and gone back to the hotel. But his bulls had been exceptional at the event tonight, and Denny Bucking Bulls was celebrating—even if he was the only employee on the roster. *Well, make that one and a half—maybe.*

He looked through the bottles of booze on the back bar to watch the crowd in the mirror. It showed a different perspective of the churning crush; as if his bar stool were a seat in a movie house. Stetsoned cowboys strutted around glittery ladies in a barroom mating dance.

The females flitted and flirted, choosing their mates for the evening.

Jaded tonight, aren't we? JB shook his head. Months ago, he'd been a part of the scene, swaggering with the best of them. *Guess that makes me hypocritical too.* He widened his focus, taking in the gouged cinder-block walls and pockmarked, blacked-out ceiling tiles that booze, raucous music, and vibrating hormones usually rendered invisible.

A large-breasted, forty-something waitress brushed past him, and he caught her look in the mirror. Her tired, sardonic smile telegraphed "How'd *we* end up here?"

He raised his beer an inch in salute and turned his attention back to the show.

"Are you JB Denny?"

He swiveled his stool to the high-pitched voice. A curvy little blonde stood, too close, behind him.

"Yes'm."

"I just wanted to meet you." Bracelets jingled as she stuck out a hand with bloodred talon-tipped fingers. "I think you and Wiley are the best. You have such a sexy voice."

He stood, sucked in his gut, and took her fingers in his hand. "Pleased to meet you."

"I'm Courtney." She turned toward two twittering girls behind her. "And this is Jennifer and Lacey."

He tipped his hat.

The blonde cocked her head and smiled, in a move he somehow knew she'd practiced in a mirror. "Could we buy you a drink?"

He looked past the cosmetics and bravado. *No way the bouncer is carding tonight.* "Thank you, miss, but I'm on my way out." He relaxed his gut and tossed back the last of his beer.

Her bottom lip protruded to a practiced pout. "Oh, come on, JB. The night is young!"

He reached for his wallet. *And so are you.* Dropping bills on the bar, he shot her what he hoped passed for a disappointed look. "I'm sorry, ladies, but this old guy is flat tuckered. Y'all have a big time tonight."

CHAPTER
16

Learn from yesterday, live for today, hope for tomorrow.

—*Albert Einstein*

JB whistled "High Cotton" along with Alabama as he made the familiar turn onto State Highway 87, stretching a hand out to steady the bouquet of roses on the truck seat. Char had always loved the white ones best. They cost him dearly, but he wanted her to know how much it meant to him, her letting him back on the ranch.

He'd gotten the idea from Wiley. Since he was living there, he couldn't miss that Wiley was always bringing home flowers to Dana, and she lit up, every time. He glanced down at the flowers. Maybe they'd be the peace pipe that would get them back on comfortable speaking terms. He'd enjoy seeing Char happy for a change. He hardly remembered what her face looked like wiped clean of worry.

A few minutes later, his arms full of conciliatory roses, he strolled into the welcome shade of the barn. Charla's trim backside confronted him as she shuffled and strained, dragging a bale of alfalfa down the middle of the aisle.

"Here, let me get that." He trotted up and, as she straightened, thrust the flowers in her gloved hands, then bent and lifted the hay bale. "Where do you want it?"

Her face drained of color, and she swayed on her feet.

He dropped the hay, grabbing her arm to steady her. "What's wrong, Char?" He lowered her to sit on the bale. When she stuck the roses out, he took them, shocked at the look of raw pain on her pallid face. He pushed her head down, lower than her knees. "Breathe. Just breathe." He patted her back.

"The funeral," she whispered.

Oh, shit. The flowers on Benje's casket had been white roses. "Here, keep your head down a minute."

He looked around, not knowing what to do with his offending armload. He tossed them into the stall behind him, to get them out of her sight. *Damn, how could I have forgotten?*

When she sat up, a minute later, some color had returned to her face. He patted her shoulder.

"I'm fine." She shrugged him off, stood, and stepped away. Her eyes narrowed, watching him as if he could be poisonous. "What are you up to, Jimmy?"

Her lightning shift from weak to angry caught him flat-footed. "What?"

She stood, hands on hips. "James Benton Denny. I washed your dirty underwear for twenty years. You think I don't know when you're up to something?"

"Jesus, Char. I'm trying to do something nice here."

She snorted. "Do you think you can waltz back in here and sweet-talk your boots back under my table?"

Dammit, he'd taken about all the kicking he was going to take. He felt blood rise to his face; the cords in his neck pulled taut. "Why don't you get it all out, Charla Rae? I'm sick of all the little digs." He lifted his boot onto the hay bale, forcing himself to relax. "Say your piece, Little Bit—have at it."

As if his words lit a fuse, her face turned red and her jaw clenched. "You puffed-up, arrogant rooster!" Her shrill voice echoed down the barn. "You're a self-centered, self-serving weasel!" She sputtered, but her mouth kept moving, clearly so mad she couldn't get it out.

Maybe this was better. Quit all the dodging and sparring and finally have it all out in the open. "Oh, come on, Charla, you can do better than that."

She shook a finger at him. "You're a mangy, good-for-nothing cur dog. You've got the manners of a baboon and the morals of a goat!"

"Is that it? After all this time, that's it?" He smiled, knowing it would fire off a bottle rocket. "You never could swear for spit."

"Oooh, you turd! You insufferable . . . dick head!"

The little hellcat stood in front of him, tail puffed and spitting. "I can do better than that without even cussing. How about disloyal, low-down cheater?"

She crossed her arms over her chest. "That's right."

"Dirty, double-crossing, two-timing loser."

She nodded. "That too."

"Lily-livered sheepherder."

The corner of her mouth curled up. "Butt-wipe."

"Yellow-bellied sod-buster."

She chuckled.

He felt a glimmer of hope.

• • •

An hour later, Char made the familiar turn onto State Highway 87. After the dustup with Jimmy, she'd run to pick her dad up from Junior's. She glanced across the bench seat to where he sat, hat pulled down, staring out the window. Was he thinking—or off wandering the jumbled labyrinth of memories in his poor, damaged mind? Hard to tell. After a while, the hum of tires on the asphalt and the familiar fence line unrolling alongside the car lulled them both into their own thoughts.

Oh, she'd been mad at Jimmy, plenty mad. In the beginning. But after the initial rush of words, the mad was gone, just like that. As if the anger were a heavy bucket of water she'd toted around; she'd gotten used to its weight. Apparently there'd been a hole in the bottom, and the anger had leaked out the past year, unnoticed. Now, without it, she felt kind of... naked.

Another crutch, Charla Rae?

Mom, you've really got to get a—doesn't *heaven* have anyone who needs advice?

No answer. She drove past a carpet of bluebonnets in a boggy section of ditch. What if Jimmy was only trying to be nice? She pictured his tentative smile as he handed her the roses, like he couldn't wait to see her reaction to his extravagant gift. The freeze-frame photo of pins atop a headstone flashed across her brain and shame burned in the blood that pounded up her neck to flush her face.

On the other hand, her Jimmy, with no agenda? She shook her head. Not likely. But just in case, she'd be watching. Closely.

Char turned into the driveway and drove to the back of the house. Jimmy stood at the rail of the front corral, watching the two-year-olds amble around, getting acquainted with the bucking chutes.

Her dad's hands jerked. Animation returned as his face lit up. "'Bout time JB got home!" He pulled the door handle before she got the car stopped.

"Daddy, he's not—" But he was gone, walking across the yard, hand outstretched, huge grin on his face. Char stepped out and stood, one foot in the car, leaned her elbows on the roof, and watched to see what would happen.

"Welcome home, son." Her dad pumped Jimmy's hand.

Jimmy shot her a confused, panicky look.

She shrugged her shoulders and smiled. *Welcome to my world.*

When her dad put his arm around Jimmy's shoulder, pointed to the bulls, and began dispensing advice, Char turned and walked to the house.

CHAPTER 17

The world is round and the place which may seem like the end may also be the beginning.

—*Ivy Baker Priest*

I'm only listening here, but it sounds to me like you're working on a plan to wrangle your way back into Charla's life, JB." Wiley prodded a hamburger on the smoking grill, then straightened and shot him a canny look. "Are you?"

Slouched in the plastic chair, JB took a pull from his longneck and tugged the feedlot cap down to block the laser rays shooting from the horizon. Had he bought the flowers as more than a peace offering? "At this point, Wiley, I think I'd settle for an amiable truce."

Wiley rolled the hot dogs to a flame-free corner of the grill. "Charla Rae is a good-looking woman, you gotta give her that."

"Yes. She is. And you're about as subtle as a shark attack, partner."

Wiley shrugged. "I always thought you two fit. Like two pieces of a jigsaw puzzle—your outies fit her innies, if you know what I mean."

And so they had. He and Char had clicked together back in high school and stayed, locked snug, until the day Benje died. He'd thought that was how things worked in a relationship. Looking back now, from the other side of fragile, JB recognized that he'd taken that fit for granted. He now knew how rare and special it had been. "She's changed, Wiley."

"Given what she's been through, it'd be strange if she hadn't, don't you think?" Wiley opened the sweating beer that Dana had left at his elbow when she brought the meat. "You saying that's good or bad?"

"Both." In JB's mind, there were three Charlas. His wife of twenty years, comfortable, solid, *known*. The grieving wraith, addicted and inconsolable. Then there was the new Charla—the delicate, plucky woman with a soft new hairdo and cutting-sharp edges.

Wiley stood, spatula poised, waiting for an explanation.

"I don't know this new Char. She spooks easy. Won't let me close."

"Sounds like you're gentling a wild horse, not getting to know a woman."

"Believe me, partner, they're not so different." JB took another sip of beer. One by one the connections clicked in his brain, and, suddenly, he had the answer. "The flowers were a big move. That was my mistake."

Wiley waved away the smoke and squinted at JB. "What the heck are you talking about? A woman is not a horse, JB. You can't—"

"Wiley, don't you see?" He rushed on, the idea clean and perfect in his mind. "You can't make big moves around a spooky horse. Even if it's the right thing, it scares 'em." He stood and paced the weed-strewn grass of the backyard. "It's like bull riding too."

Wiley looked at him like he'd been at the locoweed.

"When you're in trouble, during a ride, you want to make a big move, to pull yourself out of the well on the inside of a spin. But that's too much. You end up butt first in the dust, the bull doing a dance on your dangling parts. Small moves. That's what gets you back to center and keeps you there till the buzzer. Why didn't I see this before?"

"JB, I don't want to discourage you, but—"

He clicked his bottle to the one hanging, forgotten, in Wiley's hand. "Thanks, buddy. I got it now." He drained the beer.

"Sounds to me like you went from an 'amiable truce' to courting in the time it took to cook a hamburger." Wiley laid slices of cheese on the burgers. "Just remember while you're making all those smooth moves, it isn't the flowers that women love. It's the caring behind them—knowing that you took time out of your day to think about her and what would make her happy."

JB snorted. "Now, don't you go all cuddly on me, partner. You make me wonder about you sometimes."

"Hey, screw you. I've got a warm, willing woman in bed next to me every night. You're the one sleeping like a hound on my back porch."

"You got a point there, Wiley, you truly do."

Dana called from the window. "Wiley, that meat's got to be boot leather by now. Come on in, you two. Supper's ready."

The kid hung on the fence, watching the bull riders, same as he had every practice for the past two weeks.

JB walked up behind him. "So, when are you going to try it?"

Travis jerked as if he'd been caught looking at dirty magazines. "What makes you think I want to try it?"

JB took off his hat, wiped his sweaty face in the crook of his elbow, and settled the hat back on his head. "I've been a bull rider since I was younger than them." He waved at the high school team, huddled around the coach in the arena. "I train bulls for a living, and on most weekends, I'm at a PBR event. Do you think I don't recognize the look?"

Travis's too-cool slouch gave nothing away. "What look?"

"The look of somebody who wants to put themselves up against an animal a hundred times stronger than they are, just to see if they've got the guts. To be on top of a force of nature, to see if you can ride it—because if you can, it shows you something about yourself that no one can ever take away from you." The words surprised JB. He hadn't known he'd felt that way until he heard them. "The coach is a friend of mine; I could introduce you."

A naked bolt of wanting flashed across Travis's face before the mask of studied teenage indifference fell once more. "Yeah, like I'm gonna hang with those HJs."

"Huh?"

"*Hitler-Jugend*. Nazi youth party."

JB glanced to the arena. "What're you talking about? They're just a bunch of country kids."

Travis snorted. "Yeah, and they march in lockstep. Trust me, it's a closed society." He nodded at the crowd. "Even the uniform. Notice how they're all wearing white hats?" He shook his head. "Stupid. They watch too many Duke movies."

JB looked Travis over. Backward cap, oversized T-shirt, untied Skaters. "Yeah, like you're any different." He pointed to the kid's oversized pants, held on his skinny hips, God knew how. "You gonna tell me that's not a uniform? Besides, that isn't the point. Riding isn't about such foolishness."

Travis shook his head. "You don't get it. Do you think I'm ever gonna fit with that crowd?" He snorted. "Like I'd want to, anyway."

"Oh, well, I guess that excuse is as good as any." JB turned to leave, took two steps, and tossed back over his shoulder. "Ask yourself, though: Is that crap gonna hold up in ten years, when you've wished you would've tried it?"

Twenty minutes later, JB turned in at the ranch to see Char driving toward him, Ben riding shotgun. She braked and rolled her window down as they pulled alongside each other.

"Hey, Ben." Blank stare. Bad day. "Afternoon, Charla Rae." The sunlight fell sharply on her face, aging her. She looked overworked and overburdened. He felt a pang of regret. He should have been here for her, they could have shared the burdens, instead of where they both were— alone.

"I'm taking Daddy to the doctor, then to the hospital, for a PET scan. We'll be back in a couple of hours." Without waiting for a reply, she rolled on, making the turn at the bottom of the drive.

God, how did she keep it up? There was Rosa, but still...His tires crunched gravel as he accelerated up the driveway. He noticed a hoe propped against the house amid the half-weeded garden, and he got an idea. He smiled, threw the truck into reverse and scattered gravel, heading for the garden supply store in town.

Char pulled the brush through her hair, watching a blush advance from the collar of her rayon pajamas. It was one thing to cry when she'd found her raggedy garden made perfect, but to blubber on the phone when she called to thank Jimmy, that was flat embarrassing.

He'd weeded, fertilized, and spread cedar bark to keep down the weeds. The roses were pruned, the tomatoes were planted, and a big section was reserved for her favorite: cucumbers. A riot of colorful perennials marched around the border, a cheerful splash of color against her white house. Her smile wobbled. She'd have never let him do it, if he'd asked. He'd just gone ahead and done the one thing that would make her happy. Despite all the chores he had to do, he'd done that for her. This was the Jimmy she'd fallen in love with. Was he back? She didn't know. But she'd be watching.

She stood tall and smoothed the rayon down her sides. "It's not fair. How can you be underweight and still have a belly?" The unrelenting fluorescent light spotlighted her pasty face, finding every wrinkle, freckle, and line. She thought of Jimmy, with his ex-cupcake, naked. She shuddered. How could a middle-age single woman ever let a man see her naked, with all the firm, shapely sexpots out there?

She looked into her own eyes in the mirror. *Are you really thinking of going to bed with Jimmy?* She took one more swipe at her hair and put down the brush. *Heavens, no.* But someday, going to bed with a man sure would be nice. She lifted her hand to the not-so-tight skin of her neck. "Maybe I could find a blind one." She clicked the light off and walked to the bedroom.

The light of the lamp on the nightstand made the fresh bed an inviting haven. She shuffled to the edge and kicked off her slippers. Sliding under the covers, the cool of the sheets sent a shiver up the sensitive skin of her backside. She reached for the book *Healing Wisdom: Easing a Path through Grief*. She'd gotten into the nightly habit of choosing a quote at random, always surprised at how often it touched close to home.

Forgiving others is the first step on the path to forgiving yourself.

Oh well, it couldn't be right every night. She thumbed a few more pages, ran her finger down the page without looking, stopping near the middle.

Forgiveness is me giving up my right to hurt you for hurting me.—Anonymous

"What a load of bull hockey!" Char slammed the book shut and tossed it to the nightstand. It skittered off the edge to land on the hardwood floor with a thump. "I'm not surprised the author didn't sign his name to that." She snapped off the light and snuggled into the covers. In spite of the tiredness that tugged at her limbs, her brain kept churning.

Funny, how she still slept on "her" side of the bed. Unconsciously, her hand slid to the relinquished half. The smooth, taut sheet made her wish for the rumpled mess that she'd always nagged at Jimmy for making.

This had always been her favorite time of the day. Whether they'd made love or not, she always ended up in Jimmy's arms, his strong chest at her back, her rear snugged up against him. She'd lay, head cradled on his bicep, and they'd talk, about everything, about nothing. Char smiled into the dark. The subject was just as likely to be politics as local gossip; it was their way of winding down and finding their way back to each other after a day spent apart. Regret-tinged longing squeezed around her heart. God, how she missed that: the rumble of Jimmy's deep voice, so close that it reverberated through her own chest. She'd lie safe and sheltered and listen to that voice as she drifted off to sleep, knowing all was right in her world.

Would the world ever be that safe again? How could it be, when children could die, spouses could leave, and you could discover a dark side of yourself you hadn't known existed?

CHAPTER 18

It is very easy to forgive others their mistakes; it takes more grit and gumption to forgive them for having witnessed your own.

—*Jessamyn West*

JB looked up from the beef futures report when Travis slouched into his office at the feedlot. The laces on his untied tennis shoes slapped the linoleum as he crossed to the only guest chair and plopped into it.

"So let's say I *do* want to try bull riding." His gaze roamed the bookshelf, the bulletin board, out the window. Anywhere but to JB.

JB leaned back and steepled his fingers. "Why are you telling me?"

Travis held the disinterested pose for a few seconds, but then the bravado evaporated and his shoulders slumped. "I really want to do this. But I've got a problem, and, um, I was hoping—"

"First, if you're man enough to be a bull rider, you're going to have to act like it." Travis looked puzzled. "Sit up straight, look me in the eye, and ask me. There's no shame in asking for help, and you're a damned sight more likely to get it if you're polite about it."

Travis sat up and leaned forward, elbows on the chair arms. "I want to learn to ride, but there's no way I can walk out there and ask to get on a bull. I'd be laughed out of school. This isn't something my friends would understand, and I'm sure not going to fit in with the team either." Shrugging his shoulders, he held JB's stare. "And in between is no-man's land. See what I mean?"

"Yeah, I guess I do. Back when dirt was invented, I was in high school myself. I don't imagine it's changed all that much."

"Would you teach me?" Without the cocky attitude, his face looked all of his sixteen years.

JB'd always been a sucker for a kid. God knows, Benje managed to wrangle almost everything he'd wanted out of him. *Except he never did get that tree fort.* The acid-etch of guilt bit deep.

"I know you were a great bull rider. I looked you up. You rode Rock Em Up to a standstill in the PRCA finals back in ninety."

"You don't have to suck up. I'll help you. Just give me your mom's phone number so I can get her okay. I'm going to need her written permission too." He jotted down the number Travis rattled off. "Now get out of here. I've got to think about how I'm going to make this happen."

Travis jumped up as if he'd been granted a hangman's reprieve, a huge grin on his face. He leaned over the desk to pump JB's hand. "You'll see, when I really want something, I work hard for it. You won't be sorry." He walked to the door, then turned. "Thanks, JB."

JB sat back in the chair and stared out the window a few minutes. Then he picked up the phone and hit speed dial.

"Denny Bucking Bulls, Charla speaking." Her business voice was so cute, he had to smile.

He raised his voice three octaves to disguise it. "Yeah, I was wondering, how *do* you collect semen, anyway?"

"James Benton, I don't have all day to play games with you on the phone. I'm busy here."

"Hey, Charla Rae, have you seen my hat?"

"What hat?" Her voice went all skinny.

"You know, my champion softball cap. I've searched everywhere, and I can't find it."

"Um. I haven't seen it recently."

"Keep your eye open for it, will you?" He paused. "That's not really why I called. I wanted to ask you a favor." At her sigh, he added, "Not for me. See, there's this kid at the feedlot. He wants to be a bull rider. He's a bit unconventional and—"

"Why are you calling me?"

"Well, he's embarrassed to buck in front of the high school team. He's never been on a bull. I thought I'd bring him out to the ranch and run a couple of practice bulls under him, to see what he's got. I didn't know how you'd feel about having a kid on the place. I don't want to make you sad, or uncomfortable."

"Who is it?"

"Nobody you know. His name is Travis, and he works in the feed store."

"Oh, the Dumpster monkey!"

"Huh?"

"Never mind, I know him."

Her throaty chuckle reminded him how long it'd been since he heard it. And how much he missed it.

"You can bring him out, JB."

"I appreciate it, Charla Rae. Underneath all the attitude, he's a good kid."

"Oh, and JB? Thanks for asking."

Her voice was as soft as the *click* that followed it.

Char hung up the phone and, holding the material together, pressed the foot pedal of her mother's sewing machine. The garish pink-and-black tiger-striped cotton fabric almost hurt her eyes. She held up the garment. A ruffle, maybe? Yes. Definitely.

Cutting a strip of material, she absorbed Jimmy's call. The past handful of years, he wouldn't have given a thought to how his actions might affect her. The fact that he had now was a balm to her chafed heart. *So sweet.*

This would be good for Jimmy. He loved kids, and they gravitated to him, sensing that a part of him had never grown up. It made him aggravating lots of times, but it was also the source of his playful, fun side.

Dang it, if Jimmy could evolve to a point that he considered her feelings, what excuse did she have for not growing up and facing her own sins? She snapped off the iron, then the sewing machine. Her nerves jangled. The Valium's tired one-note song ran through her head, as it did whenever she contemplated the mess she'd made of her life. Ignoring it, she strode the hall to the living room.

Rosa sat across the table from her dad, their heads bent over a jigsaw puzzle.

Char glanced at the clock on the mantel. "Rosa, don't you need to get on the road?"

The round-faced woman looked up. "I've got another hour or so free today. I can stay."

It's an omen. Char gritted her teeth. Once she committed herself, there was no going back. "Do you mind if I step out for a bit? I promise I won't be more than an hour."

"We're fine. Go, go." Rosa waved a hand at her, attention already back to the puzzle.

Char walked to the kitchen, thanking God that she lived in a county with such a rich support system for its residents. She'd have to remember not to complain, the next time her property tax bill arrived in the mail.

Checking to be sure she had the address, and before she could talk herself out of it, Char grabbed her purse and headed for the back door.

Ten minutes later, she turned in at an apartment complex on the older side of town. She trolled the labyrinth of narrow drives, scanning the redbrick buildings for the correct number. Within a few numbers of the building, she pulled into a parking space, turned off the engine, and sat, marshalling her courage. She felt open, vulnerable, as if her skin had been stripped off.

After the funeral, Reverend Mike had told her about the grief group offered by Saint Luke's Hospital. When Jimmy left, she'd become a robot: going through the motions to get through each day. After a few weeks, the echoes of happier times rang through the empty rooms, and the Valium stopped blocking it. She knew she had to do something or go mad.

Not that she'd added to the discussions at group. She sat like a lump most days, tears rolling down her cheeks.

Yet being there seemed to quiet the sounds in her head a bit. So she kept going every day. They were typical group therapy sessions led by a gentle, sensitive young man who taught them the stages of grief and how to get through the tough times. Members stayed as long as they needed to, drifting away when they moved to the final stage: acceptance.

Char got to know the members through their stories. Husbands, siblings, parents—a phalanx of dead people, kept alive through the memories of those who loved them. Telling the stories appeared to help the others. But for Char, panic welled at the thought of speaking, and she'd find herself standing in the parking lot, hands shaking so badly she scratched the paint on the car door, trying to get the key in the lock.

Typical too, she supposed, were the dynamics of the group. Most had been members long enough to get comfortable. Sometimes that support took a harsh tone, to snap the person out of a stuck place.

She shouldn't have pushed me.

Looking back now, Char could hardly believe the crazed woman who'd stood screaming into that old lady's face had been her. She could hardly blame them for asking her to leave and not return. Char snatched the scrap of paper with the address scribbled on it and got out. Peering at apartment numbers, she rounded a corner to a quadrangle of grass between buildings. A rusted swing set and neglected sandbox stood testament that these buildings hadn't always been retirement quarters. Dirty paper lay tangled in the weeds, and grass sprang from the cracks in the sidewalk. Echoes of children's shouts from another time came to her in the wind drifting over the empty playground. She hunched her shoulders and broke into a trot.

At the next building, breathless, she forced her feet to slow, then stop, before the paint-chipped door. *I shouldn't have come.* Pushing herself was one thing, but what if she pushed herself over the edge back into the pit of Valium despair?

You're made of sterner stuff than that, Charla Rae. Trust yourself.

"Thanks, Mom." She smoothed her newly shortened hair behind her ears and took a deep breath to slow her galloping heart. One hand in a death grip on her purse, she forced the other to knock.

The sound echoed in the empty courtyard. She heard a rustling behind the door. The woman who opened it looked smaller than Char remembered. Older too. Not a dragon, just a bent, gray-haired old lady in a cheap lavender pantsuit, a hopeful look on her face.

When the lady recognized her visitor, hope flashed to fear. She slammed the door.

Char stepped closer and leaned her ear to the door. "Ms. Armstrong?" In the quiet beyond, she sensed the woman standing on the other side. "Please, Ms. Armstrong, I just want to talk."

Nothing.

The truth squirmed up from her chest and out of her throat. "To apologize."

The knob turned, and the door opened a crack, displaying a red-rimmed eye and a sliver of silver hair.

"Sincerely apologize." Saying the words eased an ache that had been hurting in her for so long, she'd forgotten it.

The door opened, and watching carefully, the woman ushered her in without a word.

It was a small space, full of the old-person smell of cough drops, stale breath, and ancient dusting powder. Char walked into a living room of heavy drapes and dark corners. The old woman sat in a hardwood rocker and gestured Char to an early-American print sofa.

Expecting to be turned away, Char hadn't planned past the front door. "Are you getting on all right, Ms. Armstrong?"

"Miriam." Her mouth pursed. "If you know me well enough to get up in my face and scream me down, we're on a first-name basis."

Char sat, fingering the crocheted doily on the couch arm. "I don't know what happened that day, Miriam. I was not myself." She made herself meet the old woman's gaze. "I had problems. We all did, but I had an extra one. I was addicted to Valium." At Miriam's frown, she hurried on. "I'm not using that as an excuse. There is no excuse for what I did. I've carried the shame of it ever since." Char cleared her throat and sat up straight. "I'm better now, though. I know you were only trying to help." She took a breath.

"I felt like if I put away the grieving and went on with life, I'd be abandoning my son. I tuned out everyone, trying to stay in that place with him. Nothing was too dear, even my husband.

"Then here you came, prodding and pushing, telling me to move on, go live my life. I snapped." Char looked down to see the doily wadded in her hands. She'd been picking threads, one by one. She made herself smooth it back onto the arm of the couch and put her hands in her lap. "I hurt you. I ruined whatever good I had left in my life, all for the sake of an impossible dream."

Char looked up. The old lady's chin wobbled, her shoulders shaking. Char reached across the gulf between them and laid her hand over Miriam's.

The little woman's tremulous whisper was fierce. "And I *wanted* to prod you. There you sat, shedding all the tears that I couldn't. I'm hardly one to lecture about denial." She took the tissue that Char offered and dabbed at her eyes. "Burt died so suddenly. I was alone." She raised her destroyed face to Char. "How could I survive in a world where something like that could happen?"

Char nodded in understanding.

"In some twisted way, I thought that by controlling you, I'd get some control over what was happening to me."

Two cups of coffee and many words later, Char stood in the hall, saying her good-byes. "You know, when I was a little girl, if something went wrong in a game, we asked for a do-over." She stood, hand on the doorknob. "I often wish I could call a do-over for the entire past year and a half."

Miriam went still, her hand on Char's arm. "Charla, are you a churchgoing woman?"

She lifted the strap of her purse over her shoulder, gently shrugging off the woman's touch. "I used to be."

"I ask, because that's what got me through. There's something about sitting in church, letting the peace settle over you. It helps." She smiled. "Okay, I'm not prodding. It's just something to think about."

When the door closed behind her, Char squinted into the brutal sunshine, feeling as if she'd stepped out of a cave. Somehow lighter, cleaner. She took in a deep breath of fresh Texas air and followed the sidewalk back to her car.

As she rounded the corner, no voices whispered in the breeze that swept through the grass of the quadrangle.

Maybe every day is a do-over.

CHAPTER 19

*The greatest obstacle to discovery is not ignorance—
it is the illusion of knowledge.*

—*Daniel J. Boorstin*

Char walked out of the barn, dusting her hands. At the sound of an engine backfire, she looked up. An old beater rounded the side of the house in a fog of oily smoke. She guessed the paint color had once been blue. Or maybe silver. The driver shut down the engine, but it fought, chugging, coughing, and sputtering as he opened the door and stepped out.

She walked over. "Hello, Travis. Are you here for your first lesson?"

He had to lift the door to close it. "Hey, Ms. Denny."

They both watched as the car completed theatrical death throes, rattling and huffing, until, with a last burp, it settled. She waited for a few seconds longer, just to be sure. "You may want to get that looked at."

He smiled. "Nah, it's all good. It always does that." His fingers beat a cadence against his leg as his gaze scanned the yard. And the three bulls standing in corral. "JB around?"

She smiled. "He's in the tack room, waiting. I'm not going to watch and make you more nervous, but I want you to know that I'm rooting for you, Travis."

"Thanks, Ms. Denny." He took a few steps, turned, and, walking backward, added, "And thanks for letting me come out."

JB lifted his old bull rope from the peg in the tack room and shook the dust off. He ran his hand over it, looking for weak spots. The leather-covered hand grip was worn, and the rope was stiff with decade-old stickum, but it would do. He picked up a flank rope on his way out the door.

Travis strode toward him, looking as riled as a Thoroughbred before a race. JB was glad to see the kid owned Wranglers and a pair of boots. No, not his. JB realized the boots were several sizes too big as the kid clumped toward him. "We're going to need to get you a decent hat."

Travis snugged the backward baseball cap tighter over his bleached-white hair. "Is there some rule says I've got to wear one?"

"Nope. In fact, rules say you've got to wear this." JB pulled his surprise from inside the tack room: a state-of-the-art bull rider's helmet. It looked like a football helmet, but with a metal cage over the face.

Travis backed up a step. "I'm not wearing that."

"You will if you want to ride on my property."

The boy shot JB a defiant stare. "You never did."

"They didn't have them when I was riding. If they had, I would have." He turned his head, to display his profile. "Do you think I was born with this nose? I broke it more times than I remember. And my cheekbone, twice."

Travis winced.

"No reason to be stupid about it. Are those the only boots you own?"

"My mom's last boyfriend forgot them when he left." His look dared JB to say anything.

"They'll do, for now." JB handed Travis the ropes and gathered his old bull-riding chaps, spurs, and padded flack vest from the shelf.

They walked to the practice paddock JB had set up, each to their own thoughts. JB looked over at Travis. *Terrified.*

Just like you were, the first time. It's going to be great, working with a kid again.

This should be Benje, walking beside me to his first bull.

Something bitter rose in him, burning his eyes, making them water.

Would there always be a hole in the world where his son should be?

Char hummed the song that had been running through her head all day, an old show tune her mother used to clean the house to.

A rock band in the 1960s had covered the song, but Char loved the original. A lilting, longing song about love in the spring. The long-handled nippers were awkward to use, but they didn't faze Pork Chop. She dozed in the stall, one foot between Char's knees, unimpressed with her pedicure.

A rich bass voice outside the stall joined in, humming. She stopped, startled, then, smiling, sang the next line.

JB entered the stall, singing. He put his thumbs in his pockets and stuck out his chest.

Char dropped Pork Chop's leg and straightened.

They finished the song together, his resonant base singing the melody, and her mezzo-soprano weaving in the harmony. They'd discovered in high school that their voices were good together.

The last note hung in the air. The sun came out in Jimmy's happy grin, and Char felt her day lighten. When he smiled, the years fell away, and he looked like the boy she'd fallen in love with all those years ago. Feeling her face heat, she retrieved the rasp from the straw and lifted Pork Chop's hoof to file the rough edges. "How did Travis do?"

Jimmy reached for the rasp, then apparently thought better of it. "Well, he's going to be sleeping on an ice pack tonight, but he did real good. The kid is small and compact, and he has good awareness of his body." Leaning against the wall, he tucked his hands in his armpits and crossed his ankles. "He doesn't know a thing about bulls though. Apparently he and his mom moved here not long ago from Ohio."

"No dad?"

"Just a steady stream of boyfriends from what I gather. He said his mom chose Fredericksburg because of his great-uncle Junior. Sounds like she's been down on her luck."

Char put the final touches on the hoof, dropped it, and straightened. "Then she's lucky that she's got family close."

"If Travis wants to stick with this and work hard, I think he could be ready to join the high school team by fall."

She gathered her armload of tools and, looking up at

him, tried to smile. "You know, Jimmy, you should find a woman who can give you kids. You're good with them, and they're good for you."

"No kid is going to take Benje's place." He walked up to her and looked down, the pain stark on his face. "You think I'm so shallow that I'd lose my son and then go make another?" He strode to the stall door, then turned back. "I *had* my boy," he said before he stalked out.

God, the pain in his face. He'd looked like she'd just torn out his guts. Char stood stunned a moment, then dropped everything and followed him. "Jimmy, wait!" She trotted to catch up. "I'm sorry. I didn't mean to hurt you." When she touched his arm, he stopped. "I only meant that you're so good with kids, it'd be a shame if you didn't have more of your own."

Silence descended as he studied her face, to see if she was telling the truth. That hurt. But she supposed she'd earned it. She'd closed herself off from him for so long. Why should he believe her?

She'd taken for granted that Jimmy was hard, that he didn't hurt as badly as she did. The wariness in his eyes now made her ashamed of herself. Just because he couldn't show his feelings didn't mean he didn't have them. Yet the thought of apologizing, exposing her vulnerability to the man who'd run the last time she really needed him? It felt like stepping off the curb in front of a car. But if she'd learned anything in the past year, she'd learned that the road to denial ended at a box in the garage.

Jimmy hadn't so much run as gotten out of the way. She'd been so crazy back then, could she blame him for that?

The muscles in her torso tightened, forming a shield, just in case. "I've been self-absorbed and selfish, Jimmy.

I've hurt you, and I'm so sorry." She tried with her gaze to tell him how much. "You and I have changed a lot in the past year. We don't know each other anymore. Let's make a pact. From now on, we both give each other the benefit of the doubt. If there's two ways to take a comment, we'll take it the good way, and leave it at that. Okay?"

She knew the gears of his mind turned from his intent expression. His face slowly relaxed. He sighed heavily. "Okay, Little Bit."

He walked away, his voice gruff. But she took hope from the sound of her pet name on his lips.

JB figured he had the pick of the litter as far as the bedrooms went. He couldn't get enough of the night-released smell of grass drifting into the screened porch, and in the coolness, the humidity felt almost refreshing. He reached down to pull the drawstring of the long cotton pants—his sleepwear concession to living with a woman who was not his wife. Something seemed different. He realized he had an unobstructed view of his feet. He ran his hand over his recently flattened belly, able to feel the muscle beneath for the first time in years. *Guess worry does have one good use.*

The brick floor felt cool on the soles of his feet as he crossed to turn off the lamp at the head of his cot. He stripped back the covers to lie down, one arm under his head, feeling the familiar poke of the torture bar in the center of his back.

He missed having a bed large enough to sprawl in. He missed having walls around him while he slept. He missed the familiar routine of bedtime, when Charla would come out of the bathroom, smelling of the cucumber skin cream she'd used on her face. He scrubbed his knuckles across his breastbone, to ease the ache there. Hell, he even missed her old-fashioned pajamas. After they were married, he'd bought her little scraps of lace to wear to bed, but they seldom found their way out of the dresser drawer. He came to appreciate Charla in flannel, transforming from stodgy frump to his willing, curvy sexpot with the unwrapping.

He and Jess had always been separate in bed. She'd kept a delicate distance between them, a demilitarized zone he was not welcome to pass. Saying she felt smothered by his arms at night, she sprawled on her half of the bed, and he lay curled in a ball on his.

Not Charla. She'd snuggle close, head on his arm, almost purring, while he told her of his day. He loved the smell of her hair spread on the pillow and the feel of it wrapped in his hands.

He didn't care that she fell asleep while he talked. He kind of liked that his voice was the last thing she heard as she drifted off.

Days later, JB strode for the Peterbilt, parked on the far side of the house. Why hadn't he thought of this before? He must have left his champion softball cap in the truck the last time he drove it. Opening the door, he used the handle to haul himself up.

"Hoooboy." Liquid heat poured over him. "Hotter'n the hubs of hell in here," he grumbled, eyes scanning the interior. He pulled the seat forward to riffle through the flotsam behind it.

Nothing. Kneeling on the driver's seat, he dug behind the passenger seat. Nope.

When he sat, his knee cracked against something

hard. "What the heck?" He wiped a rivulet of sweat out of his eye and scanned the floorboards. Bolted to the brake, accelerator, and clutch pedal were metal footplates on welded extensions. So that's how Charla drove the Peterbilt solo. He scratched at the sweat that rolled from the back of his cowboy hat. Very clever. He took one last hopeful glance around. No cap. He climbed from the cab and closed the gate to hell. Ninety-five in the shade, but it felt comparatively cool out here.

He heard Travis's rattletrap long before it made the turn at the corner of the house and settled, coughing and sputtering, in the yard.

They were standing by the car, talking, when Ben opened the back door of the house and stepped out. He looked from JB to Travis and back. "Who's this, JB?"

"Ben Enwright, meet Travis Beauchane. Bull rider in training."

Travis wiped a hand on his jeans, then stuck it out. "Pleased to meet you, sir."

Ben broke into a huge grin. "Well, it's good to see the next generation step up. Welcome, son. Ya'll come on in and get washed up for dinner."

Shit. JB hated this. The awkwardness, the embarrassment, for himself and for Charla. But most of all, he hated it for Ben. Travis looked at JB, unsure of what to do. "We just ate, Ben, but we appreciate—"

"Oh, hogswallop. How long you been here, JB? You know dinner is at noon. Now get yourselves inside and cleaned up. I'll tell Charla Rae to set two more plates." The screen door slapped behind him.

He grabbed Travis's arm when he would have started toward the barn. "Oh no, you don't. I'm not going in there alone." He dragged Travis to the door by the sleeve of his T-shirt. "We'll just smooth it over with Little Bit, then we'll get at those bulls."

Travis grumbled but followed.

Charla was setting extra places as they walked in the kitchen. Ben sat beaming from his usual chair at the head of the oval table. "You boys wash up now."

JB watched Char walk toward him. "We didn't—"

"I know," she muttered out of the corner of her mouth. "Just eat. It's easier this way, trust me."

He trailed her to the kitchen, Travis in his shadow. "No, really, Charla, I'll make an excuse—"

She made that universal female *tsk* of irritation and turned on him. "If you don't stay, he won't let it go. He'll be after me all afternoon about how rude I've been and that he raised me better. So please, just wash up, and sit down. It's only leftovers, but there's plenty." She stepped to the stove and lifted the lid on a large pot.

Is that Charla's chili? His mouth watered, making up his mind. "Well, Travis, don't stand there with your face hanging out. You heard the lady."

Within minutes, his boots were back under Charla's table. Without thinking, he sat in his usual place at the other head of the table, across from Ben.

Ben reached out his hands, one to Charla on his left, one to Travis, on his right. "Let us pray." He bowed his head.

Charla's eyes skittered away, but she held out her hand. JB took it, then Travis's, and bowed his head. As Ben said grace, JB focused on the soft skin of Charla's hand, until he encountered the calluses. He ran his fingers across the rough pads at the base of her fingers, knowing the hours of manual labor it took to develop them.

The second Ben said "Amen," Charla snatched her hand away as if he'd bitten it. She passed the cornbread—the lightly browned, bits of heaven she was famous for. JB's stomach growled.

Ben took the tureen of chili that Travis offered. "Well, son, what do you think of our bulls?"

That's all it took. Once Ben found out Travis enjoyed bull riding, he started in, regaling him with stories of past exploits and dispensing advice. JB watched from across the table, mouth full of Char's chili, swamped by déjà vu, It was as if he were watching himself at this table twenty years ago. Ben had taken him under his wing the same way, ushering him into the world of bull riding with stories and laughter. He'd stepped in as a father figure to JB and, even given Ben's Alzheimer's, Travis wouldn't find a better mentor.

The sad smile on Charla's face as she watched the pair told JB she was remembering too. He had to give it to Little Bit. When she'd thrown him off the property that day, he'd expected her call the next. A call that had never come. She did everything herself; if she couldn't do it the conventional way, she figured a way around it, like rigging the truck. All by herself. JB smiled. *Downright resourceful*. He'd put Charla up against lots of ranchers he knew, and she'd show better. He realized with a start that he admired her. At her wary look, he realized he'd been staring.

Char attempted to flip her too-short hair over her shoulder, trying to keep up the calm façade. Jimmy. Back in the house. It helped to have Daddy and Travis chattering like long-lost friends. But Jimmy's familiar gestures, his smell, his hulking presence had her nerves jumping. *Holy poop, how do I get into these messes?*

And now, here he sat, staring at her with a goofy grin. "Bella bought a ranch," she blurted, for something to say.

"New York owns a ranch? Surely not."

"Surely so." She gave up the appearance of eating and set her fork beside her plate. "She and Russ bought the old Koehler place."

"You met this phantom husband?"

"He's not a phantom, he just travels a lot. He's very sweet." Jimmy chased a piece of hominy around his plate with his fork. Well, at least she wasn't the only one dancing in that frying pan. The minefield yawning between them made even simple small talk, not simple. She tried again. "I'm helping her move in tomorrow."

"Oh, yeah?"

His studied gaze was starting to irritate her. "What?"

"I was just thinking. I imagine that her tenderfoot husband could use some help. He's bound to know less than nothing about ranching. I'm not working tomorrow. I could ride out with you."

She thought about Jimmy's offer. Russ would need someone to show him the ropes. And Jimmy could probably use a friend. It was about time she stopped being selfish. "I'm leaving around nine."

"Good. I'll be here." His chair squealed on the linoleum as he scooted back from the table. "Thank you for lunch, Charla Rae. I surely miss your cooking." He scrunched his napkin, as he always did and, setting it beside his plate, stood. "Come on, Travis, daylight's burning. At some point you have to stop talking about riding bulls and actually do it."

JB walked to the door of the mudroom but then turned back. "You coming, Ben? We can't do this without an expert."

Smiling big, her father scrabbled out of his chair like it was on fire, and snatched his hat from the counter. "We'll teach this Yankee whippersnapper a thing or two, JB, see if we don't."

She caught Jimmy's eye as he settled his hat on his head and mouthed *Thank you.*

He shot her a shy grin, winked, and walked out.

Danged if she hadn't always been a sucker for that grin.

CHAPTER 20

To forgive is to set a prisoner free and discover that the prisoner was you.

—Louis B. Smede

JB pulled open the door to Keller's Western Wear. "No one's going to throw you out for being a poser."

"But I don't need a cowboy hat." Travis hovered, scanning the shop window.

JB let the door fall closed. He looked at the faded, saggy-crotch skater shorts and dingy T-shirt, not wanting to imagine this kid's home life. Travis had gobbled lunch at the diner so fast it had him wondering when the boy had last eaten. "Come in and look, that's all I'm saying. Believe me, I'm not wasting money on a hat you're not going to wear."

A frown creased Travis's brow, but he followed. JB's boots made a satisfying hollow thumping sound on the old wooden boards as he took in his favorite smell: the heady scent of new leather and saddle soap.

Hats hung on the back wall, their brands conjuring the history of the American West: Resistol, Bailey, Stetson. "A straw hat is more practical." JB reached for a pinch-crowned Panama in natural ivory. "It's going to get dirty, and these are pretty easy to clean. See how it's ventilated? Not as hot that way."

Travis grimaced and looked away. "Isn't there something not so... old?"

JB scanned the merchandise. "Well, in case you hadn't noticed, cowboys aren't real big on change."

"Duuude!" Travis hurried away, focused as a hawk spying a rabbit kabob. JB trailed him to a sale table tucked under the stairs to the second floor. There, on top of a stack of boxes, sat a hat. But it wasn't like any cowboy hat JB'd ever seen. The black felted wool had been airbrushed with a pale gray skull and iron cross on the high crown and front brim. A hand-painted red flame circled the crown, and the black leather band sported silver studs protruding a good half inch. Travis lifted the hat off the pile as if it were a crown.

JB snorted. "That's not a hat. It's an abomination."

Travis walked to a full-length mirror, settled the hat on his short white spiked hair, and grinned ear to ear. "Maybe. But it's me. See? It fits."

JB had to admit it matched the kid's look, but he was going to get stares wandering around town in that thing. "Damned thing's wool, Travis. It'll be hotter'n the firebox on a steam train."

Travis removed the hat and looked inside. "It's marked down to twenty dollars!" He ran his finger reverently over the airbrushed cross. "Can you believe that, a piece of art like this?" He looked at JB, little-boy want on his face.

"Yeah, kid, you can have it." Travis's whoop fired a warm spot in JB's chest as he pulled out his wallet.

A few days after their trip to the store, JB sat leaning on his saddle horn, watching Travis practice. "God dang it, Kid, how many times I gotta tell you? You're looking off again!" It had been a long Sunday afternoon, and they were only an hour into it. Travis seemed distracted and out of sorts. The humidity was up today, and JB could feel the sun burning his skin, right through his shirt. A veil of dust hung in the air, stirred by bull's hooves.

JB nudged his horse to the bull's side, hazing him to the exit. When the animal cleared the gate, he closed it and trotted to the center of the corral. Travis had picked himself out of the dirt and was dusting himself off. "You do that every time you get in trouble. I keep telling you, you go where your eyes look. If you're staring at the dirt, you're sure'n hell going to end up there. *Before* the buzzer." He dismounted.

Travis pulled off the helmet and pulled out his mouth guard. His lips twisted in a pout, he frowned and looked away.

"At this rate, you won't be ready when the season starts. Is that what you want?" Travis shrugged. JB'd had it with the sullen attitude. "I'm out here sweating my guts out because you asked for my help. I'm not wasting any more of my time on someone who doesn't care." He spun on his heel. "I'm done."

Ben's sharp voice brought him up short. "Now you just hold up a minute, JB." Ben stalked toward them, bent, bowlegged. Angry, from the look.

"Ben, I'm sorry to drag you into this. It's been a waste of our time. The kid's too scared to make a bull rider."

"Well, good on him. Shows he's got some sense. More'n you, I'd wager." Ben smacked dirt from the sleeve of the Western shirt JB had loaned the boy. "You're doing fine, son. Any bull rider who isn't afraid is either loco or headed for a box in a hurry." He cut his eyes to JB. "And I seem to remember you, standing in this corral, bottom lip a-wobblin' and me telling you the same thing."

His icy blue eyes burned right through JB's anger. He *did* seem to remember...

Ben turned to Travis and grasped his shoulder. "You're trying to think of too many things at once and not getting any of 'em done. Forget about looking pretty up there." He drilled JB with another disgusted stare. "Just forget all that crap." He fingered the whistle hanging from a hank of twine around his neck. "We're going to a ten-second ride instead of eight. Your job is to stay 'holt of that rope till you hear the whistle. The only thing you have to remember is to keep your hand shut." He shook Travis's shoulder. "I don't care if you're hanging down, up close and personal with that bull's gonads, as long as you have the tail of the rope in your hand when the whistle blows, the ride counts. See?"

Travis, frowning in concentration, nodded.

"Style points don't count for spit if you don't make the whistle, and no kid on that team is going to look down on you for having bad form if you get a score.

"You've got grit, kid. Don't you doubt it." Ben patted him on the back. "JB, you go run another bull under this cowboy."

The kid's shoulders straightened and his head came up. As JB mounted, Travis looked up at him like Benje used to, expression hopeful, trying to gauge his mood. JB wasn't blind. He knew the kid looked up to him and was turning himself inside out to please. Guts twisting, he wheeled the horse away with a snort of self-disgust. What kind of man lost sight of that? *A sorry excuse for one, that's what kind.*

Outside the corral, he dismounted, tied the horse, and walked the pole fence to the holding pen. Gorge rose, and he tasted bitter regret on the back of his tongue. Why was he like that? *Push, push, push; nothing's ever good enough for JB Denny.*

He didn't need a head-shrink to know that his parents dying young and him taking responsibility for his grandparents had something to do with that relentless push. Palming the Hot-Shot from his back pocket, he prodded the two young bulls into the alleyway. *This isn't about Travis, you idiot. It's about you.* It seemed he'd always had that twitchy drive and the whisper in his brain, telling him he needed to be in charge, so he could keep control of his world.

He remembered the morning of his wedding day to Charla, feeling he'd won something far more precious than the lottery, because her strong, loving family came as a dowry. The drive hadn't lessened after their marriage; if anything, it pressed harder at his back. Every success upped the stakes, giving him that much more to control. That much more to lose.

Drive wasn't all bad, was it? He'd used it to become a champion bull rider. He worked his ass off to learn the bull business, then to grow his own operation. And, dang it, he was proud of his job as PBR announcer. He liked the spotlight. What was wrong with that?

Lots. The raw truth stopped JB in his tracks. Wrapped in a self-woven blanket of glory and ego, he'd let that drive push him too far. JB's pride leaked into the dust with every dragging footstep.

It pushed him to put his son off, when all he wanted was for his dad to build him a tree fort.

Pushed him away from his wife, who needed him, and into the arms of a hero-struck young girl.

Pushed him to put *his* wants above his family's needs.

Isn't that what Char and Jess had been telling him, each in their own way? He glanced through the pole fence to where Travis and Ben stood, heads together in the arena. There they were—the past and the future—and JB fell somewhere in between. What would life be like when he was Ben's age? *No way to know.* He urged the first bull into the chute, then climbed the fence and dropped the narrow gate behind him.

He did know one thing, though; if you were busy looking back, regretting the past, you weren't planning for the future. JB pictured himself, old and bent, sitting under a lap blanket, in a generic facility somewhere.

Alone.

Gooseflesh ripped across his skin, and he shivered in the sweltering heat, contemplating the rest of his life without Charla Rae in it. What would be the point?

Travis strode toward him, eyes steely with resolve.

There's no way to change the past, JB. Time to put it down and start shaping the future.

His family's future.

It might be battered and besieged, but the Enwright family was his, right down to the blonde whirlwind at its center.

It was time to stake his claim.

JB turned the truck into the driveway of the old Koehler place, Russ and Bella's new home.

Funny how time works, Char thought. As a little girl, she'd made this trip, Mom in a flowered dress for visiting, her purse perched on the seat between them. Later, after they'd married, she and JB had come to pick up her mom from her visits with Mrs. Koehler. Now here she sat, on another trip to the Koehler place; everything familiar yet so different.

She glanced across the seat at Jimmy. The years had etched lines in his ruggedly handsome face, but other than that...The veil of time thinned to gossamer and Char felt as if she could tear it away, returning to a better time when Benje had lay cradled, safe in a child's seat behind her. A strangled sound escaped.

Jimmy whipped his head around, fear in his eyes. "You okay?"

She cleared her throat. "Just swallowed wrong. I'm fine."

His frown looked doubtful, but he turned his attention back to the task of parking.

They emerged from the car, Jimmy carrying the butcher paper–wrapped steaks and the wine. She carried Bella's house-warming present. They wandered up the walk to the open front door.

Char stood at the door's threshold and called out, "Anybody home?"

Bella's face popped around the doorway to the kitchen, her curly hair so out of control, it defied gravity, floating almost straight up. With a huge smile, she stepped into the hallway, gesturing them inside. "Welcome to Casa di Donovan, such as it is." She yelled over her shoulder in a New York truck driver voice, "Hey, Russ, the cavalry is here!"

Bella looked like a ranch wife in her Wranglers, boots,

and Western shirt. Well, almost. Her Wranglers fit like skin on a slim sausage, and bangles clinked on her wrists. It was still Bella, after all.

JB urged Char forward with a touch at her back, then reached around her to shake Bella's hand. "I guess I'm going to have to start calling you East Texas now. Welcome to ranch ownership, Bella." He handed her the bottle of wine and the steaks. "May you find it as rewarding and wonderfully exasperating as we have."

Bella raised an eyebrow at the "we," but thank God Russ lumbered into the hall, filling it, deflecting her attention. Char shot JB the same eyebrow, but if he saw it, he ignored it, stepping forward to shake Russ's hand. "JB Denny. Proud to finally meet you, Russ."

"We appreciate you coming out." They walked the short hallway to the living room, empty save boxes jumbled everywhere on the hardwood floor. "As you can see, we can use the help."

Char handed the brightly wrapped package to her friend. "Welcome home, Bell."

Bella wiped her hands on her blue jeans and took the package. "Ooh, I love presents."

She tore the paper and opened the box, letting it all fall to the floor, revealing the black and hot pink tiger-striped bibbed apron. With ruffles.

"Oh, this is *so* me!" Bella squealed. "I love it! Where did you ever find this in Fredericksburg?"

Char snorted. "I made it, silly." She mimed a needle pulling through material. "You know, sewing?"

"I think that's our cue, Russ." JB tipped his hat back. "This is about to become a hen convention. Let's go speak of manly things."

Russ said, "I'll get us a beer and I'll show you the... spread? Is that how I say it?"

JB clapped him on the back, dropping a wink at Char. "This may take a while. If we're not back by sundown, send out the dogs."

As the men walked out, Char lifted the apron over Bella's head and stepped behind her to tie it.

Bella smoothed her hands over the fabric. "This is a perfect gift, Charla Rae, thanks. I'm going to need it soon. Russ asked me to marry him."

"What?" Char spun her friend around to face her. "You mean you weren't—"

"Are you kidding?" Bella put her hand on an outthrust hip. "Honey, I'm Italian. I had the obligatory white wedding, complete with two hundred guests, six bridesmaids, and full mass, for cripes' sakes!"

"Then what are you talking about?"

Bella fingered the rings on the delicate gold chain around her neck. "Russ figured the only way he'd get these off me to get them sized is to have a priest there when he put them back on." Bella gazed out the window, a sweet smile quirking her lips. She looked like a bride; in the soft light, her face glowed in fragile luminosity. "And he was right."

"Oh, Bella, I'm so happy for you." Char ignored the tiny needle of pain somewhere around her heart. "I can help with the plans. I know the owner of the Elks Lodge in town."

Bella shook her head. "This time I want intimate. Here, on the ranch, with just Russ, me, the priest. And you and JB as witnesses, if that's okay?"

"I can't speak for Jimmy, but I would be honored."

Char sniffed back tears. "God, I know it's sappy, but I love happy endings."

"They do still happen, Charla." Bella hugged her hard. "I have one more favor to ask."

She took Char's hand and led her to the huge country kitchen. "It would be such crime to waste all this." She touched the apron. "And this. Would you teach me to cook?"

Char laughed at her friend's worried frown. "Bella Donovan. If a city girl like you can learn to cut a calf, you can certainly learn to cook! I'll make you a deal. You call your grandma, have her send out a passel of her recipes. That way I can learn Italian cooking too."

"That's a great idea. In fact, I bet when I tell Nonna, she'll insist on a trip out, and she'll teach us both."

"You're not getting off that easy. There's one more thing." Char felt blood flood her cheeks and rushed on before she could chicken out. "Would you teach me that strut?"

Bella cocked her head, but the doorbell chimed, sparing Char more embarrassment. With a wicked smile, Bella strolled, hips rolling as if on casters, all the way to the door.

Jane Buxton stood on the other side of the screen, a wine bottle resting on either ample hip. "A little bird flew by and told me you were moving in today. I'm here to help."

Bella stood in the doorway, mouth hanging open.

Char reached around her to push the screen door wide. "Come on in, Jane. Forgive the Yankee. She doesn't understand southern hospitality."

Jane walked past them into the box-strewn living room.

Bella muttered under her breath, "More likely a witch flew by on her broom."

"Hey, don't knock it. Didn't I tell you that having Toni Bergstrom the wicked witch of the Clip 'n Curl as a realtor would be your invitation to Fredericksburg society?"

"Hold the door, Charla Rae!"

They looked up to see three couples coming up the walk, arms full of casserole dishes, cake keepers, and wine.

The furniture truck had shown up shortly after the reinforcements, and they'd slaved all afternoon, putting the house to rights. It was long after sundown when they quit, fell on the food, and opened the wine.

"You know, sometimes you have to take the bridle off, throw the skillet away, and let the panther scream." Charla raised her plastic wineglass in a salute to the couples lounging about the living room.

"I can get behind that." Sam Baldry raised his beer bottle, his other arm around his wife. He leaned over to buss her cheek.

"Looks like the panther's gonna scream at that ranch tonight." Char slapped a hand over her mouth and turned a pretty pink. Everyone chuckled.

JB leaned back in the chocolate suede chair, propped his feet on the ottoman, and, as the conversation flowed around him, studied her. Char had always been a lightweight. One glass of wine, and anything she'd been thinking fell out of her mouth. It embarrassed her no end, but he'd always found it endearing.

Char kept such a tight rein on herself. She'd always been that way. She sat on the leather couch across from him, chatting with Sam's wife. He enjoyed seeing small signs of her letting go: her head reclined on the couch's high back, one knee rested on the cushion, a stocking foot tucked under her. Catching Char still was as rare as seeing a hummingbird on a branch, resting. JB's chest muscles tightened. *Damn fine-looking woman.*

He watched emotion flicker across the face he knew better than his own. He'd traced those features in the dark, imprinting them on his fingertips and in his mind, so many times that he could sculpt that face from clay with his eyes closed. The tired lines still bracketed her mouth, probably always would. After all, what she'd been through the past year and a half was bound to leave its mark. But her skin had lost that scary gray cast, and her eyes and hair shone. She was the girl he'd fallen in love with back in high school. It was as if the years had worn away the superfluous, distilling her personality down to an essence.

And like any distillation, the result was potent. Char turned, laughing at something someone next to him said. Her shorter hair swung, brushing her open mouth. A flush of heat rushed to his groin and up his chest. He swallowed.

She's no longer your wife. He crossed an ankle over his knee to give some room in his Wranglers. Maybe not, but her pheromones still called to him from across a room, touching him places no other woman's ever had.

He wanted her. Sexually, obviously, but also in ways he'd forgotten until he found himself outside her world looking in. He missed the way she used to look at him, a corner of her mouth lifted in a girl-next-door-centerfold way. He missed the sight of her dancing in the kitchen when she thought herself alone. He missed having the home she'd created wrapped around him, giving him strength to go out in the world and do things.

Char glanced at her watch, straightened, and pulled her shoes from under the couch.

He missed all those things. It was the changes in her that kept him awake, staring out of the screened walls to the night. She was stronger now. Stronger than before the accident. Stronger than he'd ever seen her. And he liked it.

It was time he let her know, before some local buck noticed what was right under his nose.

Char stood and glanced across the room at him with that new, guarded-detached look that tore him up every time. He dropped his feet from the ottoman and pushed himself out of the chair.

God, I was blind. What difference did it make if the whole world looked up to JB Denny if the only one who mattered didn't?

They said their good-byes and walked down the porch steps, out of the warm pool of light, into the dark. When Char stumbled on an unseen lip of sidewalk, he took her elbow, grateful that, this time, she didn't flinch away.

"I know better than to have more than a half glass of wine. It's a good thing you're driving." She chattered all the way to the car about normal things: joy and happy gossip.

Just like she used to.

He opened her door and handed her in. When she reached for the handle to pull it closed, he held it, resting his forearms on it and the car hood. Were those butterflies in his stomach? Must be beer fizz. "Charla Rae, would you go to dinner with me?"

She looked up, her face porcelain pale in the light of the fingernail moon. The night was so still he could hear the faint yip-yip-howl of a coyote. She regarded him for what seemed like minutes as he hung dangling, waiting.

"I read in a *Cosmo* magazine at the Clip 'n Curl that when you sleep with someone nowadays, you're sleeping with everyone they ever slept with." Her eyes narrowed. "I think your bed would be a little crowded for my tastes, JB Denny."

He reared back, as shocked as if she'd slapped him. "Jesus, Charla. I was only talking about sharing a meat loaf plate down at the diner."

The night didn't hide her flaming blush. "Oh." She looked down, fidgeting with the handle on her purse. "I'll have to think on that, Jimmy."

CHAPTER
21

Never trust a husband too far, nor a bachelor too near.

—*Helen Rowland*

Come on, Charla Rae, we're gonna be late!" her dad yelled down the hall for the third time in ten minutes. How could he remember where they were going, but not what time? Both she and Rosa had reminded him for the past two hours that Travis's first competition didn't start until four, but it didn't seem to stick. She closed out of the American Bucking Bull's website. At first look, Bodacious's bloodlines seemed like a good match for Tricks's. She'd have to remember to ask Jimmy what he thought about that.

She stood and checked the clock on the bookshelf above the computer. Two-thirty.

"Charla Rae!" Her dad's strident tone bordered on panic.

She sighed. Well, they'd just be early then. She wasn't having Daddy working himself into a dither.

Thirty minutes later, Char turned off the farm road

onto the graveled parking lot of Junior's domain. Only a couple of battered ranch trucks sat sidled up to the feed store, but a truck and horse trailer turned in after them, rolling slowly to the arena. When her dad released his seat belt and pulled the door handle before the car came to a full stop, Rosa reached from the back seat to hold his shoulder.

Char put the car in park. "See, Daddy? We're not late." She patted his hand.

Rosa said, "Besides, they couldn't start without *el profesor*."

Attention riveted on the knot of men behind the chutes, her dad leapt out of the car and hurried away as fast as his bowed legs and gimpy knee would allow, leaving the door hanging open behind.

Char smiled. "Helping with Travis sure has perked him up."

Rosa gathered her massive purse and got out. "JB did a good thing. He gave Ben purpose. It's good for a man to have a reason to get out of bed every morning. Even if he can't always remember what it is." She stepped from the car, closed both doors, and followed Ben.

Char's mind skittered from the memory of lying in bed, reaching from under the covers for the meager comfort of Valium. "Amen to that, sister."

After locking the car, Char skirted the outside of the arena to where metal bleachers stood empty under a lip of shade provided by the metal roof. She climbed the five risers to sit at the top on the end closest to the chutes and scanned the crowd of men for her dad.

He stood with his arm around a fidgety Travis's shoulders. What was that on Travis's head? It looked like a cowboy hat, only uglier. Jimmy stood alongside, hands in back pockets, listening to something Travis said. Throwing his head back, he laughed, his teeth flashing white against his tan. He clapped Travis on the back and strode away, his broad shoulders showcased in a starched Western shirt. It was tucked into a pair of Wranglers hugging that tight butt she'd always been sweet on. From deep in her womb, something stirred, as if awakening. Char put a hand over her stomach to lull the feeling back to sleep. So what if JB Denny could still make her nether regions twitch from fifty yards away? Lacing her hands in her lap, she sat up straight. I'm a grown woman. Her good judgment trumped her body's wants.

Funny, it didn't look that way in Bella's driveway two weeks ago, Charla.

She dropped her face into her hands. Mom could always cut through a smoke screen to the fire. God, she could have crawled under the car seat that night. She hadn't meant the sexual comment about Jimmy specifically, but it sure sounded that way coming out of her mouth.

As her eyes followed Jimmy's loose-hipped walk, she twitched again. *Okay, I can admit it; I miss sex.* Sweaty, back-to-her-animal-origins sex that swept through in a wave, leaving her body spent and her mind gentled. She squirmed on the seat and pried her gaze away to watch cars pull into the parking lot.

They'd always been relaxed with each other about sex. She remembered one weekend, when Daddy traveled with Junior to a stock convention. They'd tried their best to have sex in every room in the house. JB had come up with some pretty inventive ideas. One night she'd cooked dinner in nothing but an apron. Well, she'd tried to. They ended up giggling and flour covered, making love on the kitchen counter in the middle of her biscuit dough.

As much as the sex, though, she missed the intimacy she shared with JB. Sitting silently at the kitchen table in the morning, sipping coffee, trading sections of the newspaper. Never having to search for a key, because he always hung them on the peg next to the back door. Knowing without looking, when he came in the mudroom door, he'd use the boot-jack to pry off his boots before padding in his socks to the kitchen to say "What's cookin', Baby?"

There's comfort in knowing someone as well as you know yourself.

Her new life was so precarious. At any time, a prize cow could die or a hay crop could fail. She was one bad decision, one unlucky break away from disaster. Char propped her elbows on her knees and rested her chin in one palm. Oh, she knew a relationship was a flimsy shield against life's pain. She'd learned that lesson the hard way. But it would be nice to be half a team in the traces, sharing the yoke of responsibility. The sweet burden of power is better shared.

Yeah, right. You sound like a Disney movie.

Disaster had hit them like a Kansas cyclone, and instead of her and Jimmy hunkering down together to weather the storm, it had torn them apart. She'd poked her head in a Valium bottle, and Jimmy'd lit out for another woman's bed. Worse yet, a *girl's* bed. Frozen frame pictures of Jimmy knocking boots with the little blonde shot through Char's brain like machine gunfire.

Hearing a rapid tapping, she looked down to see her foot bouncing on the bleacher. She made it stop. *Besides, I*

*like being my own woman, working outdoors, not having
to ask anyone for anything. Being my own boss.* The last
thing she needed was one more person to take care of.

JB stepped up to a desk on the opposite side of the
arena, behind a sound board. She should have known
they'd ask him to announce today's event. He picked up
the mike.

"Test. One, two. Test. Junior, can you hear me?" A fat
arm waved from the rapidly filling yard behind the chutes.
Bulls milled in the holding pens, and saddled horses
stood tied to the corral fence. Jimmy's deep, singing voice
flowed from the speakers as he fiddled with knobs.

"'I do. The day I said it to you. Turns out I meant it
much more than I knew.'"

Odd choice of songs. She'd never heard this one
before. The soft ballad continued, the words weaving a
story of happy romance.

"'Then, one day, the sun went away. Left in the dark,
I lost my way.'" Char jolted upright. *Son went away?*
Jimmy had written songs before. Was this more than a
sound check? She squinted, trying to read his downcast
expression. He frowned, messing with the electronics
as he sang stanzas of darkness. Her foot started bouncing again. It didn't have to mean anything. People got the
strangest tunes stuck in their heads. Char relaxed her grip
on the riser on either side of her thighs.

Suddenly Jimmy looked up, his eyes locking on hers
so quick that she knew he'd been aware of her the whole
time. He continued singing as her heart slammed against
her ribs; his unrelenting gaze left no doubt that his song
choice was no accident. His low-set voice slowed, coming
gentle from the speakers overhead, to settle on her.

" 'So when you look up with your eyes all blue and ask me, do I still love you? I do.' "

Char sat frozen, snared. The sounds of the arena faded until nothing existed but the tractor beam of emotion in his eyes: disconsolate, heartsick, remorseful, and hopeful all at the same time. Her heart threw short, staccato beats as JB Denny bared his soul to her with a look.

She jerked, adrenaline pumping to her nerve endings. Her foot tapped out a frantic Morse code. *SOS!* She closed her eyes to break the spell. It was a lot harder to do than it should have been.

When the bench shivered beneath her, she opened her eyes. Jimmy still stood behind the sound board, speaking with the coach of the rodeo team.

"You're probably not aware that you're eyeing your ex like he's a box of chocolates, and you've been on a diet a looooong time." Bella's boots rattled the metal as she climbed the bleachers to plunk down next to Char.

Char sat up straight and glanced around, surprised to see the stands filling around her. "Bell. What are you doing here?" She smoothed the hair back from her face, brushing her hand over her cheek in a feeble attempt to cool the heat.

Bella rested one blue stiletto-heeled cowgirl boot on the step in front of her. Her bracelets winked in the light, tinkling as she pointed to the chutes. "I've come to see Travis buck, of course. After listening to him talk about nothing but bull riding for the past three months at work, I had to see for myself what this was all about."

"You? I thought you didn't like him."

"Well, he *is* a Dumpster monkey, but he's our monkey, that's the thing."

Rosa stomped up the stands toward them, lips pursed. "Do you know Ben ordered me to leave?" She huffed. "I only wanted to see..."

"Give it up, Rosa." Char patted the seat beside her. "You don't know the secret handshake."

"Not to mention your complete lack of testosterone." Bella eyed the cowboys like an art critic at a gallery opening. "They're an aggravating species. But they sure are cute, aren't they?"

The three women scoped out the men in the arena.

"Yeah," Char and Rosa said together.

An hour later, Bella asked, "When's the bull riding? My butt bones hurt." She shifted on the bleacher. "Pole bending, steer wrestling, goat tying. Who thought up this stuff? And the 'Battlin' Billies'? Who names their high school team after goats? You people need to do something about your animal fixation."

Char patted her friend's arm. "Calm down, city girl. Bull riding is up next. See? They're loading the chutes now."

Char had to raise her voice to be heard over the babble of the crowd. The stands were filled to capacity with parents, siblings and students, the overflow lining the edge of the arena. Next to the football program, rodeo was the most popular sport at Fredericksburg High.

Rosa fanned herself with a program. "I hope that someone back there is seeing that Ben stays hydrated. I'm about to melt here, I can't imagine how hot it is in the sun."

Jimmy's voice was deep and smooth as he announced the winners of the barrel racing event. Char had always had Benje to care for, so she'd never traveled to hear him call an event. She had to admit, he was good, interspersing facts and humor into lulls in the action. He orchestrated the event with an ease that she knew was far from easy.

"Ya'll out buying a hot dog at the student council stand may want to hold the chili and hustle back here. The bull riding is about to commence. For those who don't know, I'll go over the rules. The rider is strapped to the one-ton animal by a braided rope covered in rosin. The cowbell at the bottom is there as a weight, so the rope falls off the bull at the end of the ride. To receive a score, the cowboy has to stay aboard for eight seconds, and his free arm cannot touch the bull. Piece of cake, right?" JB glanced to the chutes to gauge the rider's readiness.

"The cowboy makes up half the score, the bull the other half, for a total possible of one hundred. Those weird-lookin' dudes in the arena used to be called rodeo clowns, but nowadays we call 'em bullfighters. They're there to protect the rider after the get-off by distracting the bull." JB shuffled papers. "First up is Bubba Albright, from the Kerrville team, out of chute number one. Come on, people, this isn't easy. Let's cheer that cowboy on!"

The crowd roared as the brindled bull exploded from the chute. Char knew these bulls were amateurs compared to those at professional events, but the animal's horns were just as wicked. She held her breath.

The helmeted cowboy held one arm in the air, the other gripped the rope snugged up against his crotch as he clamped down on the bull's sides with his spurs. Dirt and saliva flew as the bull started spinning. The centrifugal force pulled the rider off his rope, a bit more with every spin. Two more jumps and the cowboy was stretched out, hand still in the rope, clinging to the bull's hips with his thighs. He lost grip with his spurs and, for a moment, was pulled vertically, legs out straight, held to the spinning animal by only the rope locked around his fingers. The buzzer sounded as the teen's hand popped out of the rope and he was launched, flying ten feet across the arena and landing in the dirt.

The bullfighters moved in as the cowboy scrabbled then sprinted to climb the fence. The crowd cheered as he pumped a fist in the air.

"Since his hand was in the rope at the buzzer, he gets a score. Good hustle, cowboy. The judges award Kerrville seventy points."

Char reached over to pry Bella's nails out of her arm. "Well, Bella, what do you think? Does that beat gang wars or whatever passes for sport in New York?"

"Oh. My. God." Bella's large eyes got larger. "You raise them crazy out here. How could a mother watch her son do that?"

"I don't know, but I'm glad I never had to find out. It was hard enough watching Jimmy ride back in the day."

Bella shifted on the seat. "I think I wet my pants."

Rosa jostled her arm. "Travis is up next." She pointed to the chute where the lanky teen was lowering himself onto the back of a huge black bull.

The face Char was able to glimpse through the helmet's facemask looked as grave and hard as a cigar store Indian's.

The coach pulled the rope taut, and the bull reared, pawing at the top of the chute, trying to climb out. Char hissed as Bella's nails bit into her upper arm again. The coach grabbed Travis around the chest and hauled him to safety. The bull, unable to escape, settled back in the chute. "Dang, Bella. Next time, file those talons, or you're sitting next to someone else." Char rubbed her misused bicep.

Bella sat on her hands. "Sorry."

The coach spoke to a clearly rattled Travis, and he climbed into the chute once more. The bull thrashed in the close confines. Someone grabbed the back of Travis's vest to keep him from hurtling headfirst onto the metal bars at the front of the gate. His head disappeared below the top of the chute.

"What's going on?" Rosa asked.

Char shot her a quick look. "The bull laid down in the chute. Some of them do that, to avoid being ridden. Wouldn't you just know that Travis would get a fractious one."

"Fractious? The damned thing is trying to kill him!" Bella's shrill voice cut through the noise of the crowd.

Char patted her back. "Welcome to bull riding, New York. It's not for the faint of heart—the riders, or the women who care about them." They watched the coach lean over the top of the chute to pull the rope. When it was tight, he handed it to Travis, to wrap around his hand.

"Actually, this isn't a bad thing. Jimmy always liked bulls that laid down. He said that at least they couldn't tear him up in the chute from that position."

Bella groaned. "This is insane. What's wrong with a tame game of rugby or something? You have a shot if it's only a human trying to kill you."

Travis must have nodded his head, because the spotter outside the chute swung the gate wide and jumped to the safety of the fence. The bull, seeing an escape route, shot to his feet and bucked his way into the arena.

Time seemed to slow as Char held her breath, fists clenched on her thighs. As the bull lunged forward, and Travis was left behind, off his rope. The bull turned in, and Travis was thrown off center, to the inside of the spin. Just as Char thought he was falling off, he shifted his hips in a brilliant move. Using the strength in the muscles of his forearm, along with his innate sense of balance, he pulled himself back to the center of the bull. He stayed perfectly balanced for the next three jumps. The crowd roared, coming to its feet around her. Char jumped up, standing on the riser in front so she could see through the bodies. Instead of continuing the spin, the bull lunged forward. Travis lost grip with his spurs, his feet came up, and his hand popped out of the rope. The cowboy flew off, to slam into the arena fence. He lay in a heap as one of the bullfighters stepped in front of him to protect him from the bull.

Char's air-starved lungs hitched a breath through the hand she'd clamped over her mouth.

The bullfighter needn't have bothered. Once the animal rid himself of the irritation, it stopped bucking and ran out of the open exit gate. Ben and the coach jumped from the fence to kneel beside Travis, where he writhed in the dirt. The team doctor ran in from the exit gate.

The crowd went silent, and JB's calm voice came from the speakers. "Travis Beauchane is down. This usually looks worse than it is, folks. Let's let the doctor do his thing."

The three men huddled around the downed cowboy and pulled off his helmet. Char felt Bella take her frozen hand on one side and Rosa the other. She drew a shaky breath and willed Travis to be okay. Anything else was unthinkable.

After a minute, Ben stood and waved to her side of the bleachers. The coach and the doctor hauled Travis to his feet.

"Looks like he just got the wind knocked out of him, folks." Relief flowed in JB's voice. "I say 'just,' but if you've ever had that happen, you know it feels like you're dying. Let's give the kid a hand."

The crowd cheered as Travis accepted his bull rope from one of the bullfighters and his hat from Ben. He settled it on his head, then tipped it to the crowd.

Char watched Jimmy watch Travis limp to the gate.

"No score, but a good effort from the newest member of the Fredericksburg team."

The sun shot golden streaks from the horizon, reluctant to give ground to the dusk. The stands emptied quickly as the crowd headed for the parking lot.

"I guess I see the attraction of the sport." Bella's boots rang on the metal bleachers as she stepped down. Char and Rosa followed. "But I'm not sure I can watch when I know one of the contestants. It's one thing to see a train wreck on the evening news, but it's a whole other thing when you know someone who took the train. You know what I mean?"

"Sure I do." Char hopped to the dirt. "But when someone you love loves this"—she swept her arm over the arena—"you don't have any choice but to show up, grit your teeth, and smile."

Rosa led the way to where the men gathered behind

the chutes. "Guess you spend a lot of money on a good health policy. And a lot of hours on your knees, praying."

Char rolled her eyes. "Honey, I had calluses on my knees from praying back then. It was almost a relief when Jimmy tore a tendon from the bone of his riding arm and had to quit."

Bella winced. "And here I thought New York was tough. Women there only join gangs and shoot each other. Much cleaner."

Dozens of men and a few girl contestants swarmed the area behind the chutes: loading horses, gathering equipment, and joking.

Char spied her men and walked to them. "I'm so proud of you, Travis!"

The teen tipped his unconventional hat and drawled, "Well, thank you kindly, ma'am."

Char squinted. He looked subtly different, as if he'd grown into his skin a bit.

The edge of JB's mouth quirked. "Hang around, kid, you may make a cowboy yet."

Ben clapped the boy on the back hard enough that he took a step forward. "Anyone who's got the guts to straddle a bull is a man, JB."

"You're right about that, Ben." He glanced at the women, but his gaze settled on Char. "Would you ladies care to join us for a celebratory dinner?"

Rosa said, "Thanks, JB, but I have to be getting home. I ran into my neighbor and I'm catching a ride with her. Good job, Travis." She stepped up and hugged Ben. "I'll see you tomorrow." She turned and walked toward the parking lot.

Bella pulled Travis into a one-armed hug. "I've gotta

work; it's my turn to close. You go have fun. I'll see you at work tomorrow, after school." She turned and sashayed in the direction of the feed store.

Travis put his hands in his back pockets and looked at his feet. "The team is meeting at Mr. Gatti's for pizza. Um. I thought I should go . . ."

Jimmy grinned. "Of course you should. You go on, and don't let any of them razz you about that hat."

Travis looked up with a smug grin. "Are you kidding? I'm legendary. They all want to know where they can get one." He shot JB a saucy grin, turned, and walked away.

"Excuse me a second." JB trotted after Travis.

Char watched him touch Travis's shoulder and slip him some money. The familiar hollow pain in her chest squeezed her heart, making it hard to breathe.

He should be doing that with Benje.

Travis looked up at Jimmy, relief in his eyes, his mouth forming the words *Thank you.* How could she begrudge a boy who so obviously needed a father figure, because her son no longer did?

I love you, Benje.

JB jogged back and stood before her. He didn't have to say anything; his frank assessing gaze settled on her as he awaited her choice.

She rooted in her purse for her keys. "Daddy and I have to get home." Her fumbling fingers dropped the keys in the dirt.

Taking his time, Jimmy bent, picked them up, and handed them to her. "You sure? I'm talking the Golden Corral. And I'm buying."

Char closed her purse, lifted the strap over her shoulder, and touched her dad's back to urge him toward the car. "We have to get home and get Daddy's pills." She ignored the longing in her chest, urging her to say yes. "But thanks, Jimmy."

She walked away, imagining the alarming normality she'd feel sitting down with Jimmy in a booth at the Golden Corral.

CHAPTER 22

Joy and sorrow are inseparable...together they come and when one sits alone with you, remember that the other is asleep upon your bed.

—*Kahlil Gibran*

The parking lot of the Holy Shepherd Church was packed with cars but empty of people. Char stepped from the car and glanced around, relishing the smell of fall in the air. Not yet a nip, but the easing of the heavy heat at dawn was a welcome precursor to it.

Sparkly shivers raced through her body as the soaring organ notes of "A Mighty Fortress Is Our God" drifted to her on the light breeze. She brushed a nonexistent speck from her sky-blue linen suit. By dropping her Dad at Junior's and arriving after the service had begun, she'd avoided having to speak with anyone, but she hadn't thought through her strategy past this point. She'd have to march into the packed church. She imagined every head swiveling, every eye trained on her, the prodigal daughter. The shivers settled into her stomach and started a party.

Get a grip. That's fear talking, not reality. She glared at the innocent sky. "Okay, God, I'm here. You happy?"

Before she could change her mind, she tossed her purse strap over her shoulder, chirped the auto lock, and stalked to the church she'd attended her entire life. Resolve ebbed a bit with every step up to the imposing wooden doors.

Hand on the iron handle, she hesitated again, her brain seesawing between opposing impressions. The organ music charged the air, so physically real that the metal beneath her fingers vibrated with it, bringing a familiar peace.

The calm melted like snow before a blowtorch blast of her seething fury. The same God who offered solace now was the one who had taken her son. Char looked up to the cold stone soaring overhead, pulling her gaze to the spires reaching toward heaven. "I'm here, God, but you are *not* forgiven."

Jerking the heavy door open, rage fueled her steps into the nave. She stalked to the only empty seat in the last pew and sat. Ignoring the congregants, she stared ahead at the apse. The choir stood at the ready, hymnals open in their hands. As the last organ note trailed off, the congregation rose to its feet.

Char didn't care a holy fig for etiquette at this point but knew she'd draw attention if she ignored it, so she stood. The organ began again, and voices rose. "Praise God, from whom all blessings flow." Out of habit, Char mouthed the words. From the off-key trembling voice of the octogenarian next to her, to the clear harmony of the choir, the music rose to the vaulted ceiling far above her head. There, the mishmash of voices wove like threads on a loom, settling over the crowd as more than the sum of its parts—complete, multifaceted, beautiful. It touched a forgotten chord in her chest, and the resonance spread a balm of peace.

Hymn over, the congregation sat. She'd missed this. Char settled in, examining that surprising nugget as the announcements were read. She didn't miss God; but she did miss the soothing rituals and being a part of the congregational fabric of the church.

Reverend Mike walked to the pulpit to begin his sermon. Char tuned it out, having no interest in the word of an Indian-giver God. Instead, she thought about the book on her nightstand, with the quotes about grief. Many of them referred to forgiveness. She knew from her reading that this was a cliff she was going to have to scale. Someday.

Char glanced to the stained glass window closest to her. The sun lit the abstract pattern of reds, blues, greens, and yellows, turning the common glass to kaleidoscope crystal.

How do you forgive the unforgivable?

An hour later, a babble rose as parishioners gathered their belongings to leave. Char clamped her jaw tight. It had to happen sometime. She might as well get it over with. She stood to face a phalanx of well-meaning friends and neighbors.

Salina was first, waiting at the end of the pew, blocking the escape route. She didn't offer platitudes. She didn't say anything, just folded Char in a soft embrace. When Char would have stepped back, Salina held on, lightly rubbing her back for a moment, whispering "Love you, Charla Rae." Char stepped back, studying her old friend's face. Nothing there but acceptance. And a tear.

Char's chest loosened a little. "Thanks, Sal. Love you too. I'll call you sometime." She turned to the next well-wisher.

Finally, thankfully, she was free to go. *One more chore*

and this will be behind me. Her heels tapped an echo as she walked to the door where Rev. Mike stood, greeting his flock.

He smiled broadly, taking her outstretched hand in both of his. "Charla Rae. I'm so glad you could join us this morning. We've missed you."

"Thank you, Rev. I actually came to apologize. With everything going on, I haven't thanked you for referring Rosa to us. She's Daddy's angel, and I don't know how I would have survived without her these past months."

The Reverend cocked his head. "Rosa?"

Char felt her face heat. "I know, it's been so long, you've probably forgotten. She's the nurse with County Outreach."

He shook his head, his face blank.

"You ran into her at Saint Luke's. You gave her my name?"

"I'm sorry, Charla, but I don't understand. Community Outreach doesn't offer home nursing services. I know, because I looked into it when Salina needed help with her grandmother. Could you have been mistaken?"

Char frowned. "I know she said . . ." She shook her head. "Sorry."

He smiled down at her, still holding her hands. "If it brought you here, I'll not question God's methods. I'm done with my sermon, so I won't lecture you. I only have one thing to tell you, then I'll let you go."

She squirmed under his warm scrutiny.

"God is waiting, Charla Rae. As long as it takes."

She jerked her fingers from his. "Yes, well." The stone wall's towering presence felt heavy on her back as she turned. "Good-bye, Rev."

She'd lingered so long with the greeting gauntlet that

her car was one of the few left in the lot. Clearly, Rosa hadn't told her the truth. Char rummaged in her Sunday purse for her keys. Then who'd hired her? *Hired*. She reached her car and opened the door. She dropped into the seat as her knees let go.

Oh my God, who is paying her? Was the entire town talking about poor Charla Denny? Had they put out a donation can at the check stand down at the 7-Eleven? Shame burned a hot path to the inside of her skin. She was hardly aware of pulling the door closed.

No way. In a town this small, you couldn't even pull off a surprise birthday party. So that left only . . .

"Jimmy." Her voice sounded loud in the closed space. Reality crashed in, shattering the fragile pride she'd garnered by herding her runaway life the past months. She slammed the key into the ignition. Oh, this was classic Jimmy Denny. Jump in and take over, assuming he had the answer. "Well, Mr. High-and-Mighty is *not* the savior of the Enwright clan."

Nose inches from the steering wheel, Char raced to the exit, then waited for a break in the Sunday parade of cars heading downtown. Her brain clicked off the little clues from the past months. The time she'd walked in on Rosa's conversation—she must have been reporting to her *employer*. Rosa and Jimmy's sliding looks when she'd introduced them.

She shot into a slim break in the traffic, ignoring the horn-bleat of the offended driver next in line. She and Daddy didn't need help.

Traffic slowed to a crawl as they hit the edge of town. "Are they giving away free beer at the Piggly Wiggly? Come on, people!"

You might want to look where that road goes before you turn down it, Charla Rae.

Char rolled her eyes. *Mom, from the crappy decisions I've seen God make the past year, can't you stay busy, giving him advice?*

"I'll just turn over the outside duties to Jimmy, and I'll take care of Daddy. Let him deal with the backaches, the cow snot, and the calamities." She stopped at the red light at the center of town and watched as a clearly exasperated mother crossed in front of the car. The toddler she dragged by one hand was having a meltdown; Char could hear his hair-raising wail from inside the closed car. Catching the woman's eye, she threw her a sympathetic smile. *I remember those days.* Benje was everywhere; there never seemed to be a spare minute in the day. The young mother hauled her boy into her arms as she stepped onto the sidewalk.

Her gut went hollow. *Those days are gone.*

Char cast her mind over the past months: helping Tricks calve, getting to know Pork Chop, the everyday chores that were now such a part of her life. She loved spending her days in the saddle, watching the subtle changes in the land with the change in season.

She pictured herself sitting at the kitchen table, listening to the ticking clock, as Daddy snoozed the afternoon away in the great room. She watched herself get up, walk to the sink, and reach for the amber-colored prescription bottle on the sill.

Beeep! Char jumped. The light had changed. Hitting the gas, she continued down West Main, hands shaky from just the memory of the iron-band tightening need.

Wait. *Why* did Jimmy do it?

Her mind flashed the picture of Jimmy, feet under her table, tucking away chili. Heat rose in her, remembering his smoking look as he sang to her from across the arena. "He did this to try to get me back!"

But Rosa had called the first time, way before any of that.

So why did he do it?

The traffic thinned as she reached the edges of downtown.

"I don't know, but I'm going to find out. Right now." She hit the gas.

CHAPTER 23

I am angry nearly every day of my life, but I have learned not to show it; and I still try to hope not to feel it, though it may take me another forty years to do it.

—Marmee, *Little Women*

Char slammed the car door. Jimmy's truck stood parked in the shade of the house, but he was nowhere to be seen. Ignoring the gnat of worry at the cost of a cleaning bill for her sky-blue suit, she walked to the barn.

Blinded by the transition from sunlight to shadow, she almost tripped over Jimmy. He sat sprawled on a hay bale inside the barn door, old towel in his hand, cleaning tack. Tack that looked suspiciously like hers. She stopped short.

He looked up, his face lit with a happy smile. "Hey, Little Bit. How was church?"

Fighting the magnetic tug of that little-boy grin, she tightened her fists. "Don't you 'Little Bit' me, James Benton. What do you mean, going behind my back to pay a nurse to take care of Daddy?" She lifted a finger when his lips parted. "And don't you try to tell me you didn't."

He sat back, face sober. "It's my job to take care of my family."

"Jimmy, you are not family anymore." She lifted her hand, pointing to her empty ring finger. "In case you've forgotten, we're divorced."

He bent his head to the bridle in his lap, rubbing saddle soap into the cheek strap.

She ignored the prick of guilt at her waspish tone. She didn't like that she couldn't read his face. "Jimmy."

He looked up. "Okay, Little Bit, have it your way. Ben didn't divorce me, so he and I are still family. I sent the nurse to help *him*."

She stomped a foot. "Oh, you are the most maddening man."

"Why, Charla?" He frowned. "Because I saw something that needed doing, and I did it? Does that make me a bad guy?"

She looked down at his open face and sinless smile. She knew Jimmy Denny. Knew when he was wheedling to get his way. She also knew when he was being honest.

He'd been working at the feedlot—hard, nasty work— for money that went to make *her* life easier. Her stomach twisted in what felt a lot like guilt. What kind of woman had she become in the past year that she would be furious with someone who was trying to help her daddy?

Even if it was JB Denny.

She swallowed a chunk of pride. "Okay, I may have overreacted a bit. But from this day on, *I'm* paying Rosa. I've got the money from my grandma's china." She lifted her chin.

"Sure thing, Charla Rae."

"And another thing. I'm taking half the responsibility

for running this operation. If you don't like it, you can get happy in the same pants you got mad in."

His smile cranked up a few watts. "That's great, but as I see it, you've already done that. Been doin' a good job too."

She narrowed her eyes. He looked back, relaxed, open. Sincere. The last of her anger whooshed out of her in a rush, its boiling heat melting all her starch. Her shoulders slumped. She tipped her head and squinted down at him. "Who *are* you?" *And what are you up to?*

He chuckled. After setting aside the bridle, he lifted a clean towel from the pile beside him, snapped out the wrinkles, and laid it on the opposite end of the hay bale. He patted it. "Sit down, Char. You look flat tuckered."

She sank onto the contrived seat, as far from him as possible. "It's been a long morning."

She put her head in her hands, almost dizzy from the hot-flash mood shift. "It's just that everything keeps... *changing*."

"That's true enough." Jimmy turned to her, his shoulder resting on the stall behind him as he studied her. "Char, I'm proud to have a partner as savvy as you."

"Don't you dare patronize me, James Benton."

"For such a smart woman, I swear." He shook his head. "Charla, you're much better with the calves than I am. This year's crop has more solid growth and weight on them than they ever have. What are you doing different?"

She blinked. "I gave them some love and fed them the vitamins I found on a shelf in the tack room."

He tipped his hat back and scratched his forehead. "I bought that last year, but they won't eat it."

She couldn't help it. Her lips twitched. "They will if you mix it in molasses."

"Now there, see? I didn't think of that." He raised his knee and rested it on the bale. "No one person can do it all, Char. Ever wonder why you don't see many unmarried ranchers? Back when Benje was little, the only reason I could take the PBR announcer gig is because you were home, holding down the fort."

"Yes, but now—" A whisper of despair echoed down her awareness, and her jaw locked, midsentence.

Jimmy must have heard it. He jumped in. "Now you've got some time to help with the operation, and like it or not, you and I are partners." He slapped his hands on his thighs and leaned in, too close. "With all these brains, talent, and hard work, we're going to make PBR stock contractor of the year one of these days. See if we don't."

He straightened and stood, resettling his hat, his eyes holding hers all the while. "Had you forgotten? We've always made a great team, Charla."

Regret lay etched in the furrows bracketing his mouth. Lines that weren't there last year. She wasn't the only one who had suffered. "Yeah, Jimmy, we did." It came out in a whisper.

A slice of sun hit his cheek, highlighting the silver in the beard stubble. His gaze lingered, considering, before he spun on his heel and strolled out of the barn whistling.

Thanks to the blazing light, his silhouette stayed burned on her corneas long after he was gone. No matter what he'd said, Jimmy hired Rosa for her. He had no more money than she, but he'd sacrificed to make her life easier.

Did she dare trust that softened spot on her freezer-burned heart?

• • •

Rosa glanced from her book as Char walked into the great room. Her father snored softly in the La-Z-Boy beside her rocker. "How was church, Charla?"

"Enlightening. But not in a religious sense." She smiled down at her father. In sleep, the confused look he wore most often nowadays melted away, leaving instead an almost cherubic peacefulness.

"You can relax, Rosa. I know that Jimmy hired you." The rest came out in a rush. "I'll be paying you from now on, but I wanted to tell you that I'm sorry. This must have been so uncomfortable for you. Why on earth did you agree to it?"

Rosa watched her with bright sparrow eyes. "I had my doubts, I will admit. Then, when I came out that night, you so obviously needed help. I couldn't say no."

Char lifted the dirty teacup from the table. "Yes, Daddy was getting to the point that—"

"I'm not talking about your father, Charla. I'm talking about you."

The teacup chattered in the saucer, and she covered it with her other hand to make it stop.

"Can I speak freely?"

Why do people ask that? Once asked, it's impossible to say no. Char nodded.

"I work with people every day who, because of disease, have lost their ability to communicate. They fall out of the current of society, to live on the shadowed edges. You're not so different from them, Charla. Except you've chosen the backwaters." Rosa set the chair to rocking, but her gaze never wavered. "I've been here for months now, long enough to see that you have people who love you standing by, waiting to help. And yet you shut them out." The rocker stilled. "Why do you do that?"

Char set the teacup back on the table. It made it easier to pace, with her hands empty.

"I've had to work through some things...inside myself, before it felt safe to let anyone in. I'm doing better with that now and—"

"Do you feel guilty, Charla?"

Her heart faltered, skittered, then settled in a gallop that thrummed in her ears. A strangled sob burst from her throat before it clamped shut. The stunned echo of the question that no one had yet asked hung lingering in the quiet room. This was the monolith that had risen from stinking mudflats left behind as the tide of anger had receded. Behind the blockage in her throat, emotion built, pressing up from her core, filling her chest with a seething, restless heat.

Rosa reached to touch her. "You know that it is natural to feel this?"

Char jerked away. "I know. They told us about it in the grief group. I've read about it in a book I have too." She tightened her lips, trying to put words to the Gordian knot she'd worked at until her mind frayed. She touched two fingers to her forehead. "I have it here." She swallowed back the pressure below her throat. Her chest felt swollen with it, hot to the touch. "But my heart isn't buying it."

Rosa cocked her head. "Then is Jimmy guilty as well?"

Char reared back, stunned. "Of course not!"

"Why not? He was on the property that day, right?"

Rosa's soft words hammered her heart. *How could anyone think it was Jimmy's fault?* Char heard a familiar buzzing in her head and an itch in her brain that only Valium would assuage. The buzz increased to the manic humming she remembered from the day of the funeral. Terrified, she squeezed her eyes shut and covered her ears to block it out. A touch at her shoulder startled a wail from her throat. "But I was his MOTHER!" The blockage in her throat gone, the pent-up sobs burst from her mouth like a confession.

Rosa enfolded her into her arms, and Char clung, terrified by the howling wind raging inside.

"Come on, JB, a badass cowboy like you can do better than that." Dana stood in front of the tilted sit-up board, stopwatch in hand, barking like a drill sergeant.

Squeezing his eyes shut to block the sting of sweat, he tried not to grunt as he forced his shaking stomach muscles to finish one last sit-up. "One fifty." He grabbed the bar anchoring his feet and sat up, panting.

"A six-pack of muscle would be easier to develop if you didn't drink the other kind, you know." She dropped a towel over his head.

When he'd first moved in with the Galts, he'd thought Dana had bought the gym for a steady revenue stream. She'd corrected that misguided opinion right off. The woman was obsessed with fitness, and no politician ever stumped harder for a cause. It started with a raised eyebrow when he opened a beer with Wiley at night. Then there were the subtle-as-a-hammer fitness sermons, spouted whenever she cornered him long enough to listen. When she'd started serving turkey burgers and tofu salad for dinner, he cried uncle and agreed to a workout.

Funny thing though. He was starting to see the draw.

Timing his workout in the late-morning lull, he and Dana were often the gym's only patrons. He pulled the towel off his head and wiped his sweaty face. "Six-pack? I drink one beer a night and you know it."

"Yeah, but herbal tea would be so much better for you."

"Jesus, woman. You've got me down here working out three times a week. Hang it up, Dana. You're not turning me into some simpering city dude, getting my nails buffed and my body hair waxed." He glanced at his profile in the mirrored wall surrounding the workout room. In a pair of sweats and a T-shirt with the sleeves torn off, he was hardly the height of fitness fashion. "Besides, you have to admit, this old body is looking better than when I showed up, fat and bedraggled, on your doorstep."

She tilted her head and studied him. "The fat is gone, I'll give you that. Speaking to that bedraggled part, how's it going with Charla?"

His hands clenched at the seemingly innocent question. He knew Dana better. Between the aerobics and weight-lifting sessions, he'd found her a good listener. Not to mention her good insight into the mysterious turnings of the feminine brain. He draped the towel over the back of his neck and moved on to the quad machine. "It's not. She's as skittish as a mustang filly, and she tends to take everything I say the wrong way." He slid the weight peg down two slots, settled his feet on the vertical platform, and pushed, liking the feel of his muscles bunching. "I've tried being subtle, I've tried being up front. She always finds a way to skirt around a deep discussion, much less let me ask her out."

"Yeah, I've heard your 'big move, small move' theory, JB." Dana tapped his foot, and he shifted it a bit to the right. "Slow the reps a bit." She crossed her arms on her chest and waited. "Are you asking my opinion?"

The muscles in his neck strained, and his leg muscles burned. "Damn, woman, you've got me sounding like a guest on *Dr. Phil* as it is. Jump in anytime."

"Well, I'd never offer an unsolicited opinion, but since you asked…" She sat on the trapezius machine next to him and leaned in, elbows on knees. "JB, this woman has listened to you talk for what, twenty years?"

"And your point?"

She rolled her eyes. "You guys kill me. The key to having a woman fall in love with you is so simple. We tell you what it is all the time, and so few of you get it. Why is that?"

He grunted. "Are we having a philosophical Mars/ Venus discussion here, or are you going to tell me?"

Dana sighed and did the hair-flip thing. Did they teach all the girls that in junior high? Must have, because every woman he'd ever been around had it down cold.

"In a word, communication." She sat back, smug, as if she'd delivered the Holy Grail.

Clang! He let the weight down hard and glared at up her.

"JB, you *cheated* on her." She held up a hand to silence his protest. "Oh, I know, you moved out before any bonking commenced. And maybe in a man's mind that carries weight. But as far as Char is concerned, you and Jess might as well have been doing it in Charla's bed. Don't you see? It's about trust. And you betrayed her in every way possible."

He ducked his head and fiddled with the weight selector. "Yeah, I see. Look, I know I screwed up." He stopped fiddling and met her gaze. "Sincerely, I do." He grabbed the ends of the towel around his neck in his fists, to have something to hang onto. "But even murderers can be pardoned. I've apologized. I've tried to make her understand how bad I feel about making things worse for her." He winced, remembering the ragged scarecrow he'd glimpsed the day he'd brought Mitzi to pick up the bulls. The downhill slide had been so evident in Charla's haunted eyes and ravaged body, it had frightened him. "I was an idiot. I'd give anything if I could go back and make it unhappen. But—"

"Yeah, JB, you told her." Dana addressed the ceiling. "And like I said, she's heard you talk for twenty years." Dana studied him as if he were a slow four-year-old. "She's not listening, JB. Not anymore."

Her level stare made him cringe, and he wasn't sure why. "That's what I've been trying to tell you!"

"She's not listening, JB. She's *watching*." She let that zinger sink in. "Women are tough, but we're vulnerable. No one can hurt us worse than someone we've allowed close. You snuggled up next to her heart and settled in for all those years."

He felt sure she didn't know that her hand stole up to cover her heart. "Then you took out the knives and diced it up into little pieces."

"I'm not saying that Char will let you in again. I'm not saying she won't. I do know the only way to get close is for her to trust you."

"Hell, Dana, I'm forty years old. I don't have enough time for that!"

The serious fled with her sunny smile. "JB, you just made me feel better about you. If you understand that, there may be hope for your black soul yet." She stood. "You need to show her that you're worthy of trust. And I'm not talking flowers and hyperbole. I can't tell you how." She touched her fingers to her chest. "That has to come from here."

"A woman holds as great a capacity for forgiveness as she does for love." Dana's doe eyes softened as she took a step and touched her fingers to his cheek. "Charla knows you're a good man. You only need to remind her of what she's forgotten."

CHAPTER 24

When you are sorrowful look again in your heart, and you shall see that in truth you are weeping for that which has been your delight.

—Kahlil Gibran

Dinnng! Char's hand jerked at the sound of the doorbell. Her finger brushed the metal spike at the middle of the hot roller. "Dang it!" She shook her hand to cool it, then inspected the angry mark. "Who the heck?" She glanced in the mirror. Rollers covered the left side of her head, the right side lay flat and lifeless. Her pre-makeup face shone ghastly in the fluorescent light. The terry zip-front robe covered her from neck to ankle but was hardly fit for company. *Dinnng!*

She hurried down the hallway. "Anyone who shows up unannounced gets the scare they deserve." Rounding the corner of the mudroom, she saw Jimmy's profile through the back door window. *Why is he here so early?* His face appeared above her café curtains.

Scrunching the neck of the robe in her fist, she opened the door a crack. "Jimmy, is everything all right? Bella's ceremony isn't until three."

He stood, dress hat in hand, cheeks smooth and pink from a recent shave, comb tracks pristine in his damp hair. "I was ready early, so I thought I'd visit with Ben while I waited for you."

"Oh. He's not here. He's spending the day with Junior." Her hand tightened on the knob. What was she going to do with him while she was getting ready? Jimmy stood there, fingering the brim of his hat, looking like he was prepared to stand on the back porch all afternoon if he needed to.

She put a hand to her work-in-progress hairdo. *Well, he's already seen the worst anyway.* His grin broadened as she stood back to let him in.

"I'll wait in the kitchen. You take your time, Char."

As he stepped around her, his familiar cologne filled her head. She'd bought it for him their first Christmas together. He'd never worn another. On Jimmy, it blended with his own scent to something stronger. Something deadly. She filled her lungs with it, abruptly aware that she was naked under the flimsy barrier of the robe. The terry-cloth nubs rubbed her suddenly too-sensitive skin.

She noted his broad shoulders and long legs as he strode to the kitchen. Jimmy'd always looked great in a suit, though it took a wedding or a funeral to get him into one. He opened the cupboard above the stove and rummaged through it, setting the pottery clinking. Standing on tiptoe, his head disappeared behind the cabinet door. She opened her mouth to ask, but before she could, he emerged with a grin and his old coffee cup in hand: a huge white mug advertising Purina Cow Chow.

He poured from the eternal pot of coffee on the stove. "You do what you need to do, Char, I'll be fine out here."

Yeah, like I'm going to relax with you in the house.
She hustled past him, head down.

"Oh, Char?"

She turned to see him, one hand in the pocket of his dress slacks, coffee cup in the other, looking like a model from a Western wear catalog.

"I've been meaning to ask. Have you run across my championship baseball cap?"

Her fist tightened in the material at her neck. "Not lately." Cheeks flaming, she scurried for the hall.

Standing in front of the mirror once more, she forced herself to take a deep breath. The butterflies living in her stomach seemed to like it, so she took another. *I'm not going to rush. If he shows up unannounced, he deserves to cool his heels.* She picked up the next roller and wound it in her shortened hair. She had her doubts about them going together to Bella and Russ's vow renewal. It felt too much like a date.

Hair cooking, she retrieved her liquid makeup from the medicine cabinet. Last year she'd had to switch from the powder she'd used all her life when it began to settle into the tiny cracks under her eyes. She dabbed it on a facial sponge, then patted her face. Besides, the liquid better hid those darker spots. She backed up for an overall view. Better.

But to a guy who's used to looking at a taut coed? Old.

Disgusted, she grabbed the blush, applying it with quick jerks. *You've got nothing he hasn't seen from every possible angle.* True. The almost two years since he'd been up close and personal had not been kind to her forty-year-old skin. She snapped out the wand and brushed mascara on her thinning eyelashes. *Is this how*

*it happens? The juices dry up and everything darkens,
slows, or sags.*

Raising her arm, she slid up the sleeve of her robe and
did a bicep curl. She pinched the skin beneath, gratified
to note that the underside of her arm didn't hang. "At least
I don't feel like a half-thawed chicken anymore." She
forced a smile. Better. She reached in the cabinet for the
eye shadow.

Twenty minutes later, primped, plumped, and poten-
tially pretty, she stepped out of the bedroom, dressy
shawl over her arm, and closed the door behind her. She
smoothed her hand over the bodice of her new dress to
calm the butterflies, but they weren't buying it. Down
the hall, light spilled from the doorway that hadn't been
opened in months. Alarmed, she forced her feet forward.

Jimmy looked huge, perched on the edge of the child-
size bed. Unaware of her, he looked down at the toy he
turned in his big hands: a stuffed bull, missing one eye,
with bare patches where the fur had been loved off.

She gripped the door frame to keep from snatching his
arm and dragging him from the room. Jimmy closed his
eyes, stark pain etched on his hard face as he lifted the
toy, buried his nose in it, and inhaled.

A tender bubble of sorrow swelled her chest, closing
her throat. She remembered the little badges, lined up on
the grave marker. The two of them had made her child
together. She didn't have a corner on grief. Clearing the
anger from her throat, she took a deep breath.

Jimmy lowered the toy and looked up with pensive
eyes. "Don't you think it's time to clean out this room,
Little Bit?"

An arrow slipped past her defenses to find her clenched

heart. She gritted her teeth and pushed past outrage to the unexplored emotion beyond it. When she could speak again, she choked out the truth. "I can't even force myself to open the door."

Jimmy laid the bull gently on the bed's pillow and stood. "You don't have to do everything alone, Charla. You let me know when you're ready, and I'll help." His wary eyes scanned her face. "If you want."

She sniffed and caught a tear on her finger. She rubbed her palms together and pushed off from the door frame. "We should go."

He stood, and as he passed, she touched his arm. "Thanks, Jimmy. I'll think about what you said."

He nodded, settled his hat on his head, and walked on.

On her way through the kitchen, she noted Jimmy's mug, washed, sitting on the drain board. She unraveled the shawl to put it on, but Jimmy took it from her and settled it over her shoulders. With his hand at the small of her back, they left the house. His hand had always rested there. She stiffened to keep from arching into it, like a cat reaching to be petted.

He'd washed his truck for the occasion. It sat sparkling in the sun of the yard. Jimmy pulled the back door closed behind him, rattling the knob to be sure it was locked.

He touched the small of her back again, but she didn't move. "Um."

"What?"

She hated the heat that flooded her face, making her feel like a debutante at her first dance. "We can't take the truck." She smoothed a hand over her shiny silk pencil skirt. She'd fallen for the dress the minute she'd spied it in the Posy Shop's window. Electric blue, the blousy top broadened her shoulders, and the tight skirt did good things for her rear end, but she now realized it wasn't very practical. There's no way she could lift her leg high enough to reach the running board of the F250.

Jimmy looked confused for a second, then broke into a grin. "No problem, Charla Rae." He held out a hand. She put hers in it, then concentrated on not wobbling as she crossed the yard in the thin, too-high heels. She should have known better than to take Bella shopping with her. At least she'd drawn the line at Bella's first choice of footwear: glittery silver stripper sandals.

Jimmy escorted her around the truck and opened the door, then bent and, before she could think, lifted her neatly onto the high seat.

Flustered, she tugged at the hem of her skirt, conscious of his vantage point. "Thanks." When she reached to pull the door closed, it wouldn't budge. She forced herself to look to where he stood, holding the door.

He whistled soft and low, staring at her legs with a look she hadn't seen on his face in years. "You are one good-looking woman, Charla Rae Denny."

Before she could react, he closed the door and strolled around the front of the truck.

On the way to the Donovans', the air in the truck seemed close, crowded with memories and potential. When she slid the window open a crack, clean air whistled in.

"I had an idea, Jimmy. What do you think of Bodacious's line? Do you think it would blend with Tricks's bloodlines?" She rushed on. "His sons are about the right size and proven buckers. He's also passing on a good rack of horns. I read that horned bulls score higher, just because they look scary."

Jimmy glanced from the road. "They don't just look scary. Don't you remember that time in Killeen, when that bull chased me down? Threw me butt over teakettle. I didn't realize until I got behind the chutes that his horn tore my jeans, and my butt was entertaining the crowd."

Char chuckled. "It may be funny now, but I about had a heart attack then." She took a deep breath of cleared air. "Remember that last trip to the finals, when you won everything? You walked right to the stands, picked me up, and carried me over to accept your buckle. I've never been so embarrassed." Jimmy glanced from the road. Their eyes locked. "Or proud." She turned her head to look out the window, surprised she'd said it out loud.

"Bella and Russell, have you come here freely and without reservation, to give yourselves to each other in marriage?" The cassocked priest stood, Bible in hand, before the French door to the patio in the Donovans' great room.

Bella's alabaster skin glowed in the unfiltered sunlight, a stark contrast to the black curls framing her face. Everyday beautiful, today her friend had vaulted to goddess status. The dove gray satin Grecian-style dress flowed like liquid metal over her curves to a fluted, asymmetrical hemline. Bella could have modeled for the cover of *Couture* magazine, except for the heavy silver Gypsy earrings. Char glanced down. And the glittery stripper sandals that Bella snatched up when Char passed on them.

Russ's florid complexion made it look as though his tie was strangling him, but there was no mistaking the look in his eye: solemn, proud, and smitten.

Char tuned out the priest and looked across the wedding couple to Jimmy, who seemed absorbed by the proceedings. The weight loss showed most in his face, erasing the bloated, self-satisfied man she remembered. *Leaving what?* She squinted, blurring the details. He looked more like the nineteen-year-old she'd married all those years ago than the stranger he'd grown to be.

Her parents had wanted to throw a large wedding for their only child, but Char knew money had been tight. Besides, big and showy wasn't her style, even back then. They'd opted instead for an intimate ceremony in the church she'd been christened in and a reception in her own backyard. At nineteen, Jimmy had been trying to make his name on the rodeo circuit, so they'd combined their honeymoon with a competition rodeo in Austin.

A first-class Hawaiian cruise couldn't have been more fun. They drove to the Holiday Inn near the arena straight from the reception. They laughed the whole way, giddy with the knowledge that sex was now not only sanctioned but encouraged. They took full advantage too, splurging on room service so they wouldn't waste time dressing to go out. Taking her time, exploring his body, she'd discovered as much about her own. That his look could make her nipples harden. That his finger trailing her hip could make her wet. That she held a woman's power, poised over his prone body. A new world opened in that generic hotel room, spinning the cocoon of physical emotion they shared in bed for the next twenty years. So intent were they that Jimmy almost missed his event. They arrived rushing and laughing, just in time for him to warm up before getting on his bull.

The weekend had been magical. Jimmy won the event, along with a belt buckle and enough money to buy their first bucking bull. Flushed with sex and success, they returned home on Monday, as sure of each other as they were their charmed future.

Char traveled from the memory to Jimmy's assessing gaze. Was he remembering their wedding? She flushed and shifted her focus to the droning priest. If she'd have known then how it would all turn out, would she do it again? The answer came to her, immediate and true. Even the pain that had almost taken her under couldn't eclipse the joy she'd found in being a mother. And in being Jimmy's wife. After all, that had been more than enough, before Benje. Surprise blossomed in her mind. Blissfully ignorant of any other possibility, she'd taken his love for granted.

Watching him from beneath lowered lashes, the empty spot in her chest reminded her of what she'd forgotten, that she'd mourned more than the loss of her son this past year.

Russ slipped the rings on Bella's finger, where they belonged.

"I now pronounce you man and wife." The end came so quickly, none of them moved, until the priest closed his Bible and said with a smug smile, "You can kiss your bride now, Russ."

Russ's large hands encircled Bella's upper arms gently, as if she'd break under them. He leaned over and touched his lips to hers. A simple kiss, but one made precious by the identical tear that ran down both their cheeks.

Russ straightened. "Whew. I thought up till the last, she'd leave me at the altar this time." The solemn moment was shattered by laughter.

A few hours and a few celebratory glasses of champagne later, Char read the hungry gazes of the newlyweds and rubbed her ear. Jimmy caught their old time-to-leave signal and, quicker than she'd have thought possible, they were walking for the truck. "Do you think they were in a hurry to get rid of us?" Char eyed the uneven sidewalk she could barely see in the dark beyond the porch light.

Jimmy took her elbow, his deep chuckle coming from behind her shoulder. "I'm not surprised. You and I were halfway to the car when your mom chased us down to remind us we hadn't cut the cake."

Oh! He'd been remembering too.

She tried to divert his attention to business on the drive home, but this time it didn't take. Conversation trailed off. Instead of the void she feared, an almost-forgotten comforting silence fell. They'd always had that from the beginning—an invisible bubble had surrounded her and Jimmy, keeping them separate from others. They'd never needed to fill the empty space with words. She sighed. Next to Benje, she missed this most of all. Her muscles relaxed into the familiar comfort of belonging.

When they reached the town limits, Jimmy asked, "We're all dressed up, and it's early yet. Would you come out to dinner with me, Charla?" His hard profile shone pale in the dash lights.

"I'd like to, Jimmy, but Junior's waiting for my call to bring Daddy home. He gets worse after dark, and I don't want to put that on Junior."

His hand relaxed on the wheel. "But you would like to?"

Would she? The butterflies nesting in her stomach certainly had an opinion—they awoke from their champagne stupor to career against her rib cage. She enjoyed spending time with Jimmy today. Maybe too much.

It wouldn't be so easy to sidestep him anymore. She and Jimmy were full partners in the business now. Time for the truth. As much as she knew of it, anyway. She turned to him.

"I'm glad we're not at war anymore, Jimmy. I'm even looking forward to being partners in the business. But I'm not sure I'm strong enough to handle what you're really asking here."

A sliver of regret slipped out with her words. Would she ever be? Where would she find the guts to put herself again in the hands of any man? Much less this one.

"For now, can we focus on getting used to being friends again, Jimmy?" Surely if she could get used to riding a horse and hanging with smelly cows, she could learn to relax around a guy she'd lived with for twenty years.

She'd seen tonight how easy it would be to fall into old, comfortable places.

Was it Jimmy she was really afraid of?

Or was it herself, afraid of falling for him again?

CHAPTER 25

I cannot say whether things will get better if we change; what I can say is they must change if they are to get better.

—*Georg C. Lichtenberg*

JB crossed his arms over the saddle horn and watched Char work cattle. She sat on the horse as if she were a part of it. Relaxed, but alert, she urged the momma cows and their babies to the gate. From halfway across the pasture, he recognized Tricks's distinctive black-and-white hide as she shot out of the pack, the splash-spotted calf at her heels.

With a burst of speed, Char and Pork Chop overtook the pair and turned them back to the herd, but the cow had other ideas. Tricks cut one way, the calf the other, eating ground faster than any nursing cow he'd ever seen.

Pork Chop spun on her hindquarters and leapt into action. Char leaned over the horse's neck, telegraphing direction changes with subtle shifts of her weight as they tore across the meadow. It was a valiant effort, but the lumbering cow was no match. Pork Chop came alongside and Char neck-reined her into the cow's side, turning her back to the herd. Defeated, her decoy calf trotted back to his momma.

Cattle bunched once more, Char sat back in the saddle. Back straight, one hand loose on the reins, she tipped her hat lower over her eyes and urged her horse forward. Point made, Tricks led the herd through the gate with one last bawl and a swish of her tail.

JB enjoyed the view of nicely formed, Wrangler-clad buns, as Char leaned down to close the gate. She wheeled the horse toward home but pulled up when she saw him in her path. His chest swelled, forcing him upright in his saddle.

He felt proud to have had the love of this fine woman all those years. By tonight, he'd find out if he'd be lucky enough to have the same with the time he had left. Fear-laced anticipation crackled under his skin. Sensing it, his horse threw its head up. JB checked the rangy gelding as he fought the bit, dancing in place.

Char sat watching him, shoulder-length blond hair stirring with the wind. How had he ever deluded himself that he could find another woman worth even half this one? He should've known the hole in his heart couldn't be filled by a bit of fluff.

Char nudged the small palomino to a trot. Details sharpened as she neared. She still had the waist of a young girl, but the years had subtly transformed her face, giving depth to the brash prettiness of her youth. Rod straight and chin high, she rode to him, her challenging gaze daring him to comment.

He coughed. "I see that danged cow is still hard to handle. If she's that big a hassle, once that calf is weaned, we can sell her."

Char fell in next to him and they turned for home. "And lose those bloodlines? Are you crazy?"

"We can harvest her eggs and use a surrogate cow—one that stays on the right side of the fence."

"Nah. Tricks is okay. She's just smarter than most cows, so she spends her time thinking up ways to bedevil me. It's a game we play."

He'd planned a day of truths, so he might as well get started. "Do you realize how much you've changed, Charla? I'm not talking about getting used to the horses and cows either." He kept his eyes trained on the horizon, as if the right words would be written there. It was always hard for him to speak the soft stuff, and he didn't want her thinking this was a snow job. "Before, you sat waiting for life to happen. Now you're riding out to meet it." He glanced over and read reticence in her narrowed eyes.

Taking a deep, shaky breath, he asked the question that held his future. "Charla, would you come with me? I have something to show you."

"Where?" She threw her head up like a spooked horse. "I've got to pick Daddy up at the feed store."

"It isn't far, and we won't be gone long." He watched emotion flash across her face, seeing precisely when she decided to say no. "Please, Char. I know you have no reason to trust me. You don't owe me, but I'm asking you anyway. I'd be beholden to you."

He held his breath, watching the war he planned to win being waged in her expression.

"All right, Jimmy."

The air left his lungs in a *whoosh*. He still had a chance.

• • •

She sat with one arm out the window. Jimmy drove the back roads, taking the curves wide and slow. Pulling the scent of old leaves and decaying tree bark into her lungs, she enjoyed the blend of gold and russet in the trees overhanging the road. Autumn had always been her favorite time of year. A time to snuggle in at home and prepare for winter. This time last year had been winter. The haunting smell of sour sheets and the spookiness of a blackout-curtained bedroom brushed the edges of her mind like a barely remembered nightmare. She pushed the darkness out with her exhale and drew the light, clean air of the present into her lungs.

Jimmy slowed, turning left at an opening in the trees, the two-wheeled track barely discernible amid the wild oats. She jerked upright. "Oh no, Jimmy."

His warm hand covered her fist on the seat between them. "Trust me, Little Bit, just a while longer. I have something to show you."

The old fire road dead-ended at the Pedernales River. They'd lost their virginity here, back in the dark ages. She freed her hand from under his. Jimmy pulled within a few feet of the drop-off and shut down the engine. *Right under that tree...*

Jimmy came around the truck, opened her door, and handed her down. When he closed the door behind her, she put her fists against the truck at her back and leaned against them. "I don't see the point in digging through ancient history, Jimmy."

He stood, hand out, letting her decide. After a few seconds, she shrugged and put her hand in his. Jimmy wouldn't take anything she didn't offer. The manic butterflies fought to get out of her stomach as they walked to The Tree, as she'd known he would. Instead of stopping, he led her to the opposite side.

"I knew that day we'd marry. That I'd never love anyone like I loved you."

She couldn't help it. She rolled her eyes. "Jimmy, it's a little late for romantic fairy tales, don't you think?"

He frowned, scrutinizing the tree trunk. "You fell asleep. Do you remember?"

She did, barely.

"I was so riled, I couldn't relax. The future was so clear to me." He ran his fingers down the tree, as if reading Braille. "Here." He lifted her hand, pressing her fingers against the trunk. She stepped closer, squinting at the heart-shape scar in the bark. The carving inside was harder to discern. She ran her finger down each letter.

F — O — R — E — V — E — R

Her fingers jerked from the bark.

"I did it while you were asleep." Jimmy's deep voice came from close behind her, his breath stirring her hair. "It was all so new, and happened so fast. You and I weren't even going steady yet. I didn't feel I had the right to carve our initials, so I carved this instead."

At his touch on her shoulder, she turned.

"I know it's corny as hell, but I liked the idea of others reading it, wondering who it was meant for." The half-smile that lifted the corner of his mouth looked painful. "I never told you." As his strong face fell, the lines in it deepened. "I never told you so many things, Charla. The fact that I don't have words for feelings is no excuse. I should have—"

She couldn't stand watching this strong man break. "Jimmy, don't. Please."

"Look, Char. I'm not angling for anything. We're divorced, and you don't owe me a thing. But I need to talk about it. This is more for me than for you. I can't go on without saying this, so I'd appreciate if you could do me the favor of listening."

She looked up. Much of the pain in those brown eyes was her doing. She owed Jimmy at least this, even if the listening would hurt more than the telling. Her stomach muscles tightened, preparing for a blow. She nodded.

JB spat out the words that had stuck in his craw for months. "I'm so sorry, Charla. Sorry that my being with Jess hurt you." He felt the muscle in his jaw flex as he searched for words. "That's not the end of it.

"It started years ago, when I forgot what I knew. Being a big man only mattered if you thought so. I got caught up in the big lights. I liked people recognizing me, the sound of my voice over the mike, the groupies. It was all about me, and I turned my focus from what was important to what was fun." He shook his head, as if to clear it. "In the end, I gave away the diamonds in my life for fool's gold. What I found out was that a big man, alone, mostly ends up in a bar, drunk. Now I understand why.

"Charla, that day, when Benje—"

She gave a panicked shake of her head and touched a finger to his lips. The grief bleeding from her eyes reminded him that her competent exterior cobbled over a fragile recovery. He reached to touch her but stopped short, afraid he'd pushed too hard. "Okay, Charla. We won't speak of that now." He forced his hand to his side.

"Breaking my marriage vows wasn't the worst of it."

He cleared his throat, to finish. "I turned and left you, knowing you needed me. There's no going back from that." He thrust his hands in the front pockets of his jeans. "I just wanted you to know that I'm sorry. For all of it.

"I lost more than my job the day you threw me off the ranch, Charla. I lost my way."

Leaving his guts steaming on the ground under the tree, he spun on his heel and walked away.

He's leaving. The same impotent panic as the first time roared through her. Char clutched the tree as an anchor to hold herself upright. And to keep herself from running after him.

You can't trust him. Not again. She'd always thought women who took back a cheater incredibly dense; if he'd done it once, he had a taste for it.

She watched as her fingers tightened on the tree trunk. They didn't look familiar. Strong, scarred, callused. Working hands. They'd saddled a horse, pulled a calf. They'd accomplished thousands of chores she wasn't aware of nine months ago, much less imagined herself capable of. Dropping her arms, she stepped away from the tree. *I'm not that dependent little housewife anymore.*

She wouldn't be putting anything in a man's hands that she didn't decide.

Jimmy strode away, spine straight,. Even from the back, she saw his chest hitch.

Besides, the man who left me wasn't Jimmy. <u>This</u> *is Jimmy.*

A strange calm radiated from her chest to fill her body, a liquid balm that cooled her hot skin and stilled the roar in her head. Sounds came to her: the drone of a lone cicada and the soft burble of water as it tumbled over rocks in the river's bend.

"You didn't leave me, Jimmy." Her voice sounded loud in the open meadow. "I drove you away." Her knees supported her after all when she walked from the shade of the tree to where he'd stopped, halfway to the truck. "I may have been under the influence, but I remember. I screamed in your face like a crazy woman, and if that wouldn't have chased you away, I'd have done something worse.

"See, your leaving turned out to be the best thing, Jimmy. Grief is a strange thing. It allowed me to stay close to the place I was when Benje was alive. It was a frigid comfort, but that winter I took what comfort I could find. It, along with the pills, got to be a habit, and I was sinking in an ocean of grief. I would have run out of air and drowned but for your leaving." She stopped a moment, to pull in air. "I hit bottom then." Seeing his stricken look, she hurried on. "I found out that the bottom can be a good thing. Something solid under your feet to push off of. You leaving turned out to be the beginning for me."

Char stopped in front of him, stunned by the truth she hadn't known until she spoke it. "It sounds crazy now, but when you tried to comfort me, it felt like I was pulling away from Benje." A shudder ran through her so hard that her hands brushed her thighs in a St. Vitus dance. "Like I was leaving him, all alone, in that dark place." Jimmy reached as if to touch but then dropped his hand.

The truth felt as clean as the breeze that kissed her face, giving her the resolve to go on. "I know I've made you feel guilty, Jimmy. I acted like the jilted wife to the entire town." When she caught herself looking everywhere but at him, she forced her gaze to his. "I'm not proud of it. The truth of it is, I gave you to that young girl."

Char inhaled a deep breath and set free her last secret. "You see, I forgot something too, Jimmy. I forgot that there was a time, before Benje, when we were enough. I was so immersed in trying to hang onto what was gone that I was willing to throw away what was left.

"I felt—" Once begun, the truth spewed from her throat unstoppable, burning as it burst out. "I feel so guilty. I'm afraid if I go on living, I'm abandoning my baby!"

The truth ended in a wail that rolled across the meadow. The birds and crickets fell into shocked silence. She saw her own fright reflected in Jimmy's tear-filled eyes as he stepped forward to pull her into his arms.

CHAPTER 26

Trust everybody, but cut the cards.

—*Finley Peter Dunne*

Her admission opened a door. Char cowered in the maelstrom of emotion, terrified she'd be swept back to the nightmare world of the days following the accident; that off-kilter, rabbit-hole world of shrouded light and foreign whispers. The fear didn't matter, because she couldn't stop the inhuman howl pouring from her throat. Jimmy stood silent through it, holding her, a solid mast she lashed herself to.

The tempest finally ebbed, leaving her limp, depleted. Still he held her, chin resting on her head, smoothing his hand lightly over her hair, murmuring words too low for her to hear. As she gulped for air, her chest loosened, absorbing the simple, powerful pleasure of being touched. It had been so long since she'd allowed more than a stranger's accidental brush of a hand on the street in passing or a cashier's touch while returning change. No, that wasn't exactly true. It wasn't that people hadn't touched her. After all, Bella had, and Sal hugged her in church last Sunday. The difference was that now, the touch didn't end at her skin. She was accepting of it. As she drank in the comfort, it swelled to a warm, glowing puddle in her chest, like a shot of Bailey's on a frostbitten day. She wanted to stay like this forever and not have to face whatever came next.

If she'd learned anything the past year, it was that you can't stay in one place, be it heaven or hell. She lifted her head from Jimmy's damp shirt and looked up at the quiet strength that resided in his brown eyes.

"Better?"

She nodded, holding his gaze for a moment before stepping back. "Thank you, Jimmy."

He touched the brim of his hat. "My honor, Little Bit." He pulled the white handkerchief from the back pocket of his jeans and handed it to her. She dried her tears and blew her nose. Hand under her elbow, he guided her to the truck, opened the passenger door, and settled her in as if she were made of spun glass.

He watched Char close. God, he'd hated to see her like that. Give him something solid to vanquish, someone to punch out for hurting her, anything but to stand there like an impotent fool while she fell apart. He walked around the truck grille. She hadn't really needed him. Had she? He'd only been the hurricane wall at her back.

But maybe that's all a strong person needed.

He hopped in the truck and cranked the ignition. The sun had turned the cab into a warm haven. He relaxed, wrapped in the well-known ease of riding somewhere with Charla. They didn't speak as he made a three-point turn and drove through the meadow.

Her hand wandered across the bench seat now and

again to touch him, as if, without looking, she wanted the reassurance of his presence. Maybe the affirmation was for him. Maybe for them both.

Time to finish this. He took a deep breath, and a chance. "Charla, I'm going to be honest with you from now on. If I feel it, I'm telling you. It's not easy, but it's easier than dealing with what happens if I don't."

"I'm glad, Jimmy."

"So, I have to tell you." Hands tight on the wheel, he made the turn from the dirt fire road to the highway. "I'm glad we're partners in the business, but I want more. My life doesn't work without you beside me." He shot her a quick look before focusing on the road again. Guts squirming, he blurted, "You're a strong, independent woman. If you decide to take another husband, or even if you decide to live alone for the rest of your life, I'll respect that." He studied the road, afraid to see her expression. "I'll hate it, but I'll respect it."

At Char's warm chuckle, he turned toward her.

She tilted her head in that amused way she had. "What makes you think I'd want that, Jimmy?"

"Well, I know you need someone to lift hay bales and to chase off a crazed bull trainer now and again, but other than that, you don't need a man."

She let out an unladylike snort. "Are you kidding me? I've been scared spitless most of the time. I didn't know anything, and I was terrified to make a mistake that would hurt the stock or cost us the business. I've discovered a lot, being the responsible one. I've even remembered things I'd forgotten about myself."

She was quiet so long that he glanced over. Gaze unfocused, she watched the scenery slide by his side of the truck.

"I need to be needed, Jimmy. Cows bawling to be fed don't count. I'm not whole by myself. I never have been. Maybe that makes me a relic. It's just how I'm made." She heaved a pensive sigh. "Daddy needs me now, but some-time, in a future I don't want to think about, he won't.

"I don't know if we can be a couple again, Jimmy. That part of our lives may be behind us." Out the corner of his eye, he saw her refocus on his face. "Or maybe not. You seem different. I catch glimpses now of that driven, hum-ble cowboy I fell in love with that day in the meadow." At a feather-light touch on his bicep, he turned to her resigned smile. "*That* cowboy still has my heart, Jimmy. He always will."

He wanted to tell her he was that man still. Persuasions piled into his mouth. Dana's reminder echoed in his head. *She's not listening, JB. She's watching.* He locked his jaw against the words.

They rode the rest of the way to the ranch, windows down, lost to their individual thoughts.

The wind had picked up, and the slant of the sun in his eyes told him it was around three o'clock when he pulled into the drive. He drove around the back of the house and shut down the engine.

Silence pressed into the car, and he glanced over at Charla. She sat, staring. He followed her line of sight to the hole in the world where the tree used to be. Even the stump was invisible in the high grass waving in the wind, but that damned tree still stood solidly between them. He tried to decipher her blank stare. "Are you ready to talk about it, Little Bit?"

She shook her head. "No." Her mouth twisted as if she tasted something nasty. "Though that doesn't seem to matter. I think we have to, Jimmy." Her hands twisted in her lap. Her mouth opened. Then closed. She shifted her feet, scrubbing palms over the thighs of her jeans, as if to dry them. Still she said nothing.

When he couldn't stand it any longer, he began for her.

"He was crazy for a tree fort that summer, remember? God knows where he got the idea, but he pestered me for weeks. I promised we'd build it together." The familiar dog-bite pain ate into the lining of his stomach. "I was getting to it, I swear I was. Why couldn't he wait?" He took a deep breath to make himself calm down, his eyes glued to the barn door.

"I was repairing tack in the barn when I heard you scream." His swallow clicked loud in the quiet truck. "I knew then. Not what had happened, but that inhuman howl told me that life had taken a bad turn." He still jerked awake nights, in a pool of sweat, hearing it echo from a fading nightmare.

He'd dropped everything and run, to find Char, on her knees under the huge maple tree, looking up, screaming. He didn't want to look—the utter devastation on her snot-streaked face told him he was too late—but he pried his eyes off her and looked up, through the leafed-out branches. His son hung limp and unmoving, one arm and his neck caught in a noose. JB didn't remember climbing that tree. The next thing he knew, he was sitting on a branch, holding Benje in his arms, rocking him. He didn't know how long he did that, except when he came back to himself, Char's screams were only a hoarse keening.

He choked out the rest past the tight wad in his throat. "I must have cut that damned gold rope with my jack-knife."

• • •

Gold rope? She jerked as a freight-train memory slammed into her brain. She saw every detail as if her vision had become a microscope: the dust on the dash of the pickup, the sun glinting cruelly off the metal on the windshield wiper. The sound of the wind, moaning through the truck's weatherstripping. Her stomach plummeted through her frozen guts.

The gold rope! She'd known this. Hadn't she?

She'd been making new curtains for the great room. Soft green plaid curtains, with pencil pleats and tie-backs. Material strewn across the floor, mouth full of upholstery pins, it occurred to her that she hadn't seen Benje since she griped at him to go outside, out from under her feet. Char raked her hands through her hair, trying to tug the details from her head.

Benje was a ranch kid; he knew how to entertain himself, making fun out of whatever was at hand. Gold rope. Her tie-backs.

My fault. It was my fault!

She scrabbled at the seat belt with unfeeling fingers. "I have to go, Jimmy." Her fingers seemed to have forgotten the steps to releasing it. Grunting, she fought it for several seconds until, with a snap, it came open. It retracted like a rifle shot in the cab.

"Charla, wait." He reached for her arm but she recoiled. "What is it?"

Panic screamed in her head, vaporizing rational thought. She had to get away. Somewhere she could bury the truth back wherever it had been all these months. Her lips pulled back from her teeth. "I have to *go*, Jimmy!" She pulled the door handle and almost fell out of the truck when the wind pulled at the door. Her legs wouldn't hold her.

Suddenly Jimmy was there, reaching down to lift her by her arms. The fear in his eyes told her what she looked like. "You have to talk to me, Charla Rae. I can't help you through this if I don't know—"

"Leave it. Just *leave* it!" She clamped her hands over her ears to block it, but it made no difference to the angry bee buzz in her head. *Myfaultmyfaultmyfaultmyfault.*

Jimmy still held her arms, but she shook him off, her air-starved chest heaving. "Just get away, Jimmy!"

She jerked from him, stumbling toward the back door. *I can't live. Not like this.* She remembered something else about that day. Jimmy carefully climbed down the branches, Benje in his arms. At the bottommost branch, he'd handed him down to her. Her son was warm and boneless, like when he was little and fell asleep in her arms. She cradled him, rocking, waiting for the delicate blue-veined skin of his eyelids to flutter, for his eyes to open, revealing the fractured blue irises that always reminded her of cat's-eye marbles.

Jimmy grabbed her arm and spun her around. "Char, you're scaring me."

"Get away!" She whipped her arm from his grasp, sobbing "Can't you see?" She fisted her hands at her sides, fighting the urge to slap at him. "You are not welcome here, Jimmy. Get away from me!"

Jimmy's face froze, his mouth opened in the prim scandalized *O* of a church lady. That look might have mattered to her, ten minutes ago. He ducked his head and strode back to the truck.

Watching his back recede, another insight hit like a slap.

He'd known what her brain managed to block out all these months.

He knew she killed Benje. That's why he left her.

A moan rumbled from the lava pit in her chest. How could he stand to look at her? How could she stand to look at herself?

Only one way. The wind pushed her as she ran for the garage.

CHAPTER 27

*I do not want the peace that passeth understanding. I
want the understanding which bringeth peace.*

—*Helen Keller*

Char barreled through the back door to the garage. She
wasted a few precious moments catching her breath while
her eyes acclimated to the shadows, listening to the wind
whistle around the corner of the house and the recriminations whipping around the corners of her mind. The
first object to appear out of the gloom was her father's
prize possession, the 1959 El Camino he'd owned since
he and Mom married. It sat, a forgotten ghost shrouded
in a pale gray dust cover. Yet another reminder of things
lost.

Silence met her shuffling steps as she squeezed
between it and the row of storage boxes against the wall.
At the last tier, she stopped and pulled the first box from
the pile. Seeing no free space to set it down, she turned
and dropped it. The *splat* echoed. Manila files spilled
under the car. The next box followed, and the next. Jerking the top off the bottommost box, she scrabbled through

registry papers of cattle long dead, to the bottom. Rooting for a glimpse of amber.

JB stopped in his tracks, turned, and watched Char disappear into the garage. He couldn't get his brain in gear. The shift in Charla's demeanor was so sudden it caught him flat-footed. Today he thought they'd tapped into the thick, braided-wire connection they'd always had, from high school right up to the day of the accident. Then this. She'd come at him, baring her teeth, driving him away, just like last time.

Acid burned at the back of his throat. He watched the wind push a scrap of paper across the empty yard. Here he was again, on the outside. No family, no real home. He settled his hat on his head and turned for the truck. Maybe he'd call her later, after she'd calmed down.

Hand on the door handle, he hesitated. This didn't feel right. Déjà vu ants crawled over his brain, leaving a trail of unease. Isn't this what he'd done last time? Walked out when she needed him the most? He'd allowed his own pain and insecurities blind him to why she'd attacked him. Char told him just this afternoon that it hadn't been about him. It was about her.

Forcing his own feelings out of it, he looked again at what happened. When the greedy wind threatened to take his hat, he jerked the brim down.

Char was upset. He'd expected that, but it wasn't until he talked about cutting the rope that her eyes had gone wild, exposing that crazed woman he'd hoped to never see again. Why? It didn't make any sense! Agitation amped, until a fine hum of electricity ran right under his skin, making him want to jump out of it.

He was done running.

He'd been a self-centered fool to get chased off like a stray hound last time. The jitters calmed. A solid weight of rightness settled over him.

He tossed the keys on the hood of the truck and turned back to the house. "You may be stubborn, Charla Rae, but you got nothing on this old bull rider." His words were snatched away by the wind, but not his determination.

It didn't matter if it made sense. Char needed him. He jogged to the garage door.

There! With a strangled cry, she pulled out her small bottle of oblivion and rushed as fast as the squeezed space would allow to the kitchen door.

Myfaultmyfaultmyfaultmyfault. The taunting litany chided her as she groped her purse for her keys. Finding them, she dropped the purse, scattering former essentials of her life onto the cement floor. After a few fitful tries, her shaking hands managed the lock. She crossed the kitchen linoleum to the sink.

While the water ran, she tried with palsied fingers to pry the lid off the plastic bottle. She was about to reach for her meat mallet to break it, when she remembered the childproof cap. Snorting at the stab of irony, she pressed on the lid and turned. It opened easily. She shook two tablets into her palm.

Myfaultmyfaultmyfaultmyfault. She added one more.

A child's heartsick sobbing echoed from down the hall. *Benje?* She cocked her head, listening.

Son? The sound trailed off, moving away. Her chest collapsed in on itself, the air whooshing from her lungs.

I can't live like this anymore. Ghosts aren't enough to live for.

Her chest spasmed, her lungs having forgotten the skill of breathing.

If Benje can't come to me . . .

She shook the rest of the pills into her hand. Decision made, the band around her chest slackened and her lungs pulled in a burden of air.

JB's fingers tightened on the door frame. Char's back was to him, but he knew she had those damn pills; he could hear them rattling in the bottle.

Save her! The cowboy code screamed in his head.

You can't save her. She has to save herself, whispered the contemporary voice he'd heard lately.

Charla cocked her head, listening. To what? The water ran gently in the sink, and the ticking clock in the great room contributed to the silence more than broke it. "Ahhhh!" She folded over, leaning on the sink as her knees gave way.

His hands jerked from the sill and he mounted the last step. The need to shelter a woman was a part of his genetic fabric.

You could take them from her. But the world is full of pills, isn't it?

He forced his hands to clench the frame again, feeling the wood give under his fingers. Doing nothing was the hardest thing he'd ever done.

She grabbed the edge of the sink, the delicate tendons standing out on the backs of her bloodless hands. Slowly she straightened. Her head came up. Staring through the window where the tree used to be, she blindly groped on the wall next to the sink. The silence shattered with the deep growl of the garbage disposal.

Without looking down, Char upended the bottle over the black hole in the sink. The grinder's pitch changed as it chewed.

Joy rocketed from JB's core, releasing him. He stepped into the room.

"I love you, Charla Rae."

At the deep voice, she jolted, shock coursing down her legs. She spun to the door. He was there, towering over her, enfolding her in clean, simple strength.

"You're not alone, Little Bit. I'm right here," he murmured, his breath stirring the hair at her ear as his hand came up to cradle her head.

Of course he was. She looked up into the deep brown eyes that had anchored her to the earth for the past twenty-one years. He had never left. Not really. His love spoke by way of the nurse he'd sent to save her when she was drowning. In the sweat he earned in the hot sun of the feedlot, to pay Rosa. In the money he'd left in the checking account for her, when she knew he went without. He'd hovered outside her direct sight for the past year, yet with a simple shift of focus, she could clearly see the threads of the safety net he'd woven. A net that kept her from the rushing dark waters beneath her.

Which only made her feel worse. She didn't deserve any of it. She pried her hands from his waist and took a reluctant step back.

"*Talk* to me, Charla." He frowned down at her. And waited. He leaned one hand on the sink, looking as if he'd wait for as long as it took. "I'm not leaving. So you might as well tell me."

"It's my fault!" The sobbing admission burned like

drain cleaner as it burst from her throat. "I didn't know. I didn't remember. How could I not remember?

"The gold rope, Jimmy, it was mine!

"I bought it to make tie-backs for the curtains. Benje must have taken it to make a swing." The poison burst from her mouth in an explosive sob. "I *yelled* at him. Told him to get out from under my feet." When black dots shot across her vision, she remembered to breathe. "I know why you left, Jimmy. How can you look at me? How could you love me? How can I live?

"I killed our son!"

He extended his hand slowly, as he would to a frightened horse. The deep rumble of his voice was like water chuckling over rocks. "Oh, Little Bit. You've carried that guilt all this time?" His eyes filled. With pain. With tears. "Don't do this, Hon. You didn't kill Benje." His fingers on her arm were icy; she shuddered.

The corner of his mouth twisted in a bitter parody of a smile. "If I'd have taken the time to build the fort he wanted, he'd have had no reason to be messing with your pretty rope." His gaze wandered to the window, to the stump that lurked in the grass, lethal as a coiled snake.

"Do you know how many times I've built that damned fort in my head? I can smell the sawdust from the sawn planks. I can see the sun shine off the red in his hair as I lean down to show him how to pound a proper nail—" His deep voice broke, and he swallowed. "Maybe we're all guilty. Benje too. Or maybe none of us is."

He turned to her, tears coursing down his long face. "It was an accident, Charla. A stupid random accident. And I miss him so bad it's like a piece of my heart tore off."

His gaze on her was soft as butter on a burn. "It's time

to forgive it all, Charla Rae. We can't have him back. We're gonna have to wait until we die for that. I'm trying to learn how to live without him." He raised his hands to hold her upper arms as she hugged herself to hold her guts in. "But there's another hole in me because you're not there. Between the two, there's not enough left to make a life." He squatted a bit, bringing his face even with hers. "Maybe if we stand together, we can find a way." His eyes explored hers. "What do you say, Little Bit?"

Could she? Let go of the guilt? Let go of Benje?

Benje's already gone, Charla. You've known that for some time.

Mom was right. God took Benje. She studied Jimmy's dear, hard face. Maybe if she worked the rest of her life, gave it all she had, she'd deserve the gift that God left her.

Could she, long term? No way to know. For right now...

She put it all down and lifted her hand to touch the cool skin of his face.

CHAPTER
28

The pain passes, but the beauty remains.
—*Pierre Auguste Renoir*

She and Jimmy talked until the wind stilled and the shadows in the yard lengthened. They sat drinking coffee, digging up memories from before the breakup, and filling in the holes of each other's experiences after it. They held nothing back, and in the laughter and the tears, they rediscovered each other. Like an intricate dance they'd choreographed over the years, they fell into step, knowing the other's next move almost before they made it.

Char told of her terror and pratfalls learning to run the ranch. Jimmy spoke of his time with Jess.

"That was a huge mistake, but one I learned a lot from. Hero worship is not a good basis for a relationship." His lip curled, showing more sting than smile. "For either party."

It was a hard listening, but if she expected to know Jimmy again, she needed to hear the events that shaped him since he'd been gone. After all, they'd brought the old Jimmy back to her. She hadn't known gratitude would taste bitter. "She was so young, Jimmy. Did you let her down easy?"

He threw his head back and shouted laughter at the ceiling. "Are you kidding? *She* dumped *me*!" Char tried to absorb the fact, while he got control of himself. After a minute, he heaved a breath and wiped his eyes. "Oh, Hon, thank you for assuming that." He patted the back of her hand. "If a young girl is on an old guy's arm, she's there for one of two reasons. Either she's sidling up to his money, or she's looking for a daddy." His eyes looked away. "And God knows, I was broke."

When he rubbed a hand down the thigh he'd broken in competition, she knew it must be aching. "Once I got over the ego bruise, I could see what's what. Bright, shiny paper will attract a male bird. When they get it back to the nest, they find it's not good building material." His touch on her hand became a light caress. "I've been such a fool, Charla. And like the old saw says, the old ones are the worst kind."

He laced his fingers with hers. "Are we back, Charla Rae?"

She knew without him saying that he meant "back together." She didn't have to think about what felt right. "I believe we are, Jimmy."

His eyes drew her in. Like a favorite denim shirt washed to the softness of flannel, his appreciative gaze wrapped her in the comfort of the familiar. Until it began to smolder. She knew that look. Knew exactly what would happen next. A flush of heat spread up her chest as a rush of need spread south. She wanted him. If she wasn't so distracted by his sexy looks, she'd wonder at her lack of hesitation, but as it was—

The phone rang. They jerked from each other like teenagers caught by the porch light in a lovers' clinch.

Dammit! JB released her hand and sat back, hoping to make room in his Wranglers.

Charla sprang up and took the few steps to the counter. "Denny Bucking Bulls, Charla speaking."

She leaned a hip against the counter, and she tipped her head to cradle the phone. She was small but had always been perfectly proportioned. He took advantage of her distraction to let his eyes wander. He liked her new haircut and color. It swung, thick and shiny with her every move, making him itch to bury his hands in it. Small shoulders led to a tiny waist above the slight flare of her hips. She'd lost some weight, but she looked good. Damned good.

"Oh, Junior, I'm sorry. I got wrapped up here and didn't notice the time." She shot a guilty look at Jimmy, and he grinned back. "I'll be right over. Thanks, bye."

He sighed, and heaved himself to his feet. "I'll be getting home, I guess."

"I've got to pick up Daddy at Junior's." Her eyes darted to his face, her smile twitchy. "Do you want to stay for dinner, Jimmy? It's only leftover roast, but I made bread today."

He stepped around the table to take her hand. "Darlin', if you're cooking, I'm eating."

Her smile turned radiant and he basked in it a moment, soaking up the simple pleasure of having made Charla happy. He couldn't wait any longer. He stepped closer. Her smile slipped, and her eyes widened. "May I kiss you, Charla Rae?"

Her tongue flicked over her lips, sending a shock wave to his John Henry. As she stepped up on the rung of the bar stool, her face came even with his. "Oh, James Benton, I really wish you would."

He smoothed his hands over her arms to her waist and

then to the small of her back, snuggling her to his chest. He'd waited so long for this, he planned to savor it. Her hands settled lightly on his shoulders and as he lowered his head, he held her gaze, to make sure she was sure. When everything blurred, he closed his eyes to better appreciate the input bombarding his senses.

Her familiar scent filled his head, some kind of delicate flower and the essence of Charla beneath, in a potent potion that mainlined to his brain. She relaxed, fitting against him like two puzzle pieces, same as they always had. He tipped his head and touched his lips to hers. He meant to tell her with his lips of his respect, his gratitude. But the kiss fast morphed into something different. Something hotter.

Her tongue met his in a tentative reunion and he took it without hesitation. Cupping her butt, he tugged her closer. She whimpered and captured his face between her hands as if she held something way more precious than a worn-down cowboy. She fit perfectly in his arms, filling his empty spaces. Just like that, his world shifted to the proper angle for the first time in well over a year. It was everything he could do to keep his hands gentle, when all he wanted was to rip her clothes off and take her right here on the kitchen counter.

That wouldn't do. Not with Ben waiting. He lightened the kiss, loving her ladylike groan. He set her back on her feet.

God, it was good to be home.

She flushed, and her hands fluttered to her hair. "Jeez, Jimmy, you make me forget everything." She smoothed her hands over her clothes, straightening.

"You need to be mussed up a little." He shot her a grin

as he reached for her purse, hanging on the back of the chair, and handed it over. "Why don't I take you and your dad to town? I'll buy you that meat loaf special down at the diner I've been promising you."

"I'd like that."

He puffed up as proud as the day she'd accepted his invitation to the senior prom. "Well, then, let's go get Ben." He reached for his hat on the counter and settled it on his head. "Then we'll head downtown and set the town tongues to waggin'." Orange rays of the setting sun washed the yard of the Double D in amber when he pulled up the drive. He spied Junior and Ben, standing at the corral fence, jawing. When he'd parked, Char reached for the door handle. "I'll get him, Char. You stay warm. I'll be right back." He left the truck running and stepped out into the chill.

The men watched his approach. Ben's face lit up. "You're back, JB. It's about time! Did you win you a buckle this time?"

He winced. Char had explained sundowners' syndrome to him, but it still hurt every time. Well, he'd be close from now on; he wasn't missing any more time with Ben. "I didn't, Ben, but it sure feels good to be finally home." He took the old man's gnarled hand and shook it.

Junior's beady eyes studied him. "Is that so?" He glanced to the truck, then back. "Well then. Looks like you mighta figured out how to be a big man after all." He reached for JB's hand, to shake it. "Welcome home, JB."

Char sat tucked into "their" booth beside Jimmy at the diner. Her dad perched on the vinyl seat across the table, talking a mile a minute. Trying to ignore the presence of his muscular thigh in her personal space, she smoothed her hair behind her ear and looked at the menu. Might as well have been hieroglyphics. She felt as though she'd been washed and put through a second rinse cycle. *Heck of a day.* Deep inside, heavy emotional exhaustion lurked, waiting to pull her to the oblivion of sleep. At the same time, an overlay of anticipation skittered over her taut wire nerves.

Was there such a thing as emotional whiplash? She glanced on the wall, to the sepia photo of Main Street in the early 1900s that had hung there as long as she could remember. Here she sat, once again, with Jimmy. She glanced to him. The pain of the past year and a half had weathered further the hard planes of his face, yet the essence of the brash teenager still lingered beneath—if you knew where to look.

She looked at the empty seat beside her dad, to the space once filled by her mother and Benje. Those holes would always gape, but for the first time, Char felt that maybe she'd found a way to coexist with them.

Mom, I consign my baby to your care for now. Kiss him for me. Tell him how much his mom loves him, will you?

She turned her head to the wall and brushed at the tear with a scratchy paper napkin.

Jimmy sat listening to her dad, perusing the menu. But somehow he noticed. He gently took her hand in his, and when her dad came up for air, he turned to her. "Are you all right, Little Bit?"

Jimmy had always had a gift. When he looked at you, he focused all his attention. He was really there. You knew you were special, and for that moment, you were the only person in the room. Back in high school, that gift had drawn girls to him like a season's end sale at the Posy Shop.

"I'm okay, Jimmy." As she said it, she realized it was true. She squeezed his large callused hand.

As he held her gaze, his eyes turned soft and smoky. Her thermostat clicked and the furnace in her chest fired up, spreading heat. Not like it wasn't already hot in here, what with every eye in the place trained on them. She fanned herself with her menu.

"You want to share the meat loaf plate with me, Charla Rae?"

"Sounds good," she said, grateful not to have to make a decision.

When the Olsen's girl sashayed up, JB ordered for all of them. Char sat back, appreciating a holiday from being in charge.

"What will y'all want for dessert?" the waitress asked. "Harve says it's on the house." Char glanced to the serving window behind the counter. Harvey Meister waved a spatula at her, huge grin on his face. She waved, then turned back, face flaming. "Thanks, but I couldn't." Her stomach was full of jumping beans already, and she hadn't eaten dinner yet.

Somehow she got through the meal, but between curious friends stopping by and Jimmy's hand resting warm on the inside of her thigh, she heaved a sigh when it was over.

One good thing. Eating at the diner with Jimmy was as effective as placing a full-page ad in the *Hill Country Community Press*; everyone in town would know they were back together by morning.

• • •

An hour later, Char stepped into the hall and pulled her dad's door closed. The excitement of the day seemed to have left him exhausted too. He was asleep almost before he went horizontal.

She hesitated, hand on the knob, knowing that one way or another, her world would change in the next few hours. She tucked her hair behind her ears, took a deep breath. She put one foot in front of the other down the shadowed hall to the light spilling from the kitchen.

Jimmy stood with his canvas jacket still on, turning his hat in his hand. Was he nervous too? Those danged party-animal butterflies were at it again—she didn't remember being this afraid the first time. "Jimmy, we promised to be open with each other from now on. So—" She wet her lips and forced her gaze to his stoic expression.

"Will you stay, Jimmy?" When he opened his mouth to answer, she rushed on. "Not because you feel responsible. I'll be just fine if you say no. But if you stay, I want it to be because you want *me*. All of me. You know I'm a work in progress." She tilted her head. "But I've discovered that I can take the hard truth. You don't have to feel obligated any longer."

"Jesus, Charla. *Obligated?*" He tossed his hat onto the dining room table where it landed with a hollow *thump*.

"You're smart, you're self-sufficient, and you're cute." He reached for her. "But you sure talk a lot." His head dipped, and his kiss sizzled down to her toes. He retreated sooner than she would have. "I thought that I wanted you twenty years ago, Charla Rae, but I didn't."

When she'd have looked away, he hooked a finger under her chin to bring her attention back. "What I felt for that sweet little country girl is nothing compared to what I feel for the woman in front of me." She saw the Jimmy she loved in his lopsided grin. "Hell yes, I want you, Charla Rae Denny. Always have. Always will."

JB paced the bedroom, barefoot, while Charla got ready for bed behind the closed bathroom door. His glance shifted around the room. Nothing had changed. Well, everything had, really, but the room itself hadn't. His side of the bed was unwrinkled, pristine. His fingers itched to mess it up, to prove he was back. His attention fell to a hardcover book, spotlighted in a pool of lamplight on the nightstand.

Healing Wisdom: Easing a Path through Grief

Settling on the edge of the bed, he flipped it open to a bookmarked page.

Every evening I turn my worries over to God. He's going to be up all night anyway. —Mary C. Crowley

"Amen to that, Mary." He snapped the book closed. His toes tapped a drumroll on the wood floor. What the heck was she doing in there?

I'm not going to bed in makeup. If I haven't frightened him away yet, he can take it. She pinched her cheeks to add some color to the butt-white skin and tried not to look too closely in the mirror. *Maybe that's why God makes your vision fail as you get older. It's kinder.*

She stood before the mirror, buttoning blue flannel pajamas with shaking fingers. Fluffy white cartoon sheep bounced across the material on her chest. *Oh, nice. You're a forty-year-old woman, taking a man to your bed for the first time in forever, and this is the best you can do? How sad is that? It's going to put a damper on the mood if he's laughing his head off.*

It would almost be better to walk out naked. She reached for the top button before she remembered. He's used to a twenty-year-old! Her hand dropped. Better flannel sheep than floppy boobs and a poochy belly. He sure hadn't traded up in the body department.

Her panicked gaze darted the room, searching for an alternative. *My robe!* She reached for it. Yellow terry cloth, it covered her from neck to ankle. She looked closer. In spite of numerous Shout applications, the sleeves were stained gray and snagged strings dangled everywhere; it looked like a shedding bison. A yellow shedding bison.

She groaned.

A soft tap at the door made her jump. "Charla? You okay in there?"

She shot a look to the ceiling. *You got me into this. I hope you're amused.* She pulled open the door...

And forgot all about what she was wearing. He stood before her shirtless, skin glowing in the light of the table lamp. She'd always loved Jimmy's chest. Whipcord working muscles under pale skin dusted with dark hair. She followed the line down, to where it disappeared beneath his flashy belt buckle. Her swallow clicked loud in the hushed room.

Flushing, she raised her eyes. His hair was tousled, as if he'd been running his hands through it, ruffling the curls. The hungry look in his eye told her he hadn't even noticed what she wore. He brushed a feather-light kiss against her lips, then held out his hand. When she put her shaking one in it, he turned and led her to the side of the bed. Her sheets were turned down neatly, but his side of the bed was torn up, the blankets and sheets in a jumbled mess. At the pressure of his hands on her shoulders, she sat on the edge.

He sank onto one knee in front of her, his dark eyes watching. He touched her as if she were precious. And just for this little while, she wanted to believe it. He dropped his head into her lap, his arms bracketing her thighs.

Startled, her hand went to his hair, smoothing it. "What is it, Jimmy?"

He didn't answer at first. She watched his back rise with his deep breaths. When he lifted his head, the light softened the hard planes of his face. He frowned up at her.

"I don't deserve your forgiveness, Charla. But I swear to you—on my son's grave—if you take me back, I'll spend the rest of my life making it up to you." His tortured eyes searched hers, waiting for an answer.

Hurting for him, she raised her hands to his face. "I have at least as much to answer for as you, Jimmy. I've stayed angry for a long time: at you, at God, but mostly at myself. We're going to both have to find a way to put it behind us." She smiled through her tears.

"Because living isn't about the blame, Jimmy. It's about forgiveness."

She pulled him closer, until he knelt nestled between her thighs. She tilted her head and gently touched her lips to his, to seal the unspoken vow.

Jimmy's arms came around her, and he tilted his head further and drew her into the kiss, moaning when her mouth opened beneath his. He crushed her to him, his movements frenzied, as if he were afraid he'd lose her. His breath sped up and labored. Char realized somehow her legs had wrapped themselves around his waist, and she was clinging just as tightly.

When he backed up, she tightened her legs. "It's okay, baby. I just want to see you." He unbuttoned the top button of the ridiculous pajamas with shaking fingers. Then the next.

She had a moment of panic, imagining him doing the same with his girlfriend. When he looked into her eyes, all she saw was a humble reverence.

Oh, Lord, thank you for my Jimmy.

She liked the sound in her mind so much she said it out loud. "Mine." It tasted celebratory on her tongue, like a sparkling, biting sip of champagne. She threw her head back as Jimmy smoothed the flannel from her shoulders.

Then there were only sensations: the sound of their labored breathing, the smell of his cologne, and its taste on her tongue when she licked his chest. Freeze-frame stills: the white, high arch of her foot, gliding over his calf. Her fingers, disappearing into his hair. They flashed by almost before she could acknowledge them. The pale slope of her breast, the vulnerable skin in the hollow of his neck, the small star-shape scar on his shoulder. Electricity gathered low in her belly, sizzling and arcing, building, until it burst through her in a bolt of lightning. She came apart in his hands at the same moment he came apart in hers.

Tears ran from the corners of her eyes to the pillow, mingling with his. They weren't born of sadness or regret but from the joy of letting go.

Later, Char lay cradled in Jimmy's arms. Her hand strayed to his thigh now and again, to remind herself this was real. Head on his bicep, rear snugged against him, she felt his chest rumble against her back as his deep voice wove a cocoon of peace.

"Ben and I are picking up Travis tomorrow and taking him to buy a decent pair of boots. I think by this time next year, he's going to be winning events. He says he wants to hit the circuit when he's done with high school, but I'm trying to get him to consider Austin Community for two years, at least."

"Hmmmm." She purred.

Fingers stole up the back of her neck into her hair. He absently fisted it in his hand, and at that familiar tug, her world settled.

Jimmy was home.

She drifted off, listening to his deep voice in the dark.

CHAPTER 29

In three words I can sum up everything I've learned about life: it goes on.

—Robert Frost

Char awoke like the click of a light switch, from oblivion to alert in a nanosecond. Something heavy weighted her chilled chest. She cracked an eyelid. A familiar muscular forearm lay draped across her naked breasts. A trill of lightness ran through her, matching the song of the mockingbird outside the window.

She closed her eyes and lay unmoving, listening to Jimmy's deep breathing and the *shush* of her dad's slippered step in the hall. What would he say when she and Jimmy walked in the kitchen, sleep tousled and conspiratorial? She blushed.

The bedcovers rustled and the bed bounced. She opened her eyes to Jimmy's smile. He lay, head resting on his fist. His arm tightened around her. "He'll be happy for us."

She smiled back. He always could read her mind. Or maybe the blush had given her thoughts away. "If it's a bad day, he'll think you never left."

"Either way, it's gonna be all right." He slapped her hip lightly. "Come on, Little Bit, we've got cattle to feed before church." He crawled over her and off the bed, reaching to retrieve articles of his scattered clothing. "I've got a change of clothes in the truck, and—"

She sat up, clutching the sheets to her chest. "A bit cocky about the outcome, were you?"

"Hell no, Charla Rae." He turned to her, frowning as he pulled up his jeans and zipped them. "Management or no, when you work at a feedlot, you learn pretty quickly to carry an extra set of clothes, just in case."

"Oh." She'd been awake all of two minutes and been in interminable painful blush the whole time. She fell back against her pillow.

He leaned down, and his long kiss made her want to pull him back into the warm nest of mussed sheets for a few hours. They had a lot of lonely nights to put behind them.

"You sure are adorable in the morning light, Mrs. Denny."

She squirmed. She dreaded ruining the day so early. But they'd vowed not to hold anything back from each other, so . . .

"Speaking of clothes, Jimmy," she said, focusing on the lightning bolt crack in the ceiling. "About your championship softball cap." She took a deep breath. "It's, uh . . . trashed. Beyond redemption." The rest of the story came out in a rush: her ordeal, the day Dirty Tricks had been born. She admitted to pressing it into service as a molasses trough.

"Nothing will get that stuff out. I washed it. I bleached it. I even used Bon Ami!"

Jimmy snorted. Then he threw his head back and laughed.

She watched him, surprise coursing through her. "What?"

He dropped onto the edge of the bed. Still chuckling, he leaned down, forearms bracketing her head, thumbs smoothing over her temples. "I don't give a good goddamn about that hat, Charla." The dark look in his eyes smoked her down to her toes. "I found something I lost that's a lot harder to win than a cap, or a buckle for that matter." His lips hovered, more a suggestion than a touch. "I intend to hang on for a lot longer than eight seconds."

**Aubrey Madison needs to begin
a new life.**

*Starting up a Pro Bull Riding enterprise
with an old-fashioned cowboy could be
just the ticket she needs—until her past
catches up with her...*

Please turn this page for a preview of

Nothing Sweeter.

CHAPTER 1

Her new life was going to be so much better than the last one. Aubrey Madison would make sure of that.

She savored the sight of a solitary saguaro, standing sentinel on the flat Arizona landscape. She savored the red-tipped ocotillo branches that waved in the stiff breeze of the Jeep's passing. She even savored the chilled air that swirled in, raising the hair on her body in an exquisite shiver.

God, it's good to be out of prison.

Her face felt odd. Until she realized she was smiling.

Glancing at the gas gauge, she vowed to stop soon. Only long enough to get gas and use the restroom. She had to keep putting on distance.

What if it's not possible to outrun your own conscience?

The pull of the road in front of her was as strong as the push from the view in the rearview mirror.

A weatherbeaten Sinclair sign in the distance made up her mind. She took the exit leading to a deserted corrugated building that may have once been painted white.

Pulling to the pump, she killed the ignition and sat a moment, listening to the *tick, tick, tick* of the cooling engine and the wind keening through the power lines. She stepped out, closing her denim jacket against the wind's probing fingers.

A bell over the station door jangled, and a black haired Native American teen glanced from behind the register.

She took bills from the pocket of her jeans. "I need to fill it up. Where's the restroom?"

His expression didn't change as his stare crawled over her throat. She fisted her hands to keep them still. When he finally pointed to a dark corner, she almost ran to it.

After solving the most urgent matter, she washed her hands. Her gaze locked on the black-flecked mirror. The ropy scar twisted from behind her ear to the top of her collarbone, looking like something out of a slasher movie. Shiny. Raw. Angry. She jerked her eyes away, turned the water on full force in the sink and tried once again to wash away the shame.

In her mind, she saw the sign she'd woken up to, in the prison infirmary, hanging on the wall across from her bed.

IF YOU'RE GOING THROUGH HELL, KEEP GOING.
—WINSTON CHURCHILL

In spite of her mantra, the walls closed in, as they always did. Yanking the door open, she fought to keep from running until she was outdoors, the wind kicking around her once more.

She reached for the gas nozzle, the tightness in her chest easing. When the Feds released her from eight months of perdition, her mother begged her to stay in Phoenix. But Aubrey couldn't get a deep breath there. The suburban ranch house crowded her with its memories and worried eyes. This morning she'd packed and escaped.

Holding the lever in chilled hands, waiting for the tank to fill, she turned her back to the wind. *Alone.* She pulled the luxury of the empty landscape into her solitary-starved soul and lifted her face to the sun's tentative warmth, smiling once more.

Max Jameson twisted the cowboy hat in his hands and lowered his eyes to the body in the gray satin-lined casket. His father's broad shoulders brushed silk on both sides. His face looked unfamiliar, mostly because it was relaxed. But there was no mistaking the strong jaw and high cheekbones. Max saw them in the mirror every morning.

Just like you to duck out when the going gets tough, Old Man. His mouth twisted as his father's familiar chuckle echoed in Max's mind. *Leave me holding a sack of rattlesnakes. Lotta help you are.*

No response, which, on several levels, was probably a good thing.

Max scanned the empty viewing room. He dreaded the remainder of the day: the funeral, the cemetery, the reception at the ranch. *"Your dad is reunited with your mother after thirty-five years."* The thought of solicitous friends spouting platitudes was enough to make him bolt for the barn, saddle his horse, and get the hell out of his own life.

He surveyed his father's waxen features. *Yeah, and don't tell me you wouldn't do the same, you old boot.*

"Maxie?"

The singsong cadence in that single word snatched him back, to when the man in the casket was a mountain and a little kid with worshipful eyes dogged Max's footsteps. Only one person on earth dared to call him that.

Strap yourself in, Daddy, it's gonna get bumpy. He turned to face Wyatt.

His younger brother stopped a few steps short of the casket, his gaze dropping to his father. A worried frown marred the angelic face from Max's childhood. Wyatt looked familiar, but different too. Soft cheeks had hardened to a man's and his golden locks were gone, shorn short.

Well. The prodigal returns. No points for bravery maybe, but—

"Did he suffer, Max?" Wyatt's voice wavered, his gaze locked on his father's face.

"Nope. One minute he's pounding in a post for the new fence line. The next, he's on the ground. Gone."

Wyatt's head snapped up, his eyes wide. "Jesus, Max. Do you have to be so cold-blooded?"

So much for the new and improved Max he'd committed to just this morning, lying in bed, probing the scabbed-over edges of the hole in his life. "Kinder and gentler" melted before the blowtorch that was his life lately. "Just telling you what happened. Sugar coating won't make it any prettier."

A hurting smile twisted Wyatt's mouth. "You sound just like him."

Max knew he hadn't meant the words as a compliment. "Let's grab a cup of coffee before the vultures show up." He settled his Sunday Stetson on his head. "You and I have a bucket of trouble, little brother. And trouble don't wait."

THE DISH

Where Authors Give You the Inside Scoop

♥ ♥ ♥ ♥ ♥ ♥ ♥ ♥ ♥ ♥ ♥ ♥ ♥ ♥ ♥ ♥

From the desk of Vicky Dreiling

Dear Reader,

Some characters demand center stage. Like Andrew Carrington, the Earl of Bellingham, known as Bell to his friends. Bellingham first walked on stage as a minor character in my third historical romance *How to Ravish a Rake*. I had not planned him, but from the moment he spoke, I knew he would have his own book because of his incredible charisma. He also had the starring role in the e-novella *A Season for Sin*. As I began to write the e-novella, I realized that it was almost effortless. Frankly, I was and still am infatuated with him. That makes me laugh, because he is a figment of my imagination, but from the beginning, I could not ignore his strong presence.

After *A Season for Sin* was published, I started writing the full-length book WHAT A WICKED EARL WANTS so that Bell could have the happily ever after he richly deserved. A chance encounter brings Bellingham and the heroine, Laura, together. Bellingham is a rake who hopes to make a conquest of her, but despite their attraction, there are major obstacles. Laura is a respectable widow, mother, and daughter of a vicar. Bellingham only wants a temporary liaison, but he finds himself rescuing the lovely lady. His offer of help leads him down a path he never could have imagined.

I've dreamed about my characters previously, but my dreams about Bell and Laura were so vivid that I woke up repeatedly during the writing of WHAT A WICKED EARL WANTS. Usually when I dream about my books in progress, I only see the characters momentarily. But when I dreamed about Bell and Laura, entire scenes played themselves in my head, DVD style, and sometimes a few of them in a night. While I didn't get up in the middle of the night to write those scenes down, thankfully I remembered them the next morning and some of those dreams have made their way into the book. I'll give you a hint of one dream I used in a scene. It involves some funny "rules."

This couple surprised me repeatedly when I was awake and writing, too. I was enthralled with Bellingham and Laura. Yes, I know the ideas come from me, but sometimes, it almost feels as if the characters really do leap off the page. That was certainly the case for Bell and Laura.

As the writing progressed, I often felt as if I were peeling off another layer of Bellingham's character. He is a man with deep wounds and very determined not to stir up the past. Yet I realized that subconsciously his actions were informed by all that had happened to him as a young man. I knew it would take a very special heroine to help him reconcile his past. Laura knows what he needs, and though he doesn't make it easy for her, she never gives up.

I confess I still have a bit of a crush on Bellingham. ☺
I hope you will, too.

Enjoy!

Vicky Dreiling

VickyDreiling.com
Facebook.com
Twitter @vickydreiling

♥ ♥ ♥ ♥ ♥ ♥ ♥ ♥ ♥ ♥ ♥ ♥ ♥ ♥ ♥ ♥

From the desk of Stella Cameron

Frog Crossing
Out West

Dear Reader,

My dog, Millie, doesn't like salt water, or bath water, or
rain—but it is the sight of all seven pounds of her trying
to drink Puget Sound that stays with me. Urged to walk
into about half an inch of ripples bubbling over pebbles
on a beach, she slurped madly as if she could get rid of
anything wet that might touch her feet.

That picture just popped into my head once more,
just as I thought about what I might write to you about

the Chimney Rock books and how stories shape up for me.

We were standing at the water's edge on Whidbey Island, looking across Saratoga Passage toward Camano Island. *Darkness Bound*, the first book in the series, was finished and now it was time for DARKNESS BRED, on sale now.

Elin and Sean were already my heroine and hero. I knew that much before I finished the previous story, but there were so many other questions hanging around. And so many unfinished and important parts of lives I had already shown you. When we write books there's a balancing act between telling/showing too much, and the opposite. Every character clamors to climb in but only those important to the current story can have a ticket to enter. The trick is to weed out the loudest and least interesting from the ones we *have* to know about.

The hidden world on Whidbey Island is busy, and gets busier. Once you are inside it's not just colorful and varied, sometimes endearing and often scary, it is also addictive. Magic and mystery rub shoulders with what sometimes seems…just simply irresistible. How can I not want to explore every character's tale?

That's what makes me feel a bit like Millie draining Puget Sound of water—I have to clear away what I don't want until I find the best stuff. Only I'm more fortunate than my dog because I do get to make all the difference.

Now you have your ticket to ride along with me again—enjoy every inch!

All the best,

Stella Cameron

♥ ♥ ♥ ♥ ♥ ♥ ♥ ♥ ♥ ♥ ♥ ♥ ♥ ♥ ♥ ♥

From the desk of Rochelle Alers

Dear Reader,

How many of us had high school crushes, then years later come face-to-face with the boy who will always hold a special place in our hearts? This is what happens with Morgan Dane in HAVEN CREEK. At thirteen she'd believed herself in love with high school hunk, Nathaniel Shaw, but as a tall, skinny girl constantly teased for her prepubescent body, she can only worship him from afar.

I wanted HAVEN CREEK to become a modern-day fairy tale complete with a beautiful princess and a handsome prince, and, as in every fairy tale, there is something that will keep them apart before they're able to live happily ever after. The princess in HAVEN CREEK lives her life by a set of inflexible rules, while it is a family secret that makes it nearly impossible for the prince to trust anyone.

You will reunite with architect Morgan Dane, who has been commissioned to oversee the restoration of Angels Landing Plantation. As she begins the task of hiring local artisans for the project, she knows the perfect candidate to supervise the reconstruction of the slave village. He is master carpenter and prodigal son Nathaniel Shaw.

Although Nate has returned to his boyhood home, he has become a recluse while he concentrates on running his family's furniture-making business and keeping his younger brother out of trouble. But everything changes when Morgan asks him to become involved in her restoration project. It isn't what she's offering that presents a challenge to Nate, but it is Morgan herself. When he left the Creek she was a shy teenage girl. Now she is a confident, thirtysomething woman holding him completely enthralled with her brains *and* her beauty.

In HAVEN CREEK you will travel back to the Lowcountry with its magnificent sunsets; slow, meandering creeks and streams; primordial swamps teeming with indigenous wildlife; a pristine beach serving as a year-round recreational area; and the residents of the island with whom you've become familiar.

Church, community, and family—and not necessarily in that order—are an integral part of Lowcountry life, and never is that more apparent than on Cavanaugh Island. As soon as you read the first page of HAVEN CREEK you will be given an up-close and personal look into the Gullah culture with its island-wide celebrations, interactions at family Sunday dinners, and a quixotic young woman who has the gift of sight.

The gossipmongers are back along with the region's famous mouth-watering cuisine and a supporting cast of characters—young *and* old—who will keep you laughing throughout the novel.

Read, enjoy, and do let me hear from you!!!

Rochelle Alers

ralersbooks@aol.com
www.rochellealers.org

♥ ♥ ♥ ♥ ♥ ♥ ♥ ♥ ♥ ♥ ♥ ♥ ♥ ♥ ♥

From the desk of Laura Drake

Dear Readers,

Who can resist a cowboy?

Not me. Especially a bull rider, who has the courage to get on two thousand pounds of attitude that wants to throw him in the dirt and dance on his dangling parts. But you don't need to be familiar with rodeo to enjoy THE SWEET SPOT. It's an emotional story first, about two people dealing with real-life problems, and rediscovering love at the end of a long dirt road.

To introduce you to Charla Rae Denny, the heroine of THE SWEET SPOT, I thought I'd share with you her list of life lessons:

1. Before you throw your ex off your ranch, be sure you know how to run it.
2. A Goth-Dolly Parton lookalike *can* make a great friend. And Dumpster monkeys are helpful, too.
3. Next time, start a hardware store instead of a bucking bull business—the stock doesn't try to commit suicide every few minutes.
4. "Never trust a husband too far, nor a bachelor too near." —Helen Rowland
5. If you're the subject of the latest gossip-fest, stay away from the Clip-n-Curl.
6. Life is full of second chances, if you can get over yourself enough to grab them.

7. "To forgive is to set a prisoner free, and discover that the prisoner is you." —Louis B. Smede

I hope you'll enjoy THE SWEET SPOT, and look for JB and Charla in the next two books in the series!

Find out more about Forever Romance!

Visit us at
www.hachettebookgroup.com/publishing_forever.aspx

Find us on Facebook
http://www.facebook.com/ForeverRomance

Follow us on Twitter
http://twitter.com/ForeverRomance

NEW AND UPCOMING TITLES

Each month we feature our new titles
and reader favorites.

CONTESTS AND GIVEAWAYS

We give away galleys, autographed copies,
and all kinds of exclusive items.

AUTHOR INFO

You'll find bios, articles, and links to personal websites
for all your favorite authors—and so much more.

GET SOCIAL

Connect with your favorite authors, editors, and
other Forever fans, and share what's important to you.

THE BUZZ

Sign up for our monthly romance newsletter,
and be the first to read all about it.